Vivianna's Story
Shattered Existence Book 2

Tamara White

Photo by Tamara White

ISBN: 978-1-62420-406-7

Credits
Cover Design by Ms G

Editor: Sherry Deborah C. Day

There is always more to the story.

Prologue

Raymond forced his fist through the boring green-colored kitchen wall of his two-bedroom apartment. His apartment with the paper-thin walls had gone from being his piece of paradise settled in the heart of an energetic and modest working-class neighborhood, to his nightmarish reality. Raymond wasn't able to reconcile how eight hours earlier he was a man feeding his daughter breakfast and sharing a cup of coffee with the person whom he declared the love of his life; the woman who he would give his physical heart to if she needed it, and now he was a man left with bruised knuckles and a life void of his woman and his baby girl. Raymond grabbed the yellow metal and vinyl kitchen chair and slammed it against the wall. *I did everything right. Everything she asked me to. I lived for her. I took care of her the best way I could, and she left me. She went back to that hellish horror of a family and took my daughter with her, my fucking daughter, my world. Leave me, fine. I'll get over that. I can get another woman but don't take my daughter. Especially not back there. Her love of rich people stuff finally destroyed us.* Raymond grabbed the leg of the metal kitchen table and flipped it over with ease. The sound of the plates and the glasses from earlier striking the floor created a dysfunctional melody. Raymond needed the apartment to reflect the agony he felt. If he couldn't go back in time and change things, talk some sense into her and stop her from leaving he would make every wall, and every piece of furniture pay for his inability to do so.

The sound of the familiar elderly voice of his downstairs neighbor, Mr. Borjarski, echoed through the parquet floor. "Too loud. Too loud. Please, no more noise. It's getting late. No more noise, please. Do construction in the morning. The morning is for construction, now is for relaxing and quiet."

Raymond knew the voice from downstairs too well. It greeted him with a warm hello when they first moved in. It reminded him not to work too hard and take time out for his family. The voice always had a piece of wisdom at the ready. Raymond thought about how many times Mr. and Mrs. Bojarski gleefully watched their daughter so he and Vivianna could steal a few hours alone. And with no children, the Bojarskis' cherished their surrogate grandma and grandpa time with Grayson, as much as Raymond and Vivianna valued date night. Raymond flipped up a kitchen chair and slumped down as he snatched the letter off of the floor. Raymond read the note over and over. Raymond's chest constricted as he read all the vile names Vivianna had called him. Raymond studied how the letters formed her hate, how her left-handed penmanship forced the perfectly formed words into a hard slant. Her words bruised his heart and ravished his brain. Raymond had no idea who this man was she described in the letter. Raymond knew he wasn't a perfect man, but he also knew he wasn't even close to being the man she accused him of being in the letter.

Raymond had given Vivianna not just his heart but also his soul. Raymond showed her all of the vulnerability most women claim to want in a man and with her letter she threw it all back in his face. As much as Vivianna leaving hurt, it was the thought of never seeing Grayson again that pushed him to the brink of madness. Raymond couldn't reconcile how Vivianna could take a daughter who was just as much his as hers away. Raymond knew two things: Grayson needed him as much as she needed her mother and Grayson didn't need a damn thing from Lakeland. Helpless and hopeless were the emotions that filled Raymond as he thought about his destroyed family.

Chapter One

"Raymond, you can pull over here. I'll walk the rest of the way." Vivianna put on her best happy, casual voice as she tried to act as if all the sneaking around was customary for any relationship, but especially their relationship. Vivianna stared at the moonlit glow that reflected on the large ebony-colored wrought iron gate which marked the beginning of the drive of her family's home, Lakeland Estates. Vivianna's stomach constricted as the awkward drop-off ate at her. Vivianna knew she was wrong for hiding Raymond from her family, but she didn't see any other way. Vivianna knew what was at stake if her personal life and Lakeland life collided. Vivianna hoped the date wouldn't end the way it had the past. But the nagging twist in her stomach told her differently.

Raymond shifted into park. The rough sound of the idling engine mirrored the rough conversation they had had countless times in the past. "It's late, and it's dark. I'm not gonna let you walk up there alone, *again*. I've done it too many times against my better judgment. I'm not doing it anymore, Vivi." Raymond noted the distressed look on Vivianna's face. He knew without her saying a word the problematic thoughts that filled every aspect of her mind. Vivianna's silence gave Raymond the resolve he needed to purge his feelings. "I'm a good man, Vivi. Do you hear me? I'm a damn good man." Raymond rested his large dark chocolate working man hands on the steering wheel. Raymond kept his onyx eyes focused on the darkness in front of them. "I go to work every damn day. Even when I don't feel well, if I'm not sick enough to go to the hospital, I take my ass to work. I pay my bills on time. I treat any woman I'm with better than I treat myself. I only put my hands on a woman to love her or hold her when she needs and wants it. I don't take anything that doesn't belong to me. I don't run the streets. I've never been locked up, and I don't have any children running around fatherless or otherwise. I take my liquor in moderation. I smoke a little weed when I feel the need, which only is once or twice a year. My only real vice is good loving from my woman. I don't have much but everything I have I came by the legal way. Now, if that's not enough for you let me know and we can part ways. Makes no sense to force a fit. But this dropping you off in the dark like we're doing something wrong when everything is supposed to be right is bullshit. If I'm not who you want to be with, then tell me. Tell me right now. What do you want?"

Vivianna let an anxious laugh slip past her words. "Listen, I know you're a good man baby. That's why I'm with you. You treat me better than any other man I've dated. Better than I even knew I wanted to be treated."

"The question is, do you want me?"

"Yes, I want you, Ray." Vivianna nervously pushed her hair over to one side. "I've never felt this good or this free before. And I like this feeling, and I don't want it to end. I really don't know why you're getting angry with me, Ray. There is no reason for us to be angry at each other. We had a great time tonight." Vivianna used her cute sexy voice as her last-ditch effort to soften the mood in the truck. "I don't want to end the night with an argument. I just figured it's late, I'm tired, and I know you are. There's no need for you to drive all the way up the drive to the house. You have to make a weird turn around in the dark up there. I'm just thinking about you. I want my man to go home and get some rest for tomorrow night." Vivianna winked at Ray. An awkward silence lingered between them. "Really, I think you're making this more than it is. I've been dropped off at the bottom and walked up before. I know this place in the dark better than anyone. Short of a possible bug bite nothing is going to happen to me. I'll be fine. I promise." Vivianna pushed a guilty smile across her face as she nervously wiped her sweaty palms on her jeans. She even added her famous spoiled girl pout for good measure.

Raymond let out a long frustrated sigh. Her flirty antics did not affect his frustration. "All the way up the drive." Raymond huffed in annoyance. "You act like I'm driving you to another state instead of to the front door, which, by the way, I would if you needed me to. I don't know who these other guys were you were dealing with, but I'm not cool dropping you off like this. I don't care if the worst is just a bug bite. It's a bug bite you shouldn't have to receive." Raymond shifted and turned his upper body towards Vivianna. "Why won't you let me be the man my parents raised me to be and drop you off at the front door? Why do you fight me on this? What is it, Vivi? What are you not telling me? Every time I bring you home, we end things the same way. Why? How much are you going to leave unsaid this time before you get out and walk to the house?"

Vivianna felt the disappointment emitting off of Raymond. Raymond used his large hand to push the flyaway hair back behind Vivianna's ear. "It's not you, Ray. I promise. It's just..." Vivianna lowered her head when she felt the glare of the headlights that headed towards them. Vivianna's stomach knotted from the guilt. "Sorry." Vivianna's voice was barely a whisper.

Raymond pushed her chin up. "That's what I'm talking about, Vivianna." Even upset Raymond's voice still possessed a soothing baritone sound. "You duck and dodge every time you think someone might see you, see us. It's been three months since we got together and this is the closest I have been to your parents' home. Like I said, I'm a good man and if your father is half the man you say he is then he will have no issue with me. I treat you good, and I respect you. That's what should matter to him."

"Ray, my relationship with you is more important to me than anything I can think of. More important than I can put into words, and I don't want me being a Harrow to ruin it for us. Being a Harrow has a strange way of closing as many doors as it opens. Besides, it's not my father you have to be concerned with meeting. My father is the reasonable one. But his reason is no match for my mother's ways. And Momma always gets her way, even when it's not the right way."

"How is your family going to ruin things for us? Unless your family is involved in something extremely outlandish or illegal, what is the deal about being a Harrow?"

"Raymond, you know how you say your mom is going to love me and how you can't wait for me to meet her and the rest of your family?"

"Yeah, I spoke to Momma the other night. She can't wait. My

sister is getting on my nerves asking for an exact date. But that ain't nothing new for Regina. She's always on someone's nerves about something. You'll see. Good person, but just plain irksome at times." Raymond let out a soft chuckle when he thought about his sister.

"See that's what I'm talking about Ray. Your family is—your family is for lack of a better word, *is* family. I mean mine is a family, but different, *really different*. My family isn't like your family; hell, it's actually the complete opposite. They don't welcome all with open arms. The Harrows live by these rules. I don't even know who came up with them, but they are what we all live by. The Harrows have standards, really high standards. And my mother is the type of woman who doesn't compromise on those standards for anyone or anything. My mother could find a flaw in perfection. Everything we do, Cora, Jack, myself, has to be done the 'Harrow' way. Right or wrong, it's the Harrow way, no exception, no discussion. Meeting my family isn't all let's talk and get to know each other, but more I'm going to interview you, damn near interrogate you and then I'll decide if I want to expend the effort to get to know you. I need time to prepare them for you not meeting their standards. It's going to be hard, but it could be worse if I don't prepare them, and even then there's no guarantee."

Raymond shifted again and rested his folded arms across his chest. Raymond didn't care he was sitting partway in the road and blocking the gate. "What standard ain't I meeting, Vivi? Tell me. What part of who I am doesn't meet your family's standard? Is it because I work with my hands instead of putting on a suit and tie? Because wearing a suit doesn't make a man a man. I know some well-dressed man-boys. They are as ignorant and foolish as the day is long, but they stay sharply dressed. Some of them gonna live with their mommas until the day she dies because no halfway respectable woman will have them. I don't make enough money for them, is that it? If it's that, then let me declare right now money don't make you happy. Stuff can't love you, and you can't take any of the stuff you buy with you in the end. Everybody in the graveyard is broke."

Vivianna's eyes watered as she cursed at herself. Raymond was everything Vivianna wasn't supposed to want and yet everything she needed. *This thing wasn't supposed to go this far. Slumming in the city was never supposed to be this serious. Why can't it be different? I wasn't supposed to fall in love with a casual thing.* Raymond was a reality check in dark chocolate form. "Please." Vivianna's tears flowed like water rushing towards the mouth of a river. "I, I don't do want to do this. I really want to be with you. You're all I want. But, but I can't do this with them right now. I just can't. Please, I can't. I just want it to be you and me right now. I want to say goodnight without you being mad at me. I don't want to bring the other stuff into it. I don't like dealing with the other stuff. Can't it just be you and me right now and that's it?"

"Okay, okay." Vivianna's tears made Raymond quickly surrender his position. Raymond never liked to see a woman cry, especially his woman. "Okay," he whispered again. Raymond brushed Vivianna's tears off of her flawless face. "We won't do this now. I don't like to see you so upset."

Vivianna shook her head in agreement.

"But we are going to do this at some point. Soon, Vivianna. Do you understand me? There is going to be a day where I am going to go up there, and I am going to introduce myself to your parents. I'm going to extend my hand to your father and if he's a real man he'll shake it, and if your mother is a real woman, she'll shake it too. Damn all the standards and rules. It will go good or it'll go bad. But either way, I'll still love you." Raymond's stern baritone let Vivianna know he meant what he said.

Vivianna shook her head several more times as she composed herself. Vivianna smiled as she looked at Raymond and a wave of relief washed over her. She had delayed the inevitable for at least one more night. Vivianna knew Raymond had no idea how bad or how far an introduction could escalate. "I have to go."

Raymond leaned in and kissed her. Vivianna loved the way his full lips felt against hers. Everything thing Raymond did he did it with confidence. His kisses were no exception. They were demanding and meaningful. Vivianna loved how his self-assurance made her feel. She admired how free he was in being himself. Raymond was unlike the men she grew up around. He didn't put a whole lot of stock into trends and acquiring pointless things. He could care less which actor was dating which actress. Words like Chanel, Louis Vuitton, and Mercedes-Benz carried no weight with him. Right or wrong, Raymond was the type of guy who owned his failures as well as his successes, and he humbled himself to learn there were lessons in both.

The manliness he exuded was intoxicating. Raymond was powerful and gentle at the same time. Vivianna dated boys who went to the best schools and had the best formal upbringing, yet they didn't treat her with the level of care and respect Raymond did. Vivianna didn't want to, but she knew she had to pull herself away. "I have to go, or I'll be neck high in trouble with Momma. Pick me up Saturday night?"

"Saturday night? What happened to Saturday afternoon? I can pick you up at the front door around eleven or twelve." Raymond leaned in and kissed her again. His eyes would not allow Vivianna to break his stare. Raymond gently rubbed his nose against her. Vivianna giggled back at him.

"I can't. We have to spend all day tomorrow with Momma's parents." Vivianna rolled her hazel-green eyes. "Trust me, I would rather be with you instead. Papa is okay, but Grand-Mère is another story. Her mood determines how well the visit goes. I already know I'm going to catch hell when she finds out I took the semester off. Papa is all about us being free spirits and doing what makes us happy. Grand-Mère only cares about what looks right. If it doesn't involve lineage and raise your status in society, it's not worth doing as Grand-Mère would say. It's all about how we look to the outside." Vivianna twisted her face.

"She sounds wonderful in a mean old grandma kinda way."

Vivianna couldn't control the giggle that escaped her lips.

"Your laugh is one of my favorite sounds. It lifts my spirits every time I hear it. If I could catch it in a jar and save it to listen to later, I'd have countless jars on my shelves."

"Wow, I've never had anyone so in love with my laugh. It's sweet, really sweet."

"I meant every word of it. Now, is there any way my sweet words convinced you to meet me in the afternoon tomorrow instead of in the evening?"

"I wish I could baby, but..."

"Okay. You don't have to explain it again. I understand. You can't do the afternoon." Raymond smiled before he kissed her again. "I'll wait for Saturday night. I'll pick you up at seven. Don't panic, I won't come to the door *yet*. But one minute past seven-thirty, and I'm driving up and ringing the bell. I'm only giving you thirty minutes because I know you'll need time to plan your escape."

"Thank you."

"I'll even have something special planned. A surprise."

"What is it?" Vivianna's eyes lit up.

"You wanna know what it is?"

She pushed him playfully in the chest. "You know I do! What is it? Tell me, please."

"You really wanna know? You don't want to wait for Saturday night?" Raymond's grin widened. He loved the way her eyes scintillated with excitement. "Saturday night is not that far away," Raymond teased with his broad smile.

"No, tell me. Tell me now."

Raymond loved how her face lit up from excitement. "Okay, okay, Vivi I'll tell you what I have planned." Raymond took a deliberate pause. "What I have planned for Saturday night is," he chuckled at the way Vivianna's looked like she was going to come off the seat, "what I have planned is...a surprise. That's what I have planned." Raymond let out a huge laugh that matched his velvety voice.

"Really, Ray, really." Vivianna playfully pushed him again. "You're not funny at all."

"Yeah, I am, and the look on your face, priceless." Vivianna shoved him in the chest again. Raymond kissed her again. "You had better get before I change my mind and drive off with you."

Vivianna kissed Raymond again. Raymond watched as she walked up the extended drive. He studied how her hips moved as she walked along the pebbled driveway. Even with the uneven ground under her feet, Vivianna was determined to stay poised. Raymond smiled at the bounce in her curls. Vivianna turned briefly and smiled before she disappeared into the late night.

~ * ~

Vivianna hummed softly as she quietly opened the back door. Vivianna wasn't surprised when she saw Cora at the kitchen table, her yellow nightgown peaking through her baby blue bathrobe and a head full of soft pink rollers with a flowered scarf tied around her head. Cora, with the same green eyes Vivianna possessed, barely looked up as she demolished a plate of leftovers.

"You're late." Cora crammed a fork full of mashed potatoes into her chubby smooth-edged light brown face.

"And you're eating." Vivianna sat next to her sister and snatched a chicken wing off of her plate.

"Hey, get your own. You know Momma's gonna have a fit when she finds out you came home late *again*." Cora attacked the two-day-old macaroni and cheese next.

"Who's gonna tell her? It's just you and me in the kitchen. If you out me you have to out yourself. And we both know how Momma feels about the love affair you have with the refrigerator."

"Yeah, but if it gets you in trouble, then it's more than worth it to have to deal with Momma." Cora smiled at her sister as she shoved more food on top of the already half chewed pasta in her mouth. "Or you could loan me that sweater, and I won't tell."

Vivianna tossed the chicken bones carelessly back on Cora's plate. "Cora please, you're too big to fit this sweater or anything of mine for that matter. A cashmere blanket is what you need, and even that would be tight on you. "Vivianna admired how the soft vanilla color of her sweater played against her skin tone and hugged her breast. Vivianna stopped laughing when she looked up and saw the hurt look in her sister's eyes. Cora let the fork fall out of her plump fingers. Cora fought every day to lose weight and the more she struggled, the more she ate. Most nights Cora snuck down to the kitchen and ate a plate filled with a double portion of everything from dinner while she cried. Thankfully the one time Cora fell asleep during a food binge Momma Mae found her in the morning before Emily did. Vivianna played her role as the pretty younger sister who could make any man stop in mid-stride to perfection and Cora mastered being the tubby older sister whom everyone pitied and whispered *what a waste her face is so pretty* about behind her back.

Vivianna tilted her head down to draw her sister's eyes up. "Sorry."

"No, you're not. You do it too often to be sorry about it." Anger mixed with self-pity as Cora spoke. "Fat Cora. The one you and Jack berate and torment until one of you needs a paper written or a co-conspirator in the lies y'all tell. When the two of you are sneaking in and out with God knows who from God knows where to wherever you two go. Then it's fat Cora to the rescue. Fat Cora to clean up the messes you two make and make it all look like it never happened."

"If that's really how you feel maybe we can get you a cape with a big fat F on it for your birthday. You can put it on and swoop in like a real superhero next time."

Cora shook her head and fought her tears. "Fuck you, Anna. Fuck you and everything about you."

"Oh, stop it. It was a damn joke, Cora. Why the hell are you so sensitive tonight? Are you on your period because I'm not saying anything you haven't heard before? Why is tonight the night you grow a set of feelings?"

"I've always had feelings Anna, it's just you and Jack, and everyone else in this damn house have never given a damn about my feelings. No one in this family gives a damn about me, just the number on the damn scale. I'm so tired of the whole damn family making fun of my weight. I am fat, but I'm still a fucking person. You think I like being this way?"

"Then lose the damn weight, Cora, if you don't like it. Put down the fucking fork and lose it."

"I've tried! Don't you think I've tried? It's not as easy as you say it is miss skinny and pretty without trying. It's hard really hard. I could wire y jaw shut tomorrow and be ten pounds heavier in three days."

"Well, I can't argue with your skinny and pretty comment." Vivianna's signature devilish grin raced across her face. "I am amazing."

"You never miss an opportunity to make something about me about you, do you? Once again, fuck Cora and her feelings. Just go to bed,

Anna, and leave me alone. We both know I'm not going to tell Momma you missed curfew." Cora snatched the fork off the plate and consumed another mouthful of food.

Vivianna watched in silence as Cora ate. Vivianna studied how Cora barely swallowed before she shoved another fork full in her mouth. There ore she ate the harder she slammed she fork into the plate. Vivianna noticed how Cora ate like a drug addict who didn't want to get high but had no choice because the psychological beast within her demanded satisfaction.

"Sorry." Vivianna never really considered how all of the rude comments made Cora feel. Emily had convinced Jack and Vivianna that Cora liked being spoken down to because if she didn't, she would have lost the weight. *Being fat is a choice, and Cora has chosen to be fat. If she wants kindness, she'll lose the weight.* Vivianna remembered how her mother would say that over and over to Vivianna. Those two sentences encouraged Vivianna's bullying behavior towards Cora. "Cora?"

"I don't need a fucking audience." Cora snatched her arm away. "Just go already. I said I wouldn't tell. Fat Cora won't say a word."

Vivianna lowered her voice. "I know, Cora. You never do." Vivianna put her hand over her sister's before Cora could scoop more food on it. "I'll make you a deal. When you lose the weight, you can *have* this sweater and any outfit you want in my closet."

Cora's eyes danced up with joy. Vivianna knew Cora would never lose the weight and Cora knew it as well. It was the moment of kindness and a smile that made Cora forget her reality. "Deal." Cora slid her plate over to Vivianna. Vivianna picked off of Cora's plate a little longer before she headed upstairs.

"Is he worth all the trouble you go through to be with him?"

"He's not trouble, Cora. He's wonderful, and he's so good to me. He makes me feel good about myself." Just the thought of Raymond put an uncontrollable smile on her face.

Chapter Two

Emily, the second-oldest of Delphine and Andre LaSalle's children, started the day as she always did when her mother came to visit. Emily demanded the housekeeper Mae, or Momma Mae as Emily's children called her, begin the day two hours earlier than her regular start time. Emily forced the rest of the family up at seven that Saturday morning. Emily commanded a much higher level of perfection when her parents descended onto Lakeland. Their visits were never about visiting kinfolk but more about Delphine taking inventory of what Emily had done with Lakeland. Fifteen years earlier Andre talked his wife into moving away from Lakeland. Andre sold Delphine on the idea that travel in the final years would make them a lot happier than living at Lakeland.

Andre, like the rest of the men who married into the family of Lakeland, viewed the estate as more of a prison than a home. The thick and heavy misery swept over every inch of Lakeland. No matter how loud and lavish the parties and family gatherings were, the undercurrent of desolation always prevailed. The perceived happiness at Lakeland present to outsiders was the one of the greatest illusions created.

Delphine, ripe with frustration, took her usual place in the sitting room in what was her mother's favorite chair. The chair was circa early 1900's Old South and had been passed down for several generations. The chair was a boring brown color and as uncomfortable to sit on as it was to view. No one knew why such a hideous piece of furniture had been passed down for generations instead of being put out of its misery. But there it sat, just as dismal as the people who sat in it. Delphine used the lackluster coffee-colored chair as her throne.

Delphine kept a scoffing expression on her creamy face. Delphine rarely smiled; even in family photos her face held some degree of disgust smeared across it. She equated happiness to simple-mindedness. "Only fools are truly happy, and I am no fool." Delphine said the saying so much that her husband often wondered if she was desperate to convince herself of its truth. Delphine's petite five-foot stature always made her feel as if she had something to prove to the world. Delphine had the same green eyes Cora and Vivianna possessed, an inherited gift from her father, Cairo. Her hair, which was mostly grey now, she kept pinned back in a pristine bun, which only added to her uptight appearance.

Carnations. Only Emily would be tacky enough to have carnations, the roses of the underprivileged, in a vase of such eminence. It's as if the words 'imported' and 'handmade' mean nothing to her. "These flowers could give a dead person a migraine. I wonder what grave our daughter stole them off. They scream piss-poor funeral chic." Delphine possessed a tongue that made Emily's words seem kind and caring in comparison. Delphine crossed her slender legs at the ankle and smoothed her rust-colored skirt before she folded her arms across her chest. She huffed as the grandfather clock chimed. "Unacceptable. Our daughter is fifteen minutes late. It's as if she is determined to live her life on that colored people's time instead of civilized time like the rest of us."

Delphine's husband Andre, like Emily's husband Quincy, said as little as possible. Decades of marriage made Andre a professional at avoidance when it came to Delphine's contemptuous and repugnant rants. Andre's height fell on the side of short for a man born to his generation. Andre's full beard worked well for him. He carried himself with quiet dignity. His café-colored skin tone contrasted with his wife's and Delphine never let him forget where he fell on the color spectrum in comparison to her. Andre possessed a handsome kindness that made people whisper about what he saw in Delphine.

"There is no colored people time, Delphine. Just time. Time is time, and everyone falls to lateness at some point. Does it really matter she's fifteen minutes late? Emily could have rushed in here moments after our arrival, and you still wouldn't be happy. Something else wouldn't have been to your liking. Hell, you know she's upstairs, if her tardiness is affecting you so much, go get her."

"I shouldn't have to go get her, Andre. She should have been down here waiting for me. Emily has known for several weeks we were going to be here. The constant disappointment I feel in her behavior is exhausting for me. You will never understand how exhausting it is."

Andre ran his hand over his thick beard. "If you say so, Delphine. If you say so."

Delphine took detailed mental notes of everything her eye found offensive as she seethed. *The painting will be moved back where I had it. I don't like the frame around that picture. The drapes are tacky, and I will have them switched before I leave. Where is the lamp I placed in the corner next to the chair? Emily is going to have to see if there is a different rug in storage. I don't know how I feel about this one yet. I've only been here a short time, and already I feel drained just thinking about all the things I have to fix. On my life, I swear my work is never done. No matter how well I trained her, Emily still can't seem to perform to standard. This house is a disaster. Josephine is unquestionably my better creation. Why can't she be like her sister?* "You never get tired of making excuses for our daughter do you, Andre? You have never expected better of her, so she sees no need to do better. I have yet to return home and see the house up to standard. Just look around at this place. It's obvious I gifted Lakeland to the wrong child. Her inability to run the house the way I did is really getting under my skin. I would never allow Mae to keep the house the way Emily does. Obviously, Emily doesn't know how to motivate Mae to do better. Look at how she moved the painting. I put those paintings where I put them for a reason. I don't like them there. It makes no sense to put a picture of such size where she has." Delphine pointed to the painting of a colonial mistress and her female slave in waiting. "The way she has placed the furniture makes the room look small, Andre. Those picture frames she has the girls' portraits in are just tacky and rude. Your daughter has decorated as if I raised her in a rundown shack." Delphine focused on a piece of lint on the Persian rug that a nonjudgmental eye would have easily missed. "These rugs look like they haven't been cleaned properly since the last time I was here and got on her about the upkeep of these rugs. My job as a mother is never done."

"You gifted. *You gifted,* Delphine, I thought *we* left things to Emily."

"Andre, *we* can't leave my family's property to anyone, only I can. Did you forget whose family owned the roof you sit under?"

"How can I forget, Delphine? You have reminded me almost every day for the past fifty years of our marriage."

"I only remind you because you keep using words like we and our when you speak about *my* family's land. My family's legacy."

Andre let out a long exhausted sigh. "Okay, Delphine, okay. I don't want to take that journey with you today. I came to enjoy my grandbabies. Besides, the house looks the way it did when we were here. The same old stuff splayed everywhere."

"My family's *objets d'art* are not stuff, Andre, they are antiques. They are items of value with prestige attached to them, objects that have been passed down for generations. My family's articles have respect attached to them. Not stuff, never stuff. Stuff is what you showed up with when we were first married and I promptly had it thrown out. Stuff, Andre, is what your mother had splayed all over her house." Delphine flung her hand in the air with disgust. "And of course, you don't see anything wrong. You never see anything wrong with your daughter's actions. One of Emily's biggest problems is your ability to *always* dismiss her flaws. Your dismissal of her shortcomings created an average child that halfway developed into a mediocre adult."

"Flaws? Was Emily flawed when she married Quincy and used the money his father left him to rebuild your daddy's company and save your family's property from the auction block after your daddy made all of those bullshit deals? Borrowing money at an interest rate he couldn't pay back? Your father put the balloon in the term balloon payment. It's amazing how deep of a hole banks will allow you to dig for yourself when they want what you have."

"How dare you speak about my father in such a vile manner. My father was a businessman, a great businessman, a great man for that matter. My daddy was greater than the man who raised you. He did what lesser men in this area wouldn't have been able to accomplish. God looks up to my father."

"Oh come on, Delphine. You're talking to me, me Delphine, not one of your high society friends. You and I know exactly who your father was. He was a drunk and a womanizer who gambled the deed to this property on more than one occasion. Between paying his gambling debts,

16

paying for his illegitimate children, and settling with the woman whose son he killed after he left the whorehouse sloppy drunk, I'm surprised we were able to leave here with what we did. Your father's trifling ways ran him into the grave, and his debts from his grave almost ruined us. You and the rest of your siblings have always harbored a blind spot for the delinquent you call a father."

"My father—"

"Your father tried to breed his own personal football team. It wouldn't surprise me at all if another half-sibling crawled out from under some bastard rock. And you know I'm telling the truth. I'm still trying to figure out how you could go to those stuck up women's meetings of yours when we were here. And sit across from one of them, in particular, knowing full well who is she."

Delphine gritted her teeth. "That woman is not my sister, Andre. She is not my sister." Delphine balled her fist and slammed it into the arm of the chair.

"The hell she isn't. You know she looks just like you and your sister Justine. And her age falls right in line with your father's antics. You may be in denial, but everyone knows the truth. Hell being only six months apart in age damn near makes you twins. So, all things considered, I think Emily has done a fine job with this forsaken place. The only reason I come back here is to see my grandbabies. If it weren't for them, I would have never crossed that damn threshold again once we left. I swear sometimes I think this place is cursed."

Emily feverishly tapped her finger against the side of her thigh as she listened to her father recount the less glamorous parts of their family's history. Emily looked back at the stairs. *Where in the hell are they? Every time I need my children to do one thing right, they do everything wrong. I am not going in there alone. Fuck facing mother's firing squad alone.* Emily needed her children to take some of the heat from the barrage of assaults in Delphine's arsenal. Emily clicked the heel of her shoe on the oak floor as she waited impatiently for her daughters. Her nerves were beyond bad, all of the tapping stopped her body from going into a full-blown shake. When Delphine was around Emily was reduced to her child self, anxious and stressed. Emily learned at a young age that a misplaced syllable, the wrong fork used, or a hair out of place could send Delphine into a rage. "Mistakes are for the stupid. Mistakes are for the stupid." Emily mumbled her mother's motto over and over as sweat pooled under her arms. "Don't be stupid. Mistakes are for the stupid. Don't be stupid."

"Momma, are you okay? You look sick."

"I'm not sick, Cora, I'm fine." Emily snapped at Cora and back to reality. "I would be better if you two hadn't come rushing down the stairs like a tribe of savages. How many times do I have to tell you two a lady should never be heard entering a room? Light as a feather on your feet, how many times do I have to tell you two? Glide in, don't storm in, this is not the Bastille. Even fat girls like you, Cora, can be light on their feet." Emily snarled. "What took you all so damn long to get ready? Because I don't see where the extra time went. Really, Cora, you couldn't find anything in that closet to make you look less fat?" Cora pulled her royal blue sweater down and folded her arms to hide her stomach. "At least pull your hair in front of your face, so it doesn't look so damn big. And you, if your skirt were an inch shorter, it would be slut modish. You two make me sick. You two do everything wrong. Wrong. Wrong. Wrong." Vivianna smirked then flicked her hair and showed how unfazed she was by her Emily's words. Vivianna enjoyed picking outfits that would provoke Emily. "You two can't do anything right. You two act as if looking presentable is some unattainable goal."

"Do you want us to change?" Cora stared at her shoes as she spoke.

"Do you want us to change?" Emily mimicked back. "No, I don't want you to change. I wanted you to do it right the first time. That's what I want. You're already late getting down here. I don't have time for you two to go upstairs and try to get it right. Just get in there and speak to your grandparents, be pleasant and don't say anything stupid. Remember no slouching, light on your feet; smile soft, and not overpowering. And don't forget to compliment your Grand-Mère."

"Do you want us to kiss the ring, too?" Vivianna mumbled under her breath.

"Shut up before I slap the words back in your mouth." Emily walked a couple of strategic steps behind her daughters. Vivianna and Cora knew to keep the plastic smiles plastered on their faces as they engaged with their grandparents. Cora and Vivianna sat on either side of their grandfather. They knew better than to sit in the chair next to Delphine.

"One or two, Cora?"

Cora's voice shook as she spoke. "Ma'am?" Cora kept her arms folded across her stomach as she pulled at the fabric of her sweater.

"Dress sizes, dear. You have you eaten yourself one or two dress sizes bigger since I last saw you. By the looks of your chins, I would guess two."

"I, I'm not sure." A burning knot seized Cora's throat.

"The only thing worse than a woman who overeats is a woman who doesn't know how much she overeats."

"Mother, I am always on Cora about her weight. I've instructed Mae to cut her portions. I even encourage Cora to skip meals. She's not allowed any snacks. I've told her more than once obesity is a sign of weakness. I've told her a woman in control of her figure is a woman in control of her life." Emily clasped her hands together as she stood with perfect posture.

"Well, maybe you should try saying it in a different language because the child looks like she doesn't understand English. Your French was never up to par, Emily, but I'm sure you could string together a few painfully executed sentences to get the point across to her. *S'il te plaît et merci.*"

"*Oui, Madame, je vais.*"

"All of those trips to Paris and you still sound like an American twelfth grader speaking French. I guess good schooling and world travel can't benefit everyone. Although it did wonders for your sister Josephine and her children."

Andre kissed the side of Cora's head and whispered to her. Cora couldn't help but smile as she looked down at her shoes and slid her hair behind her ear. Andre cleared his throat as the roughness in his voice carried across the room. "There is nothing wrong with a woman carrying some weight, Delphine. A man would much rather have a woman with weight who has a beautiful smile and a happy disposition than a twig with a foul attitude."

Vivianna struggled to smother her giggle.

"Emily!"

Emily snapped to full attention when she heard the shrill in her mother's voice. "Yes, Mother."

"Why does your daughter dress like her education came from standing on the corner instead of the best schools in the state? Working-class cheap is a look one should never aspire to achieve. It's clear to me you have been far too lenient with both these girls. By their looks it's obvious they have not been given the proper correction of motivation to do better. But your sister is the one who excelled at being a mother."

Emily glared at Vivianna to say something.

"Grand-Mère, so nice you're still here with us." Vivianna's telltale "I don't give a damn" look splattered across her face. "I would be so sad if you passed."

"Delphine, leave these beautiful girls alone. They are just fine the way they are. They couldn't be any more perfect if they tried. There aren't words in any language to describe how perfect they are."

Delphine threw Andre her wicked side-eye as she laced her words with sweetness. "Andre, I believe you're due to have your glasses updated because you have been overlooking what's obvious since we arrived. Emily, I don't see Jackson. Am I to assume my grandson will not be making an appearance? *Again*."

"The boy is at college trying to make something of himself. Jackson can't run back here to entertain you every time we show up. Isn't that right, Emily?"

Emily allowed a rare smile to form on her face. "Daddy, Jackson—"

"Emily, I don't like what you have done with the house. Everything is wrong. When your father and I left, I left you a house with everything in its place. You have managed to turn perfection into a habitat for a menagerie. It's clear you are entirely too lax with Mae. She needs to do a better job. I didn't spend all of those years training her for you to let her become languid in her old age. There's a piece of lint on the rug. These rugs aren't cheap, Emily. Lint should never litter them. I want the paintings and furniture oved back to where I had them. And you need to start training that girl of Mae's to take her place. You know those people don't keep themselves in the best of health. You need to focus on making the transition from one to the other as smooth as possible."

Delphine always spoke about the black people who worked for them as well as black people in general as if she weren't black herself. Delphine spent her entire life dismissing her culture. She made sure all pictures and references to ancestors darker than a paper bag disappeared from the family history. Delphine saw blackness as a curse, and she would have gleefully sold her soul to the highest bidder if it meant waking up a white woman the day after. "And as for college, when is this one going back? You thought I didn't know, but I know. You forget my brother is a trustee at your school."

"Soon, Mother. Soon. It's just a semester off." Emily tried to drown out her mother's critique in her head. Emily knew better than to utter anything but compliance and apologies while her mother explained everything that was wrong with her, her husband, and her children. As small and useless as Emily felt when her mother attacked every aspect of her life. Emily had no issue exacting the same level of hate-filled words and judgment onto her children, especially her daughters.

"Well, let's make sure it's just a semester. I don't need to tell you the trouble a young woman can get into when she has too much time on her hands. And the next time I come to visit, Emily, Quincy will make himself available to greet me upon my arrival. Do you understand me, Emily?"

"Yes, Mother." Emily's tone fell flat and worn. The cycle of destructive abuse by the women in the family was always on full display when Delphine descended on them. The men picked up on it and fled to higher ground when they could, while the women, numb to the cruelty, were conditioned to perceive it as love. "Is there anything else I need to fix, Mother?"

"Yes. Your appearance is downright nauseating. I see where the girls get their lack of dress. Please do yourself a favor and burn that outfit when you're done wearing it. My eyes ache from looking at the fabric pattern; the cut is completely wrong for your figure. Your hairstyle is working against you. It does nothing to enhance your flat expression. You need to trim your nails back; they are long enough to be considered claws. And you should do a better job of staying out of the sun. We are a lot of things, Emily, dark is not one of them."

"Yes, Mother. Is there anything else, Mother?"

"For now, no, but I'll have a detailed list before I leave. You have made it abundantly clear to me you are in need of detailed direction as if you were still a scandalous twenty-something." Delphine smirked as she glanced from Emily to Vivanna.

"Delphine!" Andre hissed. "Catch your mouth before it runs away from you."

"You're right, Andre, I should stop. Furthermore, what would a family be without secrets? Isn't that right, Emily? Foolish, foolish secrets." Delphine savored the misery she poured all over Emily. "Don't stand there looking lost. Do something right and pour your mother a glass of cognac. And not the common stuff you serve your guests. I want the good stuff that you keep hidden in the back of the cabinet. Don't act surprised that I know where you keep the good spirits."

"What!" Delphine snapped at Andre.

"Nothing, I'm just a little shocked you waited this long to climb into your first bottle."

Delphine snatched the glass out of Emily's hand. "Andre, with all the exterior doors in Lakeland, I would hate for you to feel you couldn't walk out of one of them."

~ * ~

"Damnit, Cora, don't drop crumbs all over my bed."

"Sorry. I could barely eat at dinner. I swear Grand-Mère was counting every time my fork brought food to my mouth. She makes me so nervous. She's worse than Mamma."

"And don't wipe them on the floor either. Put the crumbs in the damn napkin. Grand-Mère is a dried-up wretch and nothing more. I don't know why you let her get to you. Just ignore her like I do. When she starts talking, I sing a song in my head. It drowns her right out."

"Easy for you. Grand-Mère doesn't attack you the way she attacks me. Anyway, what do you think Grand-Mère meant when she said Momma made foolish mistakes?" Cora swallowed her turkey on rye hard. "I mean, don't you think that was an odd thing for her to say?" Cora had mastered the art of talking with a mouth full of food.

Vivianna looked at Cora through her large dresser mirror. "Don't know. Don't care." Vivianna hunched her shoulders as she applied blush to her cheeks. "It's probably nothing. You know how Grand-Mère is, she'll say anything to get a rise out of anyone, and when she drinks she says a lot, and it means little. How Papa has endured her, I'll never know."

"Vivianna." Cora's eyes widened. "You shouldn't talk about our grandparents that way."

"Why not? I bet they don't even do *it* anymore."

Cora's laugher ran away from her. "Gross. How can you think about of grandparents having sex?"

"I don't, but the truth is the truth and we both know I'm telling the truth."

"Yeah, but it's still eeewww. I prefer to think of them as unisex."

"You have a point. It is kinda of gross to think of either one of them that way but especially Grand-Mère." Vivianna shook her head back and forth. "I don't apologize often, but I am sorry for bringing grandparent sex up."

"Yeah, you think. Back to the original point I was making, did you see the look on Momma's face when Grand-Mère said what she said? Momma fell two shades lighter from the comment. So you know it means something. Momma doesn't just fall silent." Cora spoke with a full mouth. "Even Papa reacted to what she said, and Papa normally doesn't react so hard to what Grand-Mère says. I'm telling you, Vivianna, there's something there."

"Well, I'm sure like a piece of pie you'll sniff out what it is. Cora, don't give me that look. I'm just playing, and you know it. I'll be nicer to you but I'm not going to treat you with kid gloves just because you're thick in the thighs. Hell, you're not an infant you know. You don't need to eat every two hours." Vivianna spun around on her black pumps. "So, how do I look?"

"Like always." Cora rolled her eyes.

"What does that mean?" Vivianna's slammed her hands on her hips.

"It means perfect. You always look perfect. Happy now, I said it."

Vivianna widened her smile. "I knew it. I just wanted confirmation."

"Of course you did. It's getting late, Vivianna, will you be leaving out of the front door? Or making your usual escape through the kitchen?"

"Will you be eating in the kitchen when I get home?"

"Whatever." Cora pulled herself off of the bed.

"Just make sure if Momma asks where I am you tell her I went to Shelia's to study."

"Study what? Did you forget you took the semester off?"

"Then tell her I have cramps so I went to bed early. Better yet avoid Momma all together for the rest of the night. That way you don't accidentally say the wrong thing. I need you to cover my story, *again*. Please. No cape needed."

"Fine."

~ * ~

Vivianna took her shoes off as she crept down the hallway to the kitchen. The last thing she needed was to bump into her mother or worse, Delphine. Vivianna exhaled when she reached the secluded kitchen. Vivianna slipped her heels back on and wiped her nervous hand sweat on her skirt.

"Now where are you running off to this time of night, young lady?" The soft voice startled Vivianna as she reached for the knob.

"Momma Mae, I thought you had left already." Vivianna glanced at the plain kitchen wall clock. The time, two after seven, reminded Vivianna of what Raymond said he would do if she wasn't at his truck no later than seven thirty.

"I'm on my way out now. I always stay late when your Grand-Mère is here. The visit goes a little smoother when I do a little extra." Mae pulled her red coat with the faux fur collar on as she walked towards Vivianna. Mae was one of those women who seemed to walk onto the

24

planet possessing a lifetime of knowledge. Mae was slightly taller than Vivianna. She had a thick, fit build. Mae kept her shoulder-length brown hair pinned up, and her dark brown eyes had a way of looking at a person and finding all their hidden truths. Mae's chocolate skin was velvety, smooth, and flawless. Her soft, natural beauty had a way of drawing people into her. She was a woman who even well settled in her late forties, almost fifty, needed no makeup. "Now, back to my question? Where are you going at this time of night, young lady?"

Vivianna's face burned with guilt. Her voice was low and quiet. "I'm just going to study."

Mae arched her brow. She never had a problem seeing through any of the kids' lies. What they could do effortlessly with Emily and the rest of the family they couldn't pull with their Momma Mae. "Study?"

"Yes, Ma'am." Vivianna's voice shook. She valued Mae and her opinion more than she did her own mother's.

"Are you sure?" Mae looked at Vivianna's bookless hands. "A semester off and you're still going to study. Studying for what, child?"

"Everything, Ma'am. Just trying to review everything so I'm ready for the upcoming semester. Shelia offered to review some things with me. She goes to the college in the city. See even though we go to different schools we're the same major, and the work is the same everywhere." Vivianna kept her eyes focused on the ground. She could feel her lie getting away from her.

"Okay, then. Come walk me to my car." Mae linked her arm with Vivianna's. "You know something?" Mae kept her voice low. "I know you're not going to study."

"Ma'am." Guilt laced Vivianna's response.

"You children always seem to forget I've been your age, which means I also know the only thing that would have a young lady willing to risk her hide and disrespect the rules of her parents' house like you're doing is a man. You know your mother would tear you apart if she caught you out like this. Remember the bind you were in when she caught you with the Ellis boy?"

"Yes, Ma'am."

The sound of the pebbles echoed as Vivianna walked Mae to her car. The cool breeze lingered over Mae's words. "And what type of boy is this that you have to sneak around with him anyhow? Why doesn't he come to the door and introduce himself? Boys who are raised right introduce themselves."

"Momma Mae, it's complicated." The door on Mae's old Cutlass made a loud squeaking noise as Vivianna closed it. Mae continued her conversation through the rolled down the window.

"There is nothing complicated about the truth. It's the lies you tell that make the truth complicated."

"Yes, Ma'am."

"Now, where are you meeting this young man?"

"At the end of the road, Ma'am. He picks me up at the gate."

Mae handed Vivianna a disproving stare. "At the gate, you young people today. Out here just any old kinda way. Get in."

"I'll walk."

"No, you'll get in right now. Or I'll march you back in the house and tell your mother what's going on. Age wise you may be grown, young lady, but you still have a lot of growing to do to be considered fully grown."

Vivianna felt her stomach drop to her toes as she slid into the passenger seat. There was nothing more than the stench of Vivianna's guilt and half-truths lingering between them as the journeyed down the estate road. Vivianna lowered her head as she had down so many times with Raymond when she saw the headlights approach. "Hold your head up, child. If you're not doing anything wrong, there is no need for all the ducking." Mae paused when she saw the familiar faded red Chevy pulled over on the side of the road.

"Okay, I'll see you later, Momma Mae. Thanks for the ride."

"No, young lady, you will sit right here, while I have a conversation with this young man." Mae recognized the tattered truck instantly.

"But—"

"But nothing. Sit still, child." Mae shook her head. "This boy." She mumbled in disgust as she slammed the car door.

Raymond casually rolled down his window when he saw Mae.

Mae didn't give Raymond the opportunity to speak. "Boy, what is going on with you? You know you don't have any business messing with this girl. My sister would have a fit if she knew what you were doing. You came down here because you said you were tired of the city life, not to stir up mess. Now, look at you, creeping around. Got her sneaking around. And picking her up at the end of the road like some loose woman. I know for a fact your Momma and Daddy raised you better than this. Boy, where is your act right?"

"Auntie Mae." There was a disappointed tone to Raymond's voice. "What are you talking about stirring up mess? I'm not stirring up anything, and I'm not messing around with her. I'm dating Vivianna. She's a good person, and I'm into her. Everything I do with her is on the right side. You know me. As for Momma, I think Momma would like her. What's the big deal? She asked me to pick her up here and I'm just following her wishes. There is nothing scandalous going on. Just honest dating. On my Daddy's grave, I swear."

"Swearing on the dead. Boy, I can't even with you. Ray, you know good and well these people aren't like us. These people stick to their own kind, and we stick to our kind. We aren't like them. Your Momma knows firsthand what happens when you mingle with these folks. No good comes of it."

"Well, maybe that's the problem, Auntie, we have all spent too long sticking to our own kind. Who comes from where shouldn't matter. It should be about the connection. Vivianna's got a lot of good in her, Aunt Mae. Her beauty is deeper than the outside, it's just that no one has ever expected her to be more than pretty. She just needs someone to show her a different side to life. She needs someone who is going to let her be more than debutante balls and stuck-up black-tie affairs."

"That is who she is. Who she was bred to be, that child's life was decided for her the day she was born. Vivianna is part of a family based on tradition, and you are not part of that tradition. She doesn't need you filling her head with nonsense about being more and seeing the world differently and being different. Then you up and leave her when you get tired of being here; her world is fragile, Raymond. Besides, you know you never stay still too long."

"Well, maybe she's what I need to keep me still."

"Raymond, I told my sister I would look after you."

"And you're doing a great job, Auntie. As a matter of fact, you're doing a better than great job."

"Boy, don't you sass me."

"No sass, I promise. I'm a grown man, I can look after myself. You and Momma worry too much. I'm not twelve anymore, Auntie." Raymond grinned. "Everything is going to be fine. I promise." Raymond's smile got even wider. "Have faith. Give it to God. Pray on it. Let me know when I say the line that calms your nerves. I could fake hum a spiritual if that helps."

"Boy, you're not too old for the switch." Mae glanced back at Vivianna then at Ray. "You two are going to drive me to an early grave with all the sneaking you two are doing. I don't have a good feeling about any of this, but you two are determined to be and me telling you not to is just a waste of my breath. I just hope you know what you're getting into with her. People who live in bubbles don't do well in reality."

"You worry too much, Auntie. Everything is going to be fine, and Vivianna will be better for it."

Mae made her way back to her midnight-blue Cutlass. Ray watched her lean in and say something to Vivianna. Vivianna paused and hugged Mae before she half walked, half ran to Raymond. Raymond couldn't control his smile as he watched Vivianna run towards his truck. Raymond leaned in and kissed Vivianna. Raymond couldn't get his fill of Vivianna. Raymond moved in closer and pressed his lips firmly against hers. Vivianna pulled back slightly and placed her hands on Raymond's chest.

"Why didn't you tell me Momma Mae was your Aunt?"

"Does it matter?"

Vivianna settled herself in a long pause.

"Does it matter?" Ray's voice had firmness in it. Raymond cut the engine off. "Does it matter, Vivianna, that my Aunt works for your family?"

"No. I guess not."

"You guess?"

"I mean no. No, it doesn't matter."

"Good." Raymond kissed her deeply. "That's good to know." Raymond started the truck and pulled onto the road. Vivianna wanted to question why he didn't tell her, but she didn't want to fight.

Chapter Three

"Where are we?" Vivianna looked out the window as the streetlights reflected against the night sky. "I thought you said dinner and a movie."

"Woman, see I knew I shouldn't have told you anything until we got there. Next time I'm going to stick to my original plan and not say anything. Now you have that look on your face."

"I don't have a look. I'm just saying this doesn't look anything like dinner and a movie. We've passed everything that looks familiar. I've never been on this side of the city." Vivianna and her friends traveled far enough into the city to seem slumming chic. They never had any desire to experience city life fully, and they always made a concerted effort to avoid the impoverished areas. The sight of urban life up close took Vivianna back. Vivianna wasn't naïve, she knew homeless and poor people existed; however, it was different being in an area where they lived. Vivianna's world of balls, private schools, and world travel significantly skewed her view of life. There was something oddly fascinating about the life Vivianna saw outside the window. Vivianna couldn't help but smile at the kids running and yelling down the sidewalk. Their clothes were well worn, a couple of the kids had holes in their pants, but the wild freedom in their eyes made Vivianna turn her head and follow them as long as she could. The kids had little and everything at the same time. They were kids experiencing childhood, not just existing in it until adulthood took over as she had.

Raymond shifted his gaze between the busy streets and the woman whom he had fallen in love with but still didn't have the nerve to tell her. Vivianna was unlike any woman he had ever dealt with; the look in her eyes told him she wanted more than the manufactured world her parents had created for her. Raymond never saw her as an over-privileged wild child whose parents had the means to buy her out of any situation she found herself in like everyone in her life did. Raymond saw nothing but endless potential in Vivianna. Raymond resigned himself to tapping into that potential and being her everything in the process. Raymond smiled as he noted the look on her face. "What do you see? What does it look like to you, my baby?"

Vivianna looked back at Raymond as she tried her best to sit in perfect debutante style, with her ankles crossed and her hands folded, resting very ladylike on top of her Chanel skirt. The jarring of the truck as it traveled over potholes was a stark contrast to the smooth ride of her father's chauffeured car. "Well, Momma would say it looks like those Negros are acting poor and classless. Showing their color, as Grand-Mère would say. Momma would also add they need to comb their hair and fix their clothes. Grand-Mère says appearance is above everything." Vivianna's Southern accent added a honey-laced sound to her ridiculous words. "Momma would say they are acting ghetto and need to stop. She would say children don't run, they walk, and yelling is for the uneducated."

Raymond threw his head back in laughter. The naïve way Vivianna spoke as if she wasn't the same race as the people she stared at out the window gave him a chuckle. Raymond swore to himself he would teach her to love the people of her race the way he loved being a Black man. "Those Negros," Raymond placed his hand on top of Vivianna's as he maneuvered through traffic, "those Negros, as you put it, aren't acting poor. Most of them are poor. Not all of them, but never the less most are. And poor or not most of them are decent people just trying to get through their day. Kids are supposed to be loud. They are supposed to be dirty from playing outside and running everywhere. But I didn't ask you what your mother and grand-mère would say. I ask you what you saw." The long pause let Vivianna know she wasn't going to get out of answering.

"I don't know. It's all a lot to take in at once."

"Well, not knowing is something we need to work on. Your mother and grand-mère are entitled to their opinion, however, you need to make sure you always have your own opinion even if it differs from theirs or mine for that matter. Always have your own mind, Vivianna." The sound of Raymond's thick velvety voice made Vivianna tingle. She could listen to him recite the alphabet and get turned on. Vivianna stared down at his hand on hers. Raymond softly rubbed her knee.

Vivianna stared at Raymond's hand. She was still amazed at the contrast in their skin tone. There was something about the way his dark chocolate skin contrasted against her beige skin that she found daring and dangerous. Raymond was everything her mother had warned her against being attracted to in a man. Raymond was dark-skinned, a proud Black man who was completely unapologetic about being black. Raymond was the complete opposite of her past boyfriends and not just in looks. Raymond's refined working-class common sense made him an intellectual giant in comparison to her last boyfriend. Raymond just seemed to know how to get through life. Vivianna's previous boyfriends only knew how to rely on their families. Vivianna learned early on that her usual spoiled 'I get what I want' and 'you do as I say' attitude followed by her pouting wasn't going to get her anywhere with Raymond.

Raymond pushed Vivianna's long light brown hair away from her face. "Baby, you know they are just like you, just people living their lives. Their clothes are old, and their homes aren't as nice as yours, but they are still people. Never let having more void your humanity."

Vivianna pulled her hair forward again. The way her mother had trained her to wear it.

"Leave it back. I like being able to see your face."

"Momma says it needs to be forward. To cover the scare on the corner of my hairline." Vivianna's voice trailed. "I had on those little patent leather shoes. And I slipped running in the foyer and caught my head on the corner stairs. Momma wore y behind out when she saw the bruise. It healed, but it never lightened back up. Momma says stands out too much and it draws the wrong type of attention. Momma gave me cream to lighten the scar when I was old enough to use it, but it burned, so I stopped." Vivianna stared back at him with a quiet sadness. "I learned the hard way children should walk and not run."

"Well, when you with me I want your hair back behind your ear. I like that tiny scar. It's part of you. Perfect like you. Besides, there's nothing wrong with having some darkness on you."

Vivianna's cheeks burned with embarrassment. Raymond's skillful way of throwing in a sexual pun always caught her by surprise.

"I've never had anyone see my imperfections as perfections." Vivianna quickly changed the subject. "Momma says we're not Negros because we're English, French, and Creole on both sides of the family and my great-great-grandmother on my Daddy's side was half Black Hill Indian. Momma considers us displaced Anglo-Saxons. She always said we would be full English and French if it weren't for those few slavery era indiscretions, which caused our bloodline not to flourish to its full potential."

"That's an interesting way to describe the enslavement of a people and the rape of the women. Is that why you have been so hesitant about introducing me to your family? I look too slavery era like?"

"Sorry. I shouldn't have told you any of those things. Talking about Momma my mouth got the better of me. I can't imagine how all of it sounded to you. You must think my family is horribly foolish. It's just we pride ourselves on certain traditions. I'm sorry."

"No need to apologize. I suspected. Baby, I've been in the South long enough to see the time warp some people are delightedly stuck in. I'm glad we have gotten to the truth, *finally*. There was no need for you to keep it from me. The whole light skin dark skin thing was here before us and unfortunately will linger on after us. If Black people cared about each other the way some of us obsess over skin color and hair texture, things would be different for all of us. One day you and I are going to have a conversation about what being Black means and self-hating ideas. But not tonight, tonight is about doing dinner and a movie the Raymond way."

"Where are we?" Vivianna couldn't hide the shock she felt as the pickup come to rest in front of a withered and wasted apartment complex.

"My place." A broad full-toothed grin rushed across Raymond's face as she exited the car.

Vivianna was still in somewhat a flustered state as she got out of the truck. In three months, she had never been to Raymond's place. They always went out and made do in the cab of his truck if things went that far, which they usually did. Vivianna jumped a little when Raymond closed the door behind her. "Raymond, is it safe? There are a lot of—"

"Baby, you're fine. The only thing that is going to happen tonight is that you're going to have fun my way." Raymond guided Vivianna towards the door. Vivianna noted everything from the graffiti on the walls to the hum of the lights in the hallway and the hiss made when they flickered. The lack of airflow created a stale aroma that assaulted Vivianna's nose. Phone numbers, more graffiti, and crude drawings of body parts littered the elevator walls. The slight shake in the elevator made Vivianna move closer to Raymond.

"You're fine."

Vivianna was utterly taken back by Raymond's apartment. She had never experienced a living space so small before. Milk crates held countless books and albums. The makeshift table constructed of cinder blocks and plywood; the old sheet thrown on top held papers and few seeds he forgot to wipe off. The sofa, an odd shade of burnt gold with washed-out cream-colored flowers engulfed the farthest wall. The tiny television with a hanger antenna sat on a small folding table. There were also several photographs in cheap frames, which Vivianna assumed were his family from Chicago. Vivianna gently brushed her foot across the horrendous low-end brown-colored carpet. Vivianna couldn't get over how the noise outside competed with the voices she heard in the hallway. Raymond threw his keys on the table and ushered her through the tiny living room, and down the narrow hall. The constricted entrance made Vivianna feel big. Vivianna could hear the toilet running behind the bathroom door as Raymond guided her into the kitchen. Raymond couldn't help but smile with pride over his place.

"It took a couple of months for me to settle in but it finally feels like home."

Oh, God. He considers this homey.

Vivianna sat on the green-colored kitchen chair with a jagged tear in the plastic seat. The rip irritated the back of her leg. *Please don't let my skirt snag.* Vivianna snatched her hands off of the tiny matching green and silver table when it wobbled under her pressure. Vivianna folded her hands in her lap. She watched Raymond pull out the frying pan. The book on the table drew her attention away.

Vivianna read the title out loud. "Who's James Baldwin?"

"You don't know who Baldwin is?"

Vivianna shook her head. "No, is he new?"

"New?" The disbelief in Raymond's voice was undeniable. "Baldwin? No baby, he's not new. I'll add him to the list of authors and books I think you should read."

"I noticed you have a lot of books. You must really enjoy reading?"

"Yep. I'll take a book over TV any day. You can never read too much. Unless the Bears are playing, then damn all the books. So, you really can't cook." Raymond looked back and smiled at her.

"No. Momma Mae is in charge of our meals. I can make a sandwich in a pinch. Why do you cook? Didn't you have—I mean. Sorry, I'm being rude again. One of these days I'll learn to catch my tongue."

Raymond chuckled softly. "No, Sweetie. We didn't have a Momma Mae. We have an Auntie Mae. And I had a momma who made sure we all learned how to cook. Everyone helped out because everyone wanted to eat."

As cramped as the kitchen was, the cleanliness and organization of it impressed Vivianna. Things may have been old and worn, but everything functioned smoothly. Vivianna couldn't get over how easily Raymond moved around the kitchen, and how good everything smelled.

Raymond bent down in the refrigerator. "I've got beer and more beer. Which one do you want?"

Vivianna giggled. "I think I'll take a beer."

"Good choice." Raymond poured the domestic beer into a plastic convenient store cup. Raymond paused and watched her sip. Vivianna held the cup as if she was holding a crystal glass. Her lips barely touched the rim of the cup as she took small controlled sips.

"What? Is there something on my face?"

"No, I just like watching you."

"Why?"

"Why not? You're fascinating to watch. And I don't mean your beauty. Don't get me wrong, your beauty can stop traffic fine. I just really enjoy watching how you move. The way your eyes light up when something excites you or the way you curl the corner of your lip when you're trying to figure something out."

Vivianna's cheeks burned.

"And that right there. The way your cheeks redden when I talk about you drives me crazy. I've loved watching you from the moment I met you."

~ * ~

"Man, please. I don't even know why you're looking over there. Ain't none of them going to give you the time of day. Especially the one who looks damn near white. What we need to do is get out of here and go to that new spot down there on Third where the ladies don't know how broke your ass is," Clarence said with a loud chuckle. Clarence and Raymond became instant friends when he relocated. Clarence got on Raymond's last nerve but if Raymond needed to bury a body Clarence would help, no information required.

"Just because she ain't gonna talk to your ashy ass doesn't mean she won't talk to me. If she didn't want to talk, she wouldn't have looked over here at me, twice."

"Man please, I'm not out here looking for nothing. I got my woman. I'm out here trying to school you. Help you find somebody. Somebody you actually have a chance with because light skin ain't here for you."

"Oh, I have a chance with her. Trust me I have a chance. You see how she keeps looking over here."

"Because you probably look like a mutha fucker who tried to sell her a fake gold watch on the corner or some bullshit like that." Clarence smirked.

"Man, fuck you."

"Truth hurt too much."

"Whatever." Raymond finished off his beer.

"I bet you five dollars she ain't gonna talk to you."

"How in the hell are you gonna bet me five when you borrowed ten to come out with me tonight? And still owe me forty."

"Damn man, why you gotta talk about my money like that? I'm

going to get you your paper when I get paid."

"You said that three paychecks ago." Raymond let out a huge laugh as he nudged Clarence. "You know I'm just busting on you, man. Tell you what if I get her to talk to me you have to wash my truck for a month."

"Truck. What truck? Oh, you mean that piece of junk that's being held together by two bolts and a timing belt."

"It got us here, didn't it? And if you don't like it next time, we'll take your ride."

"See you think you funny, but you just talking ignorant. You know damn well my ride ain't running right now."

"Exactly, and you're talking about schooling me. Just watch me do what I do. And take some notes so you can step up your romance game with Bernice."

"Whatever. Just remember that's my brother's shirt he let you borrowed when she throws her drink at you."

"What are you smiling about, Baby?"

"Thinking about the night we met. You looked absolutely beautiful and absolutely out of place at Harold's that night." Raymond let out a huge laugh. "What made you pick Harold's anyway?"

Vivianna curled her lip. "I didn't. Remember the one with the big teeth, Shelia? She chose it. She bet we couldn't be average for an evening. I almost didn't go."

Raymond slid the fried chicken on the plate next to the mashed potatoes and peas.

"Ray, it smells so good. I can't wait to eat. I'm so hungry I picked at my plate at the house. It was some strange thing only Grand-Mère likes to eat. Your chicken smells better than Momma Mae's but don't tell her I said so."

"If I ever bump into her when I come to pick you up, I'll be sure not to tell her."

Awkward silence swept into the room. "I know. I'm going to take you by the house. I promise."

"When? We've been together three months. And the only reason why you haven't met my people is because they live so far away. But trust

I'm in the process of making that happen."

"It's complicated."

"No, it ain't. It's real simple, I show up and you introduce me as your man. Simple. You're nineteen and a grown woman by law, they can't have a whole lot to say."

"You think that way because you don't know the Harrows. How come you've never taken me to Momma Mae's house? I mean she is your aunt. How come you never told me? I'm sure she has mentioned us if not to you then around you."

Raymond paused. He too had secrets held close to him. "Look, we're not going to get into this tonight. But we are going to get into this later. I've got the plates. Do me a favor and grab a couple of more beers the movie is about the start. Come on."

Vivianna look confused as they left the apartment. "Where are we going?"

"The roof."

~ * ~

Several couples occupied the rooftop, but the only ones Vivianna knew were Clarence and Bernice from the one time they doubled. The different conversations overlapped each other and created a delightful harmony.

"It's about damn time you two got there. Damn, I was about to start without you. Shit. Nothing worse than colored people who can't be on time. Colored folks will show up two hours late to their momma's funeral and get mad folks started without them." Clarence's fumbling with the projector mixed with his curse words.

"Man, please. On time, early, or late, it doesn't matter because you still wouldn't have that thing up and running."

"Don't pay him no mind, sweetheart," Bernice yelled as she elbowed past Clarence. "He got paid today, so he's really feeling himself." Bernice was a short, plump woman in her early twenties with bulging soul-filled black eyes and a gap between her perfectly shaped teeth. "You two come over here and sit by us. I'll introduce everyone to you. Oooh, look at all that pretty hair." Bernice ran her hand through Vivianna's hair cascaded down her back. "Oooh girl, you've been blessed with some hair."

"Thank you."

Vivianna followed behind Bernice. "Baby," even when Bernice spoke in her normal voice, it sounded like a yell, "I want you to get me a wig like her hair." Bernice's wig collection could rival any high-end wig shop.

"Damn, woman, I just bought you a new wig last month. I'm not buying you another one. You're going to wear what you have. Now don't bother me. You see me trying to make this movie work."

"So, what's that got to do with me? Last month is last month. I want one like her hair. I mean it, Clarence, you'd better get me a wig like her hair or you're gonna find your ass loving on yourself instead of me."

"Woman, please. The only thing you'll be denying me is a decent meal." Clarence chuckled. Clarence had a loud style of dress and an even larger personality. He never ran out of reasons to have a good time. "She had the nerve to boil the chicken she gave me the other night for dinner. Can you believe that, man? And if that wasn't bad enough said she put lemon on it. Lemon? What black person you know who puts lemon on chicken? Lemon is for ice tea and cakes. Said she was trying something new. I told her don't bring any of that white people mess back here to my house. You leave that at the job with those tired potlucks." Clarence continued to struggle to get the film to feed through the small opening on the projector. Clarence was the head janitor at the Edward Mills High School, and every other weekend he would *borrow* a projector from the school and whatever film he could find. For the couples that met on the roof every other Saturday, it was a cheap way to have a dinner and a movie.

"I was trying to broaden your horizons."

"My horizons are fine where they are at. Just keep my chicken fried, the lemon in my tea, and everything will be fine between us." Clarence snapped the case for the film closed.

Raymond made sure Vivianna was comfortable sitting next to him in the folding chair. Vivianna couldn't help but be taken in by everything going on around her. She reveled in how lively everyone was. The talking and laughing were loud and beautiful at the same time. Nothing this energetic ever happened at Lakeland. Yes, there were celebrations, but Lakeland's manufactured fun and laughter was very contained and controlled.

"Ask her. I know she is."

"You ask. Damn, you're the one who wants to know." The two women in front of Vivianna and Raymond argued in a loud whisper.

"Fine, but I bet you she isn't her."

The slender of the two women spoke. "Do you know a woman named Mae?"

"Yes." Vivianna's eyes lit up. "She has been the housekeeper at Lakeland since before I was born. How do you know her?"

"She and my Momma go to the same church. She talks about you all a lot. She brought some of your old clothes to the church so some of the girls going to college would have a couple of nice things to take with them," the woman with the short Afro said in a small voice.

"Oh." The brief conversation reminded Vivianna that she was different from the rest of them.

Raymond sensed Vivianna's discomfort, so he kissed the side of her face to reassure her. He leaned back and yelled at Clarence. "Hey man, hurry up with the movie. And it better not be that 'this is your body' shit."

"I know you aren't co-signing on what Ray just said, Bernard. You need to be thanking me. Your ignorant ass needed that movie more than anyone here. Now you can stop looking confused every time another baby pops with your last name."

There was a loud roar of laughter.

"Man, shut up. You just mad because I get women like that." Bernard's thumb and middle finger made a loud pop when pressed them together.

"Oh, I ain't mad. Just confused how someone as ugly, and ashy as you can convince women to sleep with your narrow behind. And at the rate you get women you're gonna catch something besides child support papers if you don't slow down." The laughter overwhelmed the roof. "Now let me take my foot out your ass so I can start this move. I got the hook up this time. *Canadian Wildlife.*"

A collective groan reverberated through the night air.

~ * ~

"Cora, where is your sister? Your Grand-Mère wants to talk to her."

Cora immediately stopped practicing when she heard her mother's harsh tone as she marched into the formal sitting area. Cora had been in this position too many times to keep count.

"I'm not sure. But I'm sure Anna's here somewhere in the house, Momma." Cora kept her eyes focused on her plump hands. Cora swallowed hard and prayed her mother would take the answer offered and leave her alone. The knot in her stomach reminded her that her mother wasn't that type of woman. Cora's eye twitched when she was stressed, which was more often than not.

"Cora!" Emily snapped.

"Vivianna's asleep. She, she said she had cramps. She has cramps. She told, told me." Even though it wasn't Cora's fault when Vivianna went out, Emily always made it Cora's fault. An army of men would have fallen under the weight Cora carried on her shoulders. Cora kept her eyes down; she knew if she looked up Emily would see through her horrendous attempt to cover up Vivianna's latest forget permission and damn forgiveness adventure. Emily stepped closer and placed one hand on her hip and used her nails to tap the top of the prominently displayed Steinway Piano.

"Who is he?"

"Momma, I don't know. I mean, what do you mean? I, I, I don't, don't know. He who? Maybe she's in the den reading? Did you check? I don't, don't know." Cora's voice quivered as she forced her words out. Cora could feel her body tremble.

"Cora, look at me." Emily's perfect smile had an evil undertone to it as she locked eyes with her daughter. Emily gently grazed the side of Cora's cheek. Emily had long fingers suited for a piano but never played a day in her life. "Don't play with me, young lady. You and I both know the rugs in this house lie better than you ever could. Vivianna stayed at the dinner table long enough for you to shovel food in your mouth and then the two of you scampered off. Did you forget your sister despises your fat ass almost as much as I do? She would never be around you unless there were something in it for her. So, unless reading is slang for spreading your legs for the idiot of the month, we both know your tramp of a sister isn't somewhere reading. So, what's this one's name? With any luck, he'll be an upgrade from the schoolteacher's son. I'm starting to think your sister lowers the bar on her conquests just to piss me off." Emily casually flung the lid to the piano keys closed. Cora pulled her hands back as she had done so many times. It only took once for Cora to learn to be on the ready when she was at the piano and her mother was near.

"I, I, I," Cora's hands shook. "I don't know, Momma, I don't know his name. I ssswear." Cora's childhood stutter flared up. "I dooon't don't know. I just know she shhhe she went to see him tooonight." Cora exhaled hard, closed her eyes and tried to remember the techniques for controlling her stutter. "I promise."

"See," Emily held her daughter's chin, "I knew you could answer my questions with the right motivation. You start moving your fat ass as quickly as you moved your fat hands and we'll find you a husband closer to your age than mine by your next birthday."

Cora's silent tears rolled down Emily's hand.

"Tears, Cora. Really, how many times do I have to tell you tears are like kindness? They are overrated and completely pointless. Now you are going to waddle your ass to the kitchen and remove the key from under the mat. And when you're in the kitchen tonight eating your weight in food, don't you dare let your sister in. Do you understand?"

Cora moved her head just enough to show compliance.

"Good. Now get out of my sight."

"Just like I thought. Emily, you still have absolutely no control over your family. Your children run around here like wild animals on the prowl. The way your children act makes me think I should move in for a while to get everyone straightened out. Six months should be all I need to get everyone acting right. Motherhood, another one of your failures."

"Mother, I don't need any help raising my children. I have

42

everything under control."

Cora kept her eyes to the floor as she pulled her sweater down and left the room.

Delphine gulped the last of her scotch. Delphine's words possessed a slight slur. "I see you still believe the lies you tell. Your household is in shambles and reeks of dysfunction. Your children are an utter disgrace, nothing like Josephine's children. Some whales weigh less than Cora. Vivianna is a one-woman brothel. The stories I've heard about her could fill one of those tacky slut novels." Delphine searched her glass in vain for a lingering drop of scotch. "Still making payments to *that girl's* family Jackson got messed up with." Delphine scoffed. "Really, who in the hell forces themselves on a darkie. That girl was so dark she made midnight look light. Your reckless son just had to play in a mud puddle." Delphine fell back into her usual chair.

"Are you done, Mother? Or is there ore about my life that displeases you?"

"I haven't even started." Delphine stretched her withered finger towards Emily. "Your father may overlook your bullshit, but I don't." Emily focused on the way her mother's thin finger swayed. Emily couldn't remember Delphine ever using those fingers to embrace her and show her affection or kindness. "I see every misstep you make. I'm starting to think you don't have it in you to do better. Wrong, everything you do is wrong. Wrong. How hard is it to keep your home in order and raise respectable children? And that last one, she's the worst out of the three. It's like you took all of the worst parts of yourself and turned them into a person. But what can I expect from someone who has made the careless and reckless decisions you have, Emily? You actually thought what lays between your legs was going to make that man leave his wife for you. No wonder your daughter is the way she is. She took right after her mother." Delphine slammed her glass on the side table. "What a damn fool you were. Hell, you still are. You are just a damn fool. An utter disappointment."

Emily traced the lace runner on the piano with her finger as she spoke. "You never miss an opportunity to remind me of my mistakes do you, Momma? Too bad you don't see the flaws in Josephine the way you see them in me."

"Josephine doesn't make mistakes, unlike you."

"If she's so damn perfect, why didn't you give Lakeland to her instead of me?" Emily took a defensive stance as she stood in front of her mother. "Why isn't she here having her life analyzed under your microscope? Why aren't her husband and children picked apart and judged? When is the last time you've ever seen the great Josephine or spoken to her greatness on the phone, Momma?"

"Josephine has a life."

"You're right, Momma, Josephine does have a life. And it's a life that doesn't include being bothered by her mother. Josephine goes out of her way to avoid you. Trust me, Momma, Josephine's not as busy as she tells you. Henry's parents are always at her house. Why is that, Momma? You and Daddy have only been to her home a handful of times, but her husband's parents are always at her house always spending time with their kids. Her precious, perfect children you always put above mine. Did you know that Henry and Josephine went away for two weeks? Two weeks, Momma. And you know who watched the children while she was gone last summer? Henry's mother, Momma, she had full run of their house. The only time you see your messiah daughter is where she descends on Lakeland for Christmas. And when she's here, she barely speaks to you."

"You're talking like a fool." Delphine started on another scotch. "Why are you so jealous of your sister? It's not her fault she excelled in everything you didn't. Josephine never gave me a moment of trouble. But you."

"Josephine didn't stick around long enough to give you trouble. At eighteen she was gone, and I got stuck with the mother who thinks sobriety is a dirty word."

"Who do you think you are judging, me? You don't have any right to judge me. How dare you judge me? Especially when you have never played coy around a bottle of booze either. Or a man for that matter. I drink, but I'm not a drunk."

"Who do you think taught me how to handle a bottle of scotch, Momma? Taught me to manipulate men? I didn't walk on the planet acting this way. What you're looking at is decades of being Delphine's daughter staring back at you. You are the reason I'm the way I am. Look at me, Momma, I manipulated a man who was in love with someone else into marrying me. I had children I didn't want to keep him from leaving me. I made sure I always put on the air of being a happily married wife and mother. I always present well in public as you commanded. I did everything you ever asked of me. I never wanted any of this, I wanted to go to college. I wanted to travel. I wanted more than this. But instead, I'm here living under your constant disapproving glare. It's like you come here to torture e. To remind me of all the different ways I'm flawed. Will you ever find me good enough, Momma?"

"You know what your problem is, Emily? You blame me for everything wrong in your life. Your family is failing and you need someone to blame, and that's me. You need someone to be jealous of, and that's Josephine."

"No, Momma, that's not true. I'm not concerned about Josephine or anything she does, the only time her name comes up is when you throw her in my face. And you, Momma, I'm just tired of you." Emily slid onto the sofa.

"You're tired of me." Delphine's voice grew. "You're tired of me. Were you tired of me the night you came to me and begged me to take you to Mae's mother so she could make the *thing,* as you put it, growing inside you disappear? Answer me." Delphine's shrill echoed off the walls. "Were you sick of me then, Emily. Remember how you begged and cried. How you pleaded for your Momma to make everything better. You weren't sick of me then were you, Emily? Answer me, Emily. Were you sick of me then?"

Emily's tone and posture shrank under the weight of her mother's rant. "No." Emily bit down on the inside of her cheek. Emily had used the pain of her flesh in between her teeth as something to focus on besides her mother's relentless harangue since she was a little girl.

"No what?" Delphine sneered.

"No, Momma, I was not sick of you then." Emily's voice submitted to defeat.

Delphine knew the one event in Emily's past that would humble her and force her to repentant quicker than a preacher getting caught with a hooker. "Damn right you weren't tired of me because you needed me. Needed me to clean up your mess because you were the dumb bitch who thought that white man was going to leave his wife for you. You actually thought he was going to pack you, Cora, and Jack up and run away and make a new life with you, just because you were stupid enough to get pregnant with his child. How many times did I tell you, fairy tales are for the ugly and the poor because they give hope to the hopeless. You traded your dignity for that man. You went to his office and graveled at his feet. And what did he do? Tell me, Emily, what he did?

"He told me to leave." Emily's voice was barely above a whisper.

"I want to hear you say it louder."

"He told me to leave!"

"Edward please, you said you were going to leave her. You said she didn't make you feel the way I did. You said you loved me." Emily stood in front of her lover's desk. Emily studied the cold look on Edward's fair-skinned face. She didn't understand the distance he was putting between them now. Emily's face glistened from the exasperating humidity which filled every inch of his office. "Eddie, please say something. Say you love me. Say we're going to be together. Please."

Edward Waller was a judge who believed real power isn't found in who you locked up but in who you let go free. Edward loosened his black tie and rolled the sleeves on his starched white shirt. Settled in his late middle-age years, Edward wasn't particularly handsome, but he had charisma and a fast talking mouth. Those qualities gave him the ability to captivate any woman who wasn't his wife. Waller could charm the panties off a nun, and the town gossip swore he did once. "It's Judge Waller to you, Mrs. Harrow."

Emily's heart crumbled. The only time she ever called him judge was during playful foreplay. There was a nastiness attached to the way he said Mrs. Harrow. Emily rushed to the side of Edward's chair and fell to her knees. Tears littered Emily's face as she grabbed at his arm. Emily had no issue with trading her dignity for Edward. "Why are you doing this to me. You said you loved me. More than once you said it. Why are you treating me this way? Where is all of this coming from? Why are you being so cold? You said we were soul mates. I'll do anything, anything, just ask me and I'll do it." Emily gulped hard. "We can leave, run away like you said. I'll even leave Cora and Jack. It will just be you, me, and the baby."

"Leave, darling, please. I'm not going anywhere with you. Darling, I said whatever I had to see those pretty little curls of yours and play with those nipples." Edward's malevolent smirk crushed Emily's spirit. "I also said among other things you were the best blow job I've ever had. When actually you were the second best. Little dark thing over in Edwardsburg with lips the size of a watermelon was the best. But I said what I had to say keep your lips on my dick." Edward snatched his hand away from Emily's and handed her a tissue. "It's not my fault you took the bedroom talk literally. While I love that thing, you do with your hips, I really do, I'm not going to sacrifice the life I've created to have you do it again. This thing between you and me ends today. My three boys are the only kids I will ever want or acknowledge. If you have any sense in that pretty head of yours, you would quickly get rid of that thing and go on with your life before it's too late. I know a woman. She used to clean house for my sister. She'll be very discreet. She deals with your type all the time. I can give you fifty dollars to put towards it considering everything going on. But that's it. That's all I can do for you, Mrs. Harrow."

"My type? What's my type?"

"Why, loose colored gals who prey on white Christian family men like myself."

Emily stared into Edward's cold blue-eyed stare. Emily lost all hope when she couldn't find an ounce of compassion in the eyes of the man she had spent the last six months sneaking around with and risking her reputation and marriage to have. Emily stood up slowly and smoothed down the front of her blue flowered dress. Emily swallowed hard as the reality of being nothing more than a piece of ass sunk into her consciousness. Emily wanted to hit him, she wanted to rip his hair out, she wanted to leave scratches on the side of his face. But Emily knew no matter how light she was or how much money her family had the court system would throw her under the jail for attacking a white man. Emily snatched her purse and gloves off of the chair, she was too ashamed to say anything else.

Edward stood up and grabbed money out of his wallet. "Wait a minute now. I meant what I said about the fifty dollars. "

"He gave you what twenty dollars? Shoved it in your hand like a whore. Because that's what you were to him. A twenty-dollar whore."

Emily's voice trembled. "Fifty."

"How much? Oh, I'm sorry, was it ten?"

"Fifty. It was fifty dollars. I didn't keep it either. I threw it out the window on the drive home."

"That's right, fifty. Spread that out over the six months, and you spread your legs for him for about a dollar or two a fuck."

"If you say so, Momma." Emily's voice weathered even more.

"And after all the tears and the begging you did to me, him, and Mae's mother you still didn't do what was necessary to make it go away. Now she walks around acting like a three-dollar whore making a complete fool out of you and disgracing this family. I don't know who the bigger fool is, you for not getting rid of her, or your husband for pretending she's his. As if that was going to prevent her from being an ill-gotten idiot like her mother."

"He wouldn't have had to pretend if I hadn't been forced to marry him. I didn't love him, Momma. Quincy wanted someone else. And we all know it. He loved someone else, but you had to intervene and manipulate things. And not for me I might add but for yourself. You whored me out long before I chose to have my affair."

"Whored you out, girl, please. You are so damn dramatic I see where Vivianna gets it from. If I were whoring you out you would have been in a brothel. Which hindsight being what it is, who knows, maybe it would have been better because clearly you don't understand the way things work. Love, Emily, is something else for the poor and the ugly. Wealth and status aren't created and maintained because two people fell in love." Delphine snorted as she walked back over to the liquor cabinet. Delphine filled her glass past the acceptable level for scotch. "The family was having a trying time financially and securing us financially was the least you could do, considering all of the money spent on your private schooling along with the money invested in balls, etiquette classes, riding lessons, hairstyling, and the clothes. I gave you the best of everything, and

48

I deserved a return on our investment. So, if you had to marry a man you didn't love in order to keep not only our family's status intact but also you in the lifestyle you are more than comfortable in, then so be it. So be it, Emily, because the last time I checked no one can live off of love. Do yourself, hell, do both of us a favor and cry one last tear about it, grow up and get the fuck over it. Life isn't about what you want or what makes you happy it's about survival, and you can't survive off love or any of that other bullshit they put in Hallmark cards."

"Quincy didn't want me, Momma. He didn't want me."

"Neither did Eddie Waller but that didn't stop you from screwing him."

"What do you want me to say, Momma? Tell me what I need to say to get you to stop throwing Waller in my face. Is it 'I'm sorry?' Fine, I'm sorry. I'm sorry for all of it. Sorry for keeping her, sorry for not being a better wife and mother. Sorry for not being Josephine. Sorry for every mistake my children have ever made."

"Save your pathetic apology. I will never allow you to forget the mistakes you have made. Everything you have done has been a reflection on me. And frankly, I'm tired of having to smile and endure the whispers behind my back. People judge me based on the blunders of you and the rotten branch you added to our family tree."

"Fine, Momma. I need to do a better job of reflecting you to the world. But you will never understand what you did to me, Momma."

"You still don't get it. I have no desire to understand. I care about my family name and the legacy that is left behind. And nothing more."

Cora stood stunned with her back pressed against the hallway wall. She knew she should have ignored the argument between Emily and Delphine but the desire to hear her mother being taken down and put in her place outweighed her good sense. Cora's emotions went from joy to disgust to regret. Cora wished she could un-hear all of the nasty things said. Along with all of the other issues Cora had with being oldest, her weight, she added first-hand knowledge of the generational nastiness and secrets that plagued her family to her list of issues.

Chapter Four

"I guess I'll take you home after I finish cleaning the kitchen." Raymond's voice possessed a hint of discontent as he crammed the freshly washed pink flower-patterned plate into the crowded dish rack.

Vivianna nervously paused before she spoke. "What if I told you I'm not ready to go home? That I want to stay longer." Vivianna looked up at Raymond. There was something about the way the evening played out that took away Vivianna's rush to return home. She had never experienced that level of laughter and fun before tonight. By the time the film had ended it was nothing more than background noise for the lively conversations that had taken place all around her. Once Vivianna had relaxed and allowed the concoction she drank out of a large Mason jar to take hold she flowed effortlessly between conversations about hair, makeup, and men. The level of fun Vivianna had on the rooftop seduced in her a feeling of not wanting the night to end.

Raymond rested against the counter. "So, what are you saying, Vivi?"

"I'm saying I want to wake up next to you." Vivianna positioned herself between Raymond's legs. A wave of nervousness washed over Vivianna as she pressed herself against Raymond. Vivianna couldn't understand why Raymond just stood there casually looking at her. Vivianna wasn't used to a man's hands not instantly being all over her after she offered herself. "Unless you don't want me to stay?"

"Oh, I want you to stay. Please believe me when I say I want you to say. I'm just trying to figure out why the sudden change in the routine."

"I just want to stay, that's all. Why are we debating this?" Vivianna playfully toyed with the button on his shirt. "I thought this is what you wanted."

Raymond raised Vivianna's chin so her eyes locked on his. "Yes,

I want you to stay. Yes, I want to wake up with you lying on my chest while I push your hair back softly and listen to you breathe. But I want to make sure—" Raymond stopped Vivianna from rubbing her body against him. He knew if she kept moving the way she was he would forget everything he needed to say to her. "Make sure you're staying for the right reasons, and it isn't the stuff Janice had you drinking that has you talking like this."

Vivianna stood on her tiptoes and placed her lips just in front of his. "I feel really good, yes. The stuff she gave me tasted so good. But that's not what has me wanting to stay. Trust me, I know what I'm saying and what I want to do."

Raymond took a long pause. He debated whether to take it further or not. The sight of Vivianna undressing in his kitchen made him find his resolve, quickly. Raymond's bulge pressed against his zipper as Vivianna playfully licked her lips as she slid out of her clothes. Her skirt made a soft hushing sound as it hit the floor. Vivianna teased him with every button she undid. The closer she got to her breast, the slower she moved. Raymond relaxed even more against the countertop. He wanted to drink in the entire show.

"Are you gonna just look or are you going to come play with me?" Vivianna's tongue picked through her lips as it grazed the bottom of her front teeth. A soft moan escaped from Vivianna's lips. "Please." Vivianna's groans grew as she played with her molded nipples in between her fingers.

"Leave them on." Raymond growled when Vivianna tried to slip out of her heels.

"As you wish," Vivianna oozed in a seductive tone. Vivianna had no idea how hearing her say those words turned Raymond on; Raymond had to remind himself to go slow. Vivianna removed her red lace bra with ease. The ache in his pants demanded he do more than stare. Vivianna sucked in a small breath as she peeled her matching red panties off. The coolness in the room attacked her wet womanhood as it sent a shiver down her spine. Raymond took two large steps and towered over her soft and wanting body. "Tell me what you want me to do."

"What?" There was a hint of embarrassment in her voice. No man had ever made Vivianna explain what she wanted sexually. Vivianna had always taken off her clothes, and things just went from there.

"Don't get shy with me now."

"I'm not shy. I just figured me taking my clothes off told you everything."

"Mmm-mmm. I don't just want you to show me, I want you to tell me what you want me to do to you." Raymond molded her left breast in his hand. Vivianna let out a soft moan as he kneaded her light brown nipple between his thumb and index finger.

"I want you—" As a gasp rushed past Vivianna's red lips, the pull Raymond placed on her nipple caused her to lose thoughts. The level of electricity pulsing through her body was something she had never felt before. The pulsing ache of Vivianna's wetness matched the rhythm of her heart slamming against her chest.

"Tell me." Raymond smiled as he tugged harder. He loved how the mixture of pleasure and pain left her at a loss for words. "Tell me, or I'll stop."

"No, please don't stop." Vivianna lost her thoughts as Raymond bent down and replaced his hand with his mouth. Raymond's mouth was magical. He knew the exact amount of pressure to apply as he played with her nipple in his mouth. "I want you to make love to me."

Raymond slid his other hand in between her legs. Vivianna pooled almost instantly when he moved his hand up and down the side of her entrance. Vivianna dug her nails into his shoulder. It was the only thing she could do to keep her balance. Raymond toyed with her damp curls as he made his fingerers traveled to her nub that radiated white-hot heat. Raymond used his thumb to massage her soft nub. Vivianna's moans grew with every pass. She flowed between English and French as she expressed her passion. "You mouth says make love, but your body wants something else. Say it. Tell me what your body wants." Vivianna's moans transformed into reckless breathy screams. Her climax was moments away from being her reality. Vivianna tensed every muscle in her legs; she was desperate to remain standing. "Say it." Vivianna bit the inside of her lip. Her mind was still reluctant to say the words her body begged her to say. Raymond removed his hand from her breast and moved it down to her backside, the contrast between the softness of her cheeks and the callused hands erotic as well. Devouring them would have to wait. Raymond laid a playful smack on her left cheek. That was new for Vivianna, and she instantly wanted more. Raymond grabbed her cheek like a man holding on for life. This time his words were less sensual and more rough. "Say it. Say it now." The heat from the mouth on the side of Vivianna's neck removed any shyness that stood between her and the words Raymond wanted to hear. "Fuck me. Fuck me. I want you to fuck me." Vivianna splashed her essence over Raymond's hand as she screamed her demand.

"I knew you wanted more than to make love." Raymond swatted Vivianna on her backside again. "Don't lie to me. Always tell me what you want."

Vivianna groaned her compliance as Raymond knelt down in front of her. "Yes. Yes." The pleasant smell of Vivianna's womanhood danced on his nose. Vivianna dug her nails into his shoulders as Raymond dragged his tongue from her entrance to the soft nub that rested above it. Raymond flicked his tongue back and forth over Vivianna's nub with his tongue. He blew softly over it in between the flicking. The breeze running across her clitoris caused Vivianna to gush her sweet salty fluids. Raymond felt Vivianna's thighs shake as he sucked harder and harder. Vivianna's head spun; she forgot which way was up as her mind went numb. Vivianna braced herself against Raymond. The more Raymond licked and sucked the harder Vivianna dug her nails into him. Vivianna came apart when Raymond thrust his tongue into her and drank every ounce of sweetness. Raymond felt her insides spasm twice before he dragged his tongue up her body and to her mouth. The taste of herself in Raymond's mouth made fluids pool between her legs again. "Now I'm going to fuck you." Raymond wanted to tease more but his desires overroad his original scheme.

Raymond tangled his hand in her tresses and filled his fist with her soft wavy curls. Raymond pulled her head back and devoured the soft curve of her neck. He was going to leave a noticeable mark on her light-colored skin, and neither one of them cared. Raymond could have left them up and down her neck and she would have proudly worn her hair in a ponytail the next day. Raymond removed his mouth from her neck long enough to clean his fingers off before he wrapped his arm around Vivianna's waist and pulled her up on his waist. Vivianna naturally locked her legs around him. Vivianna instantly slammed her lips on his. The taste of herself inside of his mouth turned her on even more.

As small as Raymond's apartment was, he decided the several extra steps needed to make it to the bedroom were too many. Raymond positioned Vivianna on the ill-colored sofa. The softness of the crushed velvet tickled against the slight sting that lingered from Raymond's previous swats. Raymond never took his eyes off of her flawless body as he removed his clothes and shoes. Raymond felt a brief moment of relief when he released his manhood from his blue jeans and boxers. The intense pressure that formed at the tip of his rod reminded him he needed to do more than drop his drawers to find satisfaction.

Vivianna couldn't hide the amazement in her eyes as she ogled Raymond's full manhood. Seeing it in full view as he stood before her was different than viewing it while having sex in the cab of his truck. Vivianna felt it grow in size the longer she stared, and the closer he came to her.

"You're staring."

"I know."

"You want it?"

"I want all of it."

Raymond moved with possessiveness as he positioned himself between her legs and placed himself at her entrance. Raymond used his ample lips to part Vivianna's mouth and captured her tongue with his as he crashed through her entrance and filled every ounce of her. Raymond couldn't wait a moment longer. Vivianna almost came apart from the pleasure she felt from him being inside of her. Raymond gave a couple of shallow thrusts before he moved his hips in a way that honored the request Vivianna shouted in the kitchen. The secondhand sofa squeaked and shifted under the power of Raymond's thrusts. When Raymond removed his lips from Vivianna, she let out a bellow of pleasure that was almost primordial. Vivianna couldn't force Raymond's name and screams out of her mouth fast enough. Her voice grew in volume every time she yelled his name.

"Well, someone's having a hell of a night," the female voice in the hallway uttered with amusement.

"You're just mad it's not you," a different female voice said.

Vivianna instantly lowered her moans. Raymond grabbed the side of her face sensually. "Don't you dare go quiet on me." His voice was as labored as hers.

"They can hear me in the hall." Vivianna had to force herself to concentrate on what she was trying to say.

Raymond deepened his thrusts. "I don't care if the whole building hears us. I want them to hear." Raymond wouldn't allow Vivianna to break his powerful stare. Vivianna dug her nails deep into his shoulders as she wrapped her legs around him. The pullout was not an option tonight. Vivianna felt herself reach the point where her breath quickened and the thoughts in her head blurred. Every movement of her hips was in response to the hastened thrusts of Raymond's. Vivianna's walls tightened and pulled Raymond deeper inside as his climax followed seconds after hers. Raymond plunged several more times into the depths of Vivianna. He didn't want to stop but his body had no more to give. Raymond laced her lips and face with barely-there kisses as he collapsed on her. Vivianna wiggled her body softly under his to remind him of the differences in their weight.

"Sorry." Raymond moved Vivianna's body around on the shabby sofa, so her body was lying halfway on his. Vivianna kicked her heels onto the floor. Raymond kissed the top of her head as he whispered. "Are you still okay to stay?" Vivianna nodded her response as she dozed off. "Do you want to go to the bedroom?"

"I'm fine right here." Vivianna's words were barely above a faint whisper.

~ * ~

"Where have you been? It's almost ten!"

"Emily, don't start. It's late, don't start." Quincy threw his suit coat on the chair.

"Don't start what? Asking questions? Don't ask my husband what took him so long to get home?" Emily folded her arms across her chest. "It must be nice to show up when you feel like it and have no accountability. Except to whomever you were with. Meanwhile, I'm here trying to hold this household together."

"No, don't you dare act like I've been doing something you know full well I haven't been. You know I've never done what you are suggesting. I've never acted the way you have, Emily. You know if I'm not here I'm one of two places, and neither one involves sharing a bed with another woman." Quincy shoved his hands in his pockets as he stood in front of their king-size bed with the large columns for bedposts. "Don't sit there glaring at me. If you want to say something, damnit, say it. You're determined to start with me so let's go. Say it."

"Your daughter's not home. She snuck out and is doing God knows what with this boy Cora told me she's been seeing. I needed you here to help me deal with things earlier, and you weren't here."

"Deal with what? There's nothing to deal with, Emily. Why are you acting like Vivianna not being home is news? It's not news, and it's nothing to panic about. Vivianna has been sneaking in and out of the house and doing whatever with whomever since she was sixteen. We have yelled, threatened and punished and nothing has gotten through to her. Vivianna is not going to change until she's ready to change, which could be tomorrow or could be never. I don't know which but I'm tired of trying to figure it out. There is nothing Vivianna and Jack do anymore that shocks me. If we were talking about Cora instead of one of those two, then I would be stunned and concerned. Hell, I'd be in a complete panic if we were talking about Cora. But we're not, so stop with the high drama concern. Vivianna will show up when she shows up. All we can do is hope this semester off allows her to get the last of her wild ways out so she can finally start to grow up. What else? I can tell by the way you're acting there's something else. Me coming home late or Vivianna running the streets doesn't provoke you like this."

"You weren't here when Momma arrived, Quincy. And I had to hear about it, among other things."

"There it is, your mother. I should have guessed Delphine was at the core of your sudden breakdown. Emily, I had no intention of being here when *your* mother showed up, and if I can help it, I won't cross paths with Delphine the entire time she's here. Which hopefully won't be past the weekend. You know this is how we do things." Quincy undid his tie and shirt collar as he spoke.

Emily slammed her book down on the bed. "I'm so tired of all of you doing whatever you all want to do while I suffer through holding everything together. Quincy, you know you are supposed to be here when Mother gets here. You know how she likes things. You know it falls on me when things aren't right. I'm tired of making excuses for why you're not here when she arrives."

"Then don't, Emily. Don't hold shit together, let it all fall apart. Tell your mother the truth. Tell her how I can't stand her over pertinent, *Gone with the Wind,* Old South, my family has lineage ass. Tell her how the sight of her makes my balls itch, Emily. Tell Delphine I said she is the only woman I know who can make a rigor mortis dick go limp. Tell your mother whatever the fuck you want about why I wasn't here to greet the dried-up black Scarlet O'Hara. Why I will never be here to greet her. But don't you dare tell me I'm supposed to be here when the crusty debutante shows up to take stock of the financial mess I salvaged. As for Vivianna, like I said, she's going to do what she is going to do. I'm done chasing behind our daughter trying to save her from herself. She's nineteen; hell, damn near twenty, legally she can do whatever she wants. Ask yourself, Emily, is your concern for Vivianna or merely for how Vivianna might make you look? Your silence tells me the answer. Listen, I've had a long day, and I'm exhausted. Do I need to get a hotel room or can I get undressed and go to bed in peace?"

Emily placed her book on the nightstand and turned her side light out. Emily slid the lavish cream-colored bedspread over her shoulders and moved as far as she could to the edge of the bed.

"Thank you." Quincy mumbled as he finished undressing.

Emily allowed her tears to quietly fall as she drifted off to sleep. It was a ritual Emily indulged in almost every night. Quincy knew tears soaked his wife's pillow but neither one cared enough about the other anymore to stop them from flowing. In a way, they both resigned themselves to staying stuck. Quincy distanced himself from Emily after Delphine's liquor-infused outburst exposed her affair. But when he looked down at Vivianna in her fragile state moments after her birth and still recovering from lack of oxygen, he knew he couldn't abandon Vivianna. Quincy made sure he gave enough in the way of a presence so his children had a male presence in their lives and he made enough of an appearance for Emily to give her the illusion of having a husband. For Quincy, the tiny bit of love that existed between them, in the beginning, was long gone. Their marriage was about tolerance and survival.

"If she's not home in the morning I'll make some calls. Someone has seen her. Vivianna doesn't wander too far. I'm sure she's fine. Now try to get some sleep."

"Thank you." Emily whispered through her broken tears.

Chapter Five

Vivianna engaged in a long stretch after the sound of a door closing in the hallway woke her from her deep slumber. Vivianna achieved a level of peaceful sleep sprawled across Raymond on his sofa like she never felt laying across her plush mattress. Vivianna moaned sexually and stretched again. Vivianna positioned her body so she was lying on top of Raymond. Raymond smiled as he opened his eyes. He loved the way she felt on top of him.

"Good morning." There was a mischievous look in Vivianna's eyes. Her wild hair gave her a playful look. Raymond felt his morning erection take control of the conversation.

"Come here." Raymond pulled Vivianna's head towards his. Raymond thrust his tongue into Vivianna's mouth. Raymond's kisses were more passionate and less demanding than last night. Vivianna enjoyed the feeling of her body molded to him. Raymond's manhood knocked against her. Raymond ran his hands down her spine and stroked the small of her back before he filled his hands with her backside. The sensation made Vivianna press her lips hard against his. Vivianna rocked her hips back and forth against him. Vivianna pushed herself up as she straddled Raymond and flung her head back as Raymond grabbed handfuls of her breasts. Vivianna pushed the word "yes" past her lips. Vivianna soaked Raymond's manhood with her nectar.

Vivianna's head fell forward onto his while she eased her body down his. Raymond's rod jumped when he thought about what she was about to do. Vivianna was unbothered by the stickiness that lingered from the night before. Vivianna didn't hesitate to swallow him. Raymond filled every inch of her mouth.

"Oh, my fucking god." Raymond moaned. He had never had a woman take that much of him at one time. Vivianna could feel him hitting the back of her throat. The deeper her mouth plunged down his shaft, the more Raymond cursed. Raymond knew if he didn't pull her out he was going to flood her mouth. Raymond pulled Vivianna up by her hair. Vivianna bit down on her bottom lip as Raymond shifted under her.

Vivianna moaned several times as she rocked her hips upward long enough to create enough space for Raymond to slide into her. Vivianna couldn't believe how Raymond felt harder and more prominent than the night before. Vivianna dug her nails into Raymond's chest as she rode him using long deep thrusts. She was in no rush to climax. Vivianna loved the empowerment she felt being on top. Vivianna tightened her thighs as she changed the movement of her hips. Raymond reached and grabbed a handful of her messy hair. The sensation of pleasure and pain turned Vivianna on even more. Raymond had a way of knowing what Vivianna desired sexually even if she didn't know. Vivianna kept the movement of her hips even and deliberate. The springs in the sofa made a light rocking noise as she moved up and down Raymond's long shaft. Raymond and Vivianna lost themselves in the oneness their slow lovemaking created. Vivianna gripped Raymond with a possessive prowess. His low grunts let her know he was more than pleased. Vivianna, caught off guard by her orgasm, let out a primitive erotic cry as she gushed all over Raymond. Raymond eagerly let go when he felt her satisfaction. Vivianna collapsed on his chest after he reached his climax. Raymond stayed inside her as he stroked the small of her back softly.

"I'm so glad you stayed." Raymond wrapped his arms around Vivianna. "Feels good having my Baby in my arms."

Vivianna nodded her agreement.

"I like waking up with you lying on me. It feels so good feeling your skin next to mine."

"I hope that's not the only thing that felt good." Vivianna blushed as she giggled.

Raymond squeezed Vivianna. "Trust me, baby what we just did felt better than good." Raymond laid sloppy kisses across Vivianna's forehead. "Are you hungry, baby?"

"Very."

"Good. We'll take a shower, and then I'll teach you how to make eggs."

Vivianna stared at Raymond with a question on her face. "You want me to cook? In the kitchen?"

"Yes. You're never too old to learn. Besides, anyone can learn to cook."

"We'll see how you feel about your 'everyone can cook' when the kitchen fills with smoke and the smoke alarm is blaring."

"It won't be that bad." Raymond swatted Vivianna on her behind. "You'll do fine. Let's go shower."

The steam from the shower fogged the mirror and created moisture on the small bathroom window.

"I think it's warm now." Vivianna giggled as Raymond nibbled on her neck, his hands positioned on either side of her as she rested against the bathroom door.

"I know."

"If we keep this up, it will be lunchtime before we eat anything."

"I know."

Vivianna's giggle was out of control now. "You are insatiable."

Raymond locked eyes with Vivianna. "You make me that way." Raymond pulled back the blue-and-white shower curtain for Vivianna. "You first," he said with a wink. Raymond slid in behind Vivianna. He couldn't resist kissing her neck as he reached for the bar of soap. Raymond lathered his hands and used them to massage the suds all over Vivianna's body. Raymond refused to let a washcloth come between him and his woman. Raymond lingered at the small of her back before he moved his hands to the front of Vivianna's body. What started as a light caress quickly turned into another orgasm for Vivianna. Vivianna pressed her backside against Raymond as her body became overwhelmed by the touch of his hands. It took a few moments for her to catch her breath before she spoke.

"My turn," she said in a half whisper as she grabbed the soap and faced Raymond. Vivianna loved the muscle definition Raymond possessed. Raymond casually leaned against the back of the shower as he watched Vivianna's soapy hands explore his body. Vivianna couldn't resist holding Raymond's manhood in her hands. Raymond watched

Vivianna's hand as it slid up and down his dark brown shaft. With every pass Vivianna made sure to caress the tip in a circular motion. Raymond closed his eyes when he felt his testicles tighten. There was no holding back; Raymond knew his release was moments away. Raymond clenched his jaw as seed shot through and splattered on Vivianna. Raymond opened his eyes after the last bit jerked free. Raymond looked down at the stickiness that dripped from him and Vivianna. "I guess we need to shower off again."

~ * ~

"Mae! Mae!" Emily stormed into the kitchen like a crazed woman. "Mae, where in the hell are you? The last thing I need is another inept person lingering around my house doing nothing. Mae!"

"Yes, Mrs. Emily." Mae wiped her hands on her apron. Emily's kitchen entrance didn't rattle Mae's calm demeanor.

"Where is she? Have you seen her?"

"Who, Mrs. Emily?"

"That little wench. She—" Emily paused at the distraction. "Again, with this child at my table. My home is not a daycare, Mae. It's my home." Emily flung her hand in the air as if she was waving a fly away. "If you can't find a sitter, find a backwoods for that child to play in while you're here. I don't want her lingering around my house like a bad cold anymore." The little girl with the thick braided ponytails and glasses slid even further behind her book when Emily glared at her. "Are we clear, Mae?"

"Yes, Mrs. Emily. Please accept my apology. I must have misunderstood when Mr. Quincy said my grandbaby was welcome to come with me from time to time."

"Oh, he did? Well, Mr. Quincy and I will be having a long chat about his hospitality."

"You were looking for someone, Ma'am?" Mae kept her voice calm and controlled. Mae didn't want to give Emily anymore to add to her rant. Mae knew her tranquility was essential to temper Emily's manic moments.

Emily hissed her frustration. "Yes, my daughter, and I don't mean the fat one."

"I haven't seen Vivianna."

"Figures. Mae, I want you to keep the back door locked. When my daughter decides to bring her lowly ass home, she can ring the front doorbell like a guest. Do not let her in this door. Do you understand, Mae?"

"Yes, Mrs. Emily. I'll tell her to go around to the front if she comes to the back door."

"Oh, she's going to come to the door. You just make sure you don't open it for her." Emily pointed at the little brown girl. "Last time, Mae, last time."

~ * ~

Raymond and Vivianna stayed in the shower until the water ran cold. They couldn't get enough of each other. Every time they finished one would brush against the other. Then one light touch would quickly develop into endless sensual touches and a climax that was stronger than the last. Even drying off turned into a quickie against the bathroom wall. When they were both entirely spent, Raymond and Vivianna made their way to the kitchen.

"Do you like it?" Vivianna sat with her legs tucked under her body as she nervously toyed with the middle button on the blue flannel shirt Raymond gave her to wear.

"You did good. The eggs taste like scrambled eggs, and there was only a little bit of smoke." Raymond threw Vivianna a reassuring smile as he played off the piece of eggshell he bit. Vivianna couldn't control her smile. She felt very accomplished.

"I'm glad you like it. Baby, could you do me a favor?"

"Anything thing, Baby, just ask. You know I'd do anything for you."

"Could you drop me off at the door? I don't feel like walking up the drive."

"It's morning. Someone might see us."

"I'm pretty sure someone will. I'm not ready for the big introduction, but if it happens, it happens. I don't want to hide anymore. Like you said the other night, if we're not doing anything wrong, why are we hiding?"

"And you're sure about this?"

Vivianna nodded her response.

"Then it would be my pleasure to take you home and drop my beautiful lady off at the door."

"Thank you. Nothing would make me happier than to have my handsome man drop me off at the front door."

~ * ~

"There you are. I've got some things to go *over* with you right now." Delphine snapped at Emily and gave no regard to the conversation between Quincy and Emily as she barged into his office.

Emily immediately refined her posture to suit her mother's high expectations. "Momma, Quincy and I are in the middle of something. Can you give us our moment, please?"

"No, I will not give you a moment, young lady. I have some things to say, and you're going to listen to me on my time, not yours. If you two are talking about Vivianna, I've already made some calls to try and find her. She's not at any of the usual places you have had to drag her out of. I'll arrange for someone to go out and look for her. Emily, you need to do something about this girl immediately. She needs to be put in her place. The child is running around like a savage, and it's not okay. She's making you look bad, and that's a reflection on me. I might not live here anymore, but I still have a face I need to maintain in the community. People expect better of my grandchildren. Not coming home. What type of daughter did you raise? I have been more than patient with the way you raise Jack and the fat one, but this. This is too much, I cannot and will not look the other way on this." Delphine huffed as she paced around. "What civilized person acts the way she does? I'll tell you what kind. No kind of civilized person conducts himself or herself in the manner Vivianna does? I can only imagine the caliber of boy she has probably taken up with and what she has allowed him to do to her. A small private all-girls' college in the middle of nowhere would do her some real good. It's hard to run after boys when there aren't any for miles. And if that doesn't work there are always convents. Those nuns will have her straightened out in no time. They'll beat the wildness out of her if they have to, unlike you. How many times did I tell you, you were too soft on her? I see my granddaughter heading in a direction I do not approve of at all. We are not common, Emily. And I will not allow her to conduct herself in a common manner."

Quincy toyed with the pen in his hand as he sat behind his massive wooden desk and didn't try to hide the look of disgust on his face. "Stop with the bullshit concern, Delphine. You care about Vivianna being a better person about as much as I care about you." Quincy tapped the pen on the desk in a rhythmic manner.

"Quincy, stop."

"No, Emily, I'm not going to stop. You mother is out of order. Delphine, Vivianna is our daughter and we will see to finding her. Emily and I will get to the bottom of where she is at, and if punishment is needed, we will decide that as well. You will stay completely out of all of it. That means no more phone calls. You're not arranging for anyone to find her. If and when we decide to send our daughter somewhere you will have no say. You are Vivianna's grandparent, not her parent. You're also not going to pull my wife aside when I'm not around and demand she does things your way. And my other daughter's name is Cora, not the fat one. I don't want to hear you refer to her in that vile way again. Do we have an understanding?"

"Your daughter. Your wife. Really, Quincy? Who do you think you're talking to? You have been almost nonexistent around here. You have given very little in the way of parental guidance. Hence Jack's actions and the fat one's weight."

"I'm warning you, Delphine. Tread lightly when you speak of my family."

Delphine squared her shoulders up as she faced Quincy. "Your family? Really, Quincy. Interesting how you put the word 'your' in front of daughter as if we don't all know the truth about *your* daughter. You are no more that child's father than God is Emily's."

"Momma, please."

"Don't please me, Emily. You want to please something. *Please* fix me a drink."

"It's early even for you, Delphine." Quincy sneered back. Quincy tapped the pen harder on the desktop.

"Tell me something, Quincy, was my daughter your 'wife' when she was screwing Edward Wallace?"

"Yes, Delphine, she was. The entire time Emily and he were together she was still my wife. And the point you are so desperate to make is?"

"The point is, Quincy," Delphine slammed her hands on her hips.

"Don't bother to finish your answer, Delphine. Your daughter made a choice and while I don't agree with what she did I made a decision to not only stay but to also raise Vivianna as my daughter. Period. So, I would appreciate if you would stop bring up the past as if it's new gossip. The past around here is viscous like your drinking."

Delphine snatched the glass of single malt scotch Emily quietly passed her. "Next time less ice."

"You know, Delphine, in all these years I've only seen Andre take in the occasional social drink. I wonder what his secret is? I mean, how has he managed to stay married to you and not match your drinking glass for glass? Maybe it's a testament to his character, or maybe it's because a passion for the spirits doesn't run in his lineage. I never had the displeasure of meeting your father, but I've heard the stories. Hell, everyone in our circle knows of Cairo's infamous ways. Your father is a damn legend among the pimps, gamblers, and prostitutes. Delphine, do you think all the boozing and whoring Cairo did drove your mother to her psychological collapse? It must have been a real chore getting her blood off of the floor. Whatever happened to the rug she bled out on? Oh, I remember, your father put it under the piano. Guess your daddy couldn't bear to throw out a good quality rug. Or maybe he enjoyed it being there. It reminded him of how he successfully got rid of his wife without using divorce or murder. I mean, why else would a man keep the rug his wife slit her throat and died on? The whole thing is rather macabre, if you ask me. But I guess that's how your people do things."

"Quincy," Emily stated in a loud whisper. "Quincy, stop. Please stop. We don't talk about these things."

Delphine glared at Emily.

"Don't crumple your crusty panties any more than they already are, Delphine. Emily didn't tell me anything. I knew the twisted tale long before the introduction of Emily and I, but I know you're wondering how I found out? Who do you think let that nasty story get out, Delphine? The undertaker maybe? Did your daddy not give him enough to keep quiet or did Daddy's check bounce, leaving old man Randall with no obligation to keep quiet? Or was it one of his whores? Your daddy didn't know when to stop the pillow talk. And when he was good and liquored up, which was almost always, his mouth couldn't hold a truth or a lie. I shouldn't know anything and yet I know all the grisly details. Hell, most people in these parts know how your daddy left your momma on the floor for several hours after finding her to make sure she was dead. It's been said your family doesn't do well when the dead rise. How's it feel to know that everyone who smiles in your face knows more about your family than you would like them to know? All of those stuck-up colored folk with the same counterfeit personas you have. So, they have no problem putting on a front and pretending that they don't know a thing. When they all know the truth. How they must laugh behind your back? Their perfect public smiles keep their family secrets buried deep. But their whispers at family events and charity balls make sure your family's twisted history is passed down to the next generation of pretentious idiots. So, the way I see it, Vivianna, even with all her antics, is a virginal saint compared to Cairo and his endless debauchery. Cairo stained up your family tree all by himself."

Quincy's pen slammed against the polished desktop and sliced through the silence created by his words. "And just like that," Quincy snapped his fingers, "the expired debutante goes mute."

Delphine knew her house had been constructed of the poorest quality glass and when stones shattered her windows, Delphine knew it was time to cease her verbal assaults. "Emily, let me remind you. Your father and I will be leaving early in the morning. There will be no reason to wake the children. But before then you and I are going to have a long discussion later about the things going on around here."

Quincy interjected more harsh words. "As long as your conversation doesn't include my children you can talk about anything you want with Emily. It's not like what you say is going to make a difference."

Emily bit down on the inside of her cheek. Her voice was barely audible. "Yes, Momma." Emily pulled at the stitching on her clothing the same way she did as a child. Emily sank back into the winged back chair as Delphine stormed out. Emily waited until she could no longer hear her mother's steps before she spoke. "Quincy, how could you bring grandmama up like that? I told you we don't talk about certain things. I wish you hadn't done that. Now I have to deal with her ranting and raving. It's bad enough nothing I do pleases her. I wish you hadn't said anything."

"And I wish your mother didn't make my balls itch but she does. I wish she didn't, but I can't seem to get what I want. Maybe after this last dressing down your cantankerous expired socialite mother has finally learned I'm not the one she wants to piss off. And finally backs off our children and us."

~ * ~

Vivianna rested her head on Raymond's shoulder during the journey back to Lakeland. Vivianna didn't tense as Raymond's truck made the trek up the long tree-soaked drive. Vivianna didn't care about anything except being with Raymond. Raymond placed his truck in park. What was supposed to be a quick kiss good-bye quickly turned into an impromptu mini make-out session.

Vivianna's breath labored as she spoke. "I gotta go, baby."

"I know." Raymond thrust his tongue back in her mouth. The bulge in his pants pushed against the zipper.

"I have to go." Vivianna barely forced the words out before Raymond's tongue captured hers. Vivianna giggled and pushed Raymond back. "No, baby, I really gotta go."

Raymond placed Vivianna's hand on his swell. "Or I could put the truck in reverse."

Vivianna's giggle grew. "You're bad. I have to go. Momma and Daddy will send a search party out if I'm gone any longer." Vivianna kissed Raymond again and whispered promises to him before she slammed the door shut. Raymond waited until she disappeared behind the ornate oak door before he made his journey back down the drive.

Cold shower, here I come.

Vivianna, consumed with a blissful love feeling and everything that happened the night before, didn't notice Emily glaring down at her from the window. Emily's blood boiled when she saw Vivianna draped over Raymond. Emily prayed her mother didn't see what she had just viewed.

Vivianna hummed as she bounced up the stairs and down the hall. For the first time in Vivianna's life, she felt as if her life made sense. Vivianna forgot she was a Harrow for a moment. Vivianna flung open the door to her room as if she had nothing to fear.

But the reality of being a Harrow caught up with Vivianna quicker than even she could have expected. Vivianna barely made it all the way into her room when Emily barged in and slammed the door behind her. "Have you lost your idiotic mind carrying on with that thing I saw you lip locked with, and in front of the house no less? In front of the house, Vivianna." Emily's yells transformed into an earsplitting shrill. "Who in the hell do you think you are? What if my mother had seen you? Had seen him? You know this is unacceptable, you are a Harrow. Do you hear me Vivianna, a Harrow, and you know what that means. How dare you parade that—that—that thing in front of my home. The help is probably gossiping right now. If this news ends up on the lips of the women in my circle, I will have your backside for it. It will take months for those bruises to heal, I promise you. Tell me right now, did you spend the night with him?" Emily shook as she spoke.

Vivianna scowled at her mother as her happiness faded. "He's not a thing. Do you hear me, Momma? He's not a thing, he's a man, my man and his name is Raymond. Raymond."

"How dare you. Your man." Emily snarled. "Please. I had to deal with your Grand-Mère last night and this morning because of this. How dare you call him your man? Because you were out there doing what I don't even want to think about."

"Okay, and Momma I stayed at Raymond's place last night. It's no big deal. I'm not a child. I'm just as grown as everyone else in this house. When Jack is here, he comes and goes at all hours and you don't say a word. You can't tell me when to come home."

"Leave your brother out of this. This is about you, Vivianna, not Jack. You mind your business when it comes to your brother."

"No, this is about Grand-Mère. If she weren't here you wouldn't care, and you know you wouldn't. We are all forced to suffer more than normal when Grand-Mère is here. The only person who cares what Grand-Mère thinks is you. Every time she's here you put us through hell for her. You can't tell me what to do, Momma. Like I said, I'm grown. I can do what I want, see who I want and come home when I want. You can't stop me and neither can Grand-Mère."

Emily closed the space between herself and Vivianna. Vivianna winced when Emily grabbed her arm. "The hell I can't. You're in my house. Not only will you come home at a respectable hour, you will never see him or anything that looks like him again. The last thing I need is you getting pregnant by something that looks like that thing. You're a Harrow, and it's about time you start acting like it. As for my mother, you leave her out of this. You could learn a few things from her."

"I handle my alcohol just fine. I don't need pointers."

Emily shoved her finger in Vivianna's face. "Watch your mouth."

"Or what, you'll wash my mouth out with soap? Sit me in the corner?" Vivianna locked eyes with her mother. The air filled with the stench of their hatred for one another. "Exactly." Vivianna rolled her eyes. "We both know you're just jealous because I have a man who wants to spend every moment he's awake with me, who cares about me and wants me to be happy. And you probably can't remember the last time Daddy looked at you, let alone touched you. And by your attitude, I'd say it has been several months if not years." Vivianna snatched her arm back. "Don't ever grab me like that again," Vivianna hissed. "I'm not Cora. Maybe if you and Grand-Mère worried about your pussies the way your two obsess about what I'm doing with mine those sour scowls wouldn't be splattered across your faces anymore."

Emily smacked Vivianna against the side of her head twice. The blows shocked Vivianna. Emily's hand shook as she struck Vivianna again. Emily increased the pain level with each swing. Vivianna tried her best to play off the searing pain sensation on the side of her head. Emily landed several more blows as Vivianna tried in vain to evade each one.

"I hate you!" Vivianna growled at Emily as tears pooled in her eyes.

Emily's voice was just as hate filled. "I don't care." If cold stares were all that was needed to take a life, there would have been a double homicide in Vivianna's bedroom. Emily snatched Vivianna up by her hair. Emily twisted Vivianna's hair around her hand twice to ensure Vivianna didn't shake free. "I will rip your heart out and eat it while I watch your cheap, lifeless body smack the ground if you ever speak to me that way again." Emily violently shook Vivianna by her hair like a farmer wringing a chicken's neck. "I gave you life, which means I own your high yellow ass. Even in my grave, I'll own you." Emily gritted her teeth. "Everything you have is because of me. You are nothing without me. And as long as I am the reason you live the lifestyle you live, you will submit to my every demand. Never forget I could bury your worthless ass out back and forget I ever pushed you out. You are y property. You will do as I say."

Vivianna couldn't hold back the flood of tears anymore. Only after Emily saw tears, she stopped jerking Vivianna's head. Tears were the white flag of defeat Emily craved.

"After you wash the scent of that lowlife off of you, you will change into something respectable, which means I had better not think I see your knees. You will apologize to your Grand-Mère for not coming home last night. You will lie and tell her you stayed over at Janelle's house. Even though she'll know it's a damn lie. We're all going to pretend it's the truth. You will smile. You will listen to her lecture you on what it means to be a part of our family. You will listen to her tell you about the importance of being a proper and virtuous woman. Then you will apologize some more." Emily clenched her teeth. "Afterwards, you will return to your room and stay here until I decided what the hell I am going to do about you. Do you understand me?" Emily balled her fist after the long pause. "I said do you understand?"

"Yes, Mother, I understand." Vivianna forced the word past her lips. "It's the Harrow way or no way."

"Good."

~ * ~

"I don't drink, but I'll take a glass of wine if you have a bottle on hand."

"Absolutely." Quincy poured Andre a glass of Merlot. Quincy grabbed his scotch and sank into the plush leather chair in his office across from Andre.

"Cheers. I see you spend a lot of time in here the way I did when I lived here. Or should I say when I existed here."

"There are a lot of advantages to being in here. It's easy for the fray to miss you when you're in here."

"I'll drink to that truth. I don't know if I ever told you, but you're a good man, Quincy. A good man." Andre took an extended pause before he spoke again. "It's not easy marrying into this chaos."

"True. But I chose to be here. And no matter what the rumor mill says, Andre, I have never cheated on your daughter. Emily and I may have our differences and things have been off more than on. But all that said, I wouldn't put her through that. I understand how fragile her ego is."

"And that's one of many reasons why I said you're a good man. I'm sure you already know, but I'm going to say it anyway. Delphine and I have been here long enough. So, I'm taking Delphine home in the morning. She's caused more than enough damage for one visit. Even for her, the last couple days have been extreme."

Quincy smothered a chuckle. "Sorry."

"No apology needed. No one knows better than me how hard of a pill my wife is to swallow. I thought in vain that leaving this place would soften her, but I think it has done the opposite. Every time we come back here, she falls into those habits. Those dysfunctional habits that have eroded away her family for generations, destroyed parts of their humanity. You want my advice, Quincy?"

"Please."

"Burn this place down, collect the insurance money and run. This place has a way of turning people into the worst version of themselves."

Quincy shook his head and scoffed slightly under his breath.

"But seriously, try to save your children before they self-destruct, especially Vivianna."

"I'm doing my best, Andre."

Chapter Six

Vivianna huddled on the bathroom floor with her knees drawn into her chest. She held her eyes shut and tried to block out the endless pounding on the bathroom door. Vivianna convinced herself if she stayed still everything would work itself out. The banging would stop; the strange feeling in her stomach and the truth about her body would disappear. Vivianna convinced herself stress over the past weeks was the reason she started every morning with her face in the commode. *I can't do this. I can't handle any of this. Stupid. Stupid. Stupid. How did I get in this? How do I get out of this?*

"Vivianna." Cora shouted over her incessant banging. "Vivianna, come on, you've been in there forever. Open the door. It's not fair, Vivianna. The past two weeks you've been hogging the bathroom more than you ever have. You're not an only child, Vivianna. Open the damn door."

"Stop acting like this is the only bathroom in the house, Cora. Go use another one."

"No. I don't care if we have forty bathrooms in the house. This one is as much mine as yours and I want to use it. Besides all of my stuff is in there." Cora violently shook the door handle. "I don't have to use a different bathroom. I have a right to use this one, and this is the one I want to use."

"Go away, Cora. Go the fuck away."

"No. Open the door or I swear I'm going to get Momma, Vivianna. I mean it. Open the damn door. I'm serious, Anna, I get Momma."

Vivianna crawled forward and unlocked the door. "There, are you happy now."

"What are you doing on the floor?"

Vivianna rolled her eyes. Vivianna couldn't be bothered with words. Her stillness was the only thing that kept her nausea at bay.

"Vivianna. Vivianna?"

"What? Leave me alone. You wanted in, I let you in. Brush your teeth and get the hell out. We both know you're not doing your makeup. Or combing—" Vivianna shoved her face back in the bowl.

"Vivianna, what's wrong with you?"

Vivianna heaved harder as she flung her middle finger in the air. Vivianna flushed and fell back against the tub as sweat beaded on her brow.

"You don't look good."

"Really? What gave it away, the vomit? Still, look better than you though. Vomit breath and all."

Cora wiped the cold cloth on Vivianna's face. "Stop it. Don't be an ass. I'm trying to help. Are you hung over?"

"Always to the rescue." The cloth soothed Vivianna. The few drops of water felt like nirvana sliding down the side of her face. She didn't realize how hot she was until the dampness washed over her face.

"Didn't I say don't be an ass? I can go get Momma if you would like a firmer, less caring touch."

"Sorry."

"If this isn't excess liquor, then what have you been eating you eat to make your stomach upset?"

"I didn't eat anything." The thought of food made Vivianna's stomach wrench as she reached for the bowl again. Vivianna gasp for her breath as she leaned back against the tub.

"Then do you know how many weeks are you?" Cora's voice had a sterile doctor-like tone to it. "Don't look surprised. I might be fat, but I'm far from stupid." Cora drew back slightly. "Anna, you know I've had sex before, right?"

Vivianna's eyes widen as Cora rested on her knees. Vivianna tried miserably to hold back her smirk. Cora gently smacked her sister on the leg. "My one conquest may not be as infamous as all of yours, but it's mine none-the-less. And before you say anything smart no, it was not in my dreams. And he wasn't deformed or recently paroled or mentally ill. I didn't have to pay him, and he wasn't blind either. He was nice. He said I was pretty. I liked the smell of his cologne. So, I figured, why not?"

"I hear you, Cora. I hear you. Did you love him?"

"I liked him well enough. For me, it wasn't about love. It was about getting it over with. I felt like, why am I holding on to my virginity? It's no big deal. The only people who are obsessed with virginity are parents and pastors, and most of them were doing it long before they were sporting wedding rings. Frankly, I find it creepy how they value and try to control something that doesn't belong to them. I wished they obsessed about me and worried about if I'm okay the way they are obsessed about the status of my vagina. Also, I didn't want to be the old virgin." Cora softly smiled as she thought about her first. "He was sweet about it. Patient. He made me feel comfortable and safe. It was okay, but definitely nothing like movie love scenes or what I read in romance novels. Just so we're clear, I don't feel one ounce of guilt about not waiting until marriage. Hell, the truth is I could be thirty before I'm married and I'm not waiting that long to get laid. I also got tired of Momma and Grand-Mère pressuring me not to be you. Don't stay out like you. Don't go out with the guys you did. So, I decided to do something to push back, kinda my secret protest."

"So, what happened to him? More importantly, who is he? Do I know him? Where did it happen at?"

"He went away to college. And his name is none of your business. And if you must know."

"Yes, I must."

"In my room, but that's the only detail you get."

"Look at you the refined rebel. And here momma thought she only had one wild daughter. If she only knew. Don't worry, Cora, I'll never tell. I've got my own storm to navigate." Vivianna paused and looked at her stomach. "Well, it looks like you're finally going to get the bigger room." Vivianna chuckled softly under her breath.

Cora did her best impression of Emily. "Vivianna, all the rooms are bigger rooms at Lakeland."

"Not bad. But you forgot to roll your eyes in disgust."

"Momma's a bit much, but even she wouldn't kick you out."

"No, she'll send me to live with the aunt we know doesn't exist.

Get rid of my baby and then ship me off to part unknown. I hear the arctic is nice. I'll become one of those relatives the rest of the family whispers about at all the family gathering."

"Momma's not that cruel."

"Oh please, Cora, this is a woman who would see her father's brother's children in public and walk past them like they were strangers. Momma dismisses anything thing that doesn't make her look good." Vivianna let out a long exhausted sigh. "I dread the smug look on her face. I can see the 'I own you' look smeared across her face, and the shrill in her voice. I swear Momma has had it out for me since the day I entered the world."

"Then tell Daddy first. He's always been a kinder hand."

"Daddy may have a kinder hand, but he always yields to Momma in the end. He does it in a passive disappointed silence kind of way. Where he never actually says he's taking her side, but you know he's taking her side. Either way, I'm screwed. Hate-filled stares and the shrill or disappointed silence that will eventually yield to Momma's demands." Vivianna used her hands to weigh her options.

Cora placed her hand on Vivianna's leg. "It will work out, Anna, I don't know how but it will."

"I want to believe you, Cora, I really do, but let's be real, happy endings are not the Harrow way."

~ * ~

"I can't." Vivianna slid the bowl back towards Mae. "I can't keep anything down lately. I think I have the flu."

Mae slid the bowl back. "Child, if you have the flu then I'm six feet tall. The pregnant women in my family eat this, and it always stays down."

A guilty look swept over Vivianna's face. "How did you—"

"When a woman is in tune with life and the energy around her, she can always sense motherhood in another woman. Big bellies aren't the only way a woman tells the world she's pregnant." Mae shook her head. "I told that boy don't start with you, it's not going to end well." Mae mumbled under her breath. "When his Momma gets a hold of him."

Vivianna couldn't believe how good the noodles with spicy lemon broth tasted and made her feel. It had been days since anything had successfully stayed down. Vivianna didn't realize how deep her hunger ran until she started eating. Vivianna listened to Mae as she devoured half the bowl before she spoke again. "What do you mean? You told Ray not to get involved with me. Why?"

Mae let Vivianna's questions linger in the air for a moment. The floor creaked and squeaked as she returned with a full bowl for Vivianna. "I have always looked after you kids like I looked after my own. And while we may all be created the same, our families are different, very different, baby. And you can't mix certain families, especially in these parts. I've seen what happens when you do and it's not good. I wasn't that much older than you when the courthouse was burnt to the ground because of the names of some of the fathers listed on the birth certificates around here. Some people would rather destroy everything than deal with the truth. It's not an accident that a lot of the black and white folks look so similar to each other. Genes don't lie even if people do. My sister ran North to escape the consequences of crossing certain lines. I warned my nephew not to start with you. I don't care what year it is; some people around here still live by the old South ways where color and complexion determines privilege and class. But it's not like my nephew has ever listened to anyone. Right or wrong, he has to do everything his way. Just like someone, I know." Mae smiled softly at Vivianna. "I knew you two being together was going to be a problem long before the ill-fated dinner."

"Don't remind me. I get a headache just thinking about that night. The entire mess falls on me. I foolishly thought if Momma and Daddy could meet him, they would see Ray's a good man. They would see how good he treats me and how good we are for each other. I thought they would support my decision to be with him. I'm not a child, and I haven't been for quite some time now. When is everyone going to see it? You know how many times other girls would say how special I was. And they wished they were a Harrow too because I had all the best stuff and our family looked perfect. You have no clue how many times I wanted to scream back no you don't. How many times I wanted to tell them it's all an illusion."

"You're not grown, Vivianna. I know you think you are, but there's more to being an adult than age. All families have their issues; some have more than others. Do you hear me?"

"I'm listening."

"I know you're listening but do you hear what I'm saying to you?"

"What happened to your sister? Did Momma or Grand-Mère do something?" Vivianna pivoted the conversation with ease.

"The past mess is not for you to worry about. You need to worry about keeping food down and getting rest. Babies don't grow well when the momma's body is all out of sorts. Besides we can't change what happened, so there's no reason to dwell. All we can do is keep our fingers crossed that the little girl inside of you brings out the best in everyone instead of the worst."

"A girl." Vivianna's eyes lit up at the thought of a girl. Vivianna immediately thought about her favorite childhood doll, and how she loved to dress her baby doll, fix her hair, and cradle her in her arms.

"I've got a feeling, and my feelings haven't been wrong yet." Mae made herself comfortable at the kitchen table.

"I'm going to have my little living doll. I'm going to buy her the cutest clothes, and I can't wait to put bows in her hair. She's going to have dresses like the ones I had when I was little. You know the billowy ones with the white lace trim at the bottom. I had them in all different colors. I'm going to buy her those patent leather shoes with the buckle on the side. And she'll have eyes like mine. She'll have hair like mine; she's going to look just like me. Perfect." Vivianna's face glowed at the thought of creating someone in her image.

"Sweetheart." Mae looked on Vivianna with a quiet sadness in her eyes. "You're having a baby, and a baby is nothing like a doll. Babies are more than their looks. Babies have needs, and they grow into people. The more they grow, the more they need. And if you raise them right, they become independent of you and leave."

"I know, Momma Mae. I know babies don't stay babies forever. I want her to be as doll-like as she can for as long as possible."

Mae knew there was no getting through to Vivianna. She was lost in her fairytale and had no interest in embracing the realities of pregnancy or motherhood.

Chapter Seven

"I am tired of your endless bullshit and countless mistakes. What are you dumb, stupid or just too dumb to know how stupid you are? Was I asking too much when I asked you to think with your head instead of what's between your legs? It was a simple request you were too inept to follow. What in the hell is wrong with you? I'm amazed you haven't developed chronic back pain from the amount of time you have spent lying on your back."

"Who said I was lying on my back?" Vivianna stood in front of her father's desk like an actress standing on her mark. Vivianna knew exactly where and how to stand when she received a tongue lashing for her transgressions.

Emily pulled Vivianna by her hair. Vivianna winced from her mother's domineering jerk on her hair. "Clearly, I didn't hit you hard enough the last time you ran your mouth to me. I swear this time I'm going to knock your teeth out."

"Emily, let go of her. Right now. Let her go."

Emily paused and glared at Quincy.

"I said let go of her." Quincy growled under his breath. "Unlike your upbringing, we don't beat on our children. No matter what they do."

"Maybe that's the problem with all of them, especially this one, we didn't beat them. Maybe if I had beaten the skin off of her back a couple of times, she wouldn't be in this mess now."

"Did those skin beatings work for you, Emily?" Quincy's annoyance with both his daughter and wife poured over his words and controlled tone. "Did they stop you from making some of the decisions you made?"

Emily tightened her grasp. "I'm nothing like this one." Emily shook Vivianna like a dog shakes a toy.

"That's your perception of the choices you made. Now let go of my daughter."

"I'm nothing like her, Quincy. Nothing."

"I'm not asking you to let go, Emily. I'm telling you. Let go. And I'm not going to tell you again. Please don't make me force you, Emily."

"Like you can."

"I know I can, Emily."

Emily flung Vivianna's head to the side as she released her grasp. "Why did I keep you?" Emily's words oozed hate.

"Emily, that's enough. You've said and done enough." Quincy studied Emily and Vivianna as they stood in front of him. Quincy knew Emily's hatred for Vivianna came from not being able to forgive herself even if Emily didn't realize it. Quincy also knew Vivianna was neither an angel nor a victim. Quincy had run out of words for these two women who were determined to hate each other at any cost. Quincy used his finger to push his wedding band around on his finger. The pace at which the band moved helped to focus his mind so he didn't go off on Emily or Vivianna the way he truly wanted. "If you want to hate someone, Emily, hate me. Take all of your anger out on me, but stop it with Vivianna. You've done enough and said enough."

"No, I haven't done enough." Emily stomped her foot. "It's not enough." Emily folded her arms across her chest as she slammed her foot onto the floor several more times. Emily paced around the office. "No, no, no." Vivianna quietly pulled herself up as she listened to her mother rant. "I've got one who's too fat to find a husband, this one been passed around more than a collection plate at a summer revival. And our son, if he finishes college without getting kicked out and us having to make another donation to another higher learning institute to take him, will be a miracle." Emily threw her cold stare back at Vivianna. "Stop crinkling your skirt in your hands. You're not five years old anymore."

"Clearly." Vivianna snapped back as she rolled her eyes.

"Little girl. I don't give a damn what your father said. Mouth off again and I'll knock you into next week."

"I wish you would try." Vivianna mumbled under her breath. The tingle in her stomach gave her the courage to speak up. Emily lunged towards Vivianna and squared her shoulders as if she was a stranger rather than her flesh and blood.

"If I thought for one moment flinging you down the front steps would get rid of that thing you're carrying, I would do it and save the money I have to pay the doctor."

"I'm not getting rid of my baby." The defiance in Vivianna's eyes made it clear she was not going to willing follow her mother's demand.

"You don't have a choice."

"Says who? You? I'm not like Cora, Momma, you can't make me do anything."

Emily was thrown back by Vivianna's blatant defiance. "That's where your wrong little girl. I can make you do anything I want because I supply you with your lifestyle. And the dick you've been sprung on can't give you one-third of what I can. Poverty is not going to look good on you, sweetheart. You don't have the ability to exist in a world where people aren't paid to wait on you. How to do expect to feed that thing? You don't have any real skills. Your intelligence falls on the low side of average. Your father and I sent you to the best schools and off to college with the hopes of you meeting a husband, not because we actually thought you were capable of learning something. You are nothing more than a trophy wife in training."

Vivianna's eyes started to water and her heart sank as she looked at her father. "Daddy, is that what you think of me too? Do you think I'm on the low side of average?" Vivianna's voice grew quiet. "Do you think I'm nothing more than a trophy wife in training?" Vivianna knew her family's money and status made her better than but until now she didn't know it made her. Quincy kept his eyes down. He didn't have the heart to answer his daughter. "Daddy, please say something."

"Vivianna, you are a smart girl." Quincy's sterile tone let Vivianna know he was taking Emily's side, again. "But everyone has a role to play in life."

"Everyone has a role." Vivianna huffed. "Are you serious, Daddy? Did you really just say that to me? So, you agree with everything Momma said."

"What do you want me to say, Vivianna?"

"Say what Momma said isn't true. Say I don't have to go through with any of it. Say everything is going to be okay. Say you'll fix it. Tell me it will be all right. Rescue me. Say you will protect me, Daddy. Please save me."

"That I can't do, Vivianna. I just can't. I can't undo what's done and decided."

"Please, it's not fair. I love him. Tell Momma I don't want to. If anyone can change her mind it's you, Daddy. Daddy, I'm happy for once in my life. I'm happy."

"Oh please, you're happy." Emily snarled. "Single and knocked up is not a form of happiness you idiot. Happiness can only be bought, which is why I've made the decision for you."

"Please, Daddy, say something, please." Vivianna never really asked her father for anything, but this one time she begged him. *Please be my hero.*

Quincy looked off at nothing as he continued to play with his wedding ring. The feel of the gold being pressed against his finger reminded him of how difficult decisions can be especially when every decision is the wrong choice. *Baby, I am saving you. You just don't understand. I'm rescuing from becoming your mother. If you keep this baby you are going to end up treating your baby like your mother treats you. This baby is going to be your undoing.* "Your Mother and I have made a decision. You will abide by what we have decided. And after everything is done, you'll spend a couple of months traveling. You'll come back start college again and eventually settle down with a suitable partner. Make a suitable life; it's what's best for everyone involved. I know you think you're in love, but sometimes love is only relative to the situation." Quincy glanced over at Emily. "Once the situation changes, what you thought was love quickly changes. Isn't that right, Emily?"

You bastard. "Your father has spoken, Vivianna. You will do what I tell you to do."

"Suitable partner? Suitable life? It's always about how we look to the outside, isn't it? As long as the outside thinks everything is fine that's all that matters. Never let the world know our secrets. Never let the world see that the great Harrow family is just as dysfunctional as an illiterate shack-dwelling horde. Why send me to the doctor, Momma? Why don't you send me to visit our nonexistent relatives up North and then sell my baby to the highest bidder like Aunt Margaret did to her daughter? Turn a profit the Harrow way. Or are you too afraid I will get drunk at the Christmas party like Angeline and start running my mouth?"

"Child, please, dark-skinned bastard babies don't fetch high dollar. If I thought for one moment that thing your carrying would be light like you, you would be locked away in the same cabin with the same nurse."

"Raymond was right when he said you're nothing more than an uppity light-skinned house nigger living off of massa's ill-gotten money."

Emily backhanded her daughter. "Speak to me like that again and I'll cut your tongue out. The decision has been made. It will be done tomorrow. Now get out of my sight before I forget you're my daughter and I stomp you like I would a stranger who dared speak to me that way."

"I hope you die slowly and nameless." Vivianna rubbed her side of her cheek in a vain attempt to sooth the redness as she gritted her words through her teeth.

"And I hope the same for you."

"Emily, enough. Vivianna, that's your mother. Do not wish death on your mother."

"Oh, but she can hit me and wish death on me and that's okay? How is that fair? I have to respect her and she doesn't have to respect me."

"It's not about fair, Vivianna. If it was about fair your mother would have—" Quincy caught his tongue. It shocked him how fast he almost exposed Emily. "Vivianna, go to your room before things are said out of order."

"Daddy, why are you letting her do this? Why aren't you protecting me? I'm your daughter."

"Now, Vivianna! To your room now." Quincy rarely raised his voice, but when he did his roar could make a mountain shake.

"Daddy?"

"Now!"

Vivianna stormed up the spiral staircase. She couldn't wipe the tears fast enough from her face. Her thoughts were all over the place. The only thing she was sure of was she had to contact Raymond.

"Are you okay?" Cora's meek voice barely rose to a whisper.

"I'm fine, Cora, just fine!" Tears streamed down Vivianna's face, and her mother's handprint deepened in color. "Why don't you go eat one of the candy bars you hide in your room and leave me alone!" Vivianna slammed her bedroom door in Cora's face.

Vivianna threw herself across her queen-size oak four-poster bed and pulled one of her pillows into herself. She used the pillow to muffle her cries. Vivianna took in large mouthfuls of air as she gulped and huffed in an attempt to calm herself down. Vivianna held on to the pillow until her tears slowed and her breathing returned to an almost normal state then wiped her face. She took a deep breath before she picked up the phone. Vivianna went from almost calm to full-blown frantic when she heard Raymond's voice. "Ray. Ray, I need you."

"Baby, what is it? Tell me what's going on and I'll fix it." Even stressed Raymond's voice soothed her.

"It's bad, really, really bad." Raymond could barely make out her words in between the sobs. "I don't want to do it. I don't want to get rid of the baby."

"Baby, what baby, Vivi?"

Vivianna took a deep breath. This wasn't the way she had planned on telling him. Her voice became less hysterical and quieter. "Our baby."

A mixture of joy and confusion sweep over Raymond. "Why in the hell would you ever think I would want you to get rid of our baby? You know I'm going to be there for you. Anything you need I'm going to get it. I'm not going anywhere, baby, you can count on me."

"Not you, Ray, my parents."

Raymond swore under his breath. He'd had more than his fair share of them. Rage flew over every ounce of him. "Nobody is getting rid of nothing that's mine. Pack your bags. I'm on my way. Do you hear me?"

Vivianna forced a tearful yes from her lips.

"I mean it, Vivianna. As soon as I hang up, I'm on my way and you need to be ready to leave. I'm not bullshitting around."

"Okay."

Cora opened the door to Vivianna's room. "What are you doing?"

"Packing, Cora." Vivianna snapped as she crammed clothes into her suitcase.

"Why?" Cora settled on the edge of Vivianna's bed.

"Because I have to leave. I can't stay here anymore. Because of our mother. *Your* mother now is evil in the flesh. I really don't even think she's human. It all happened the way I said it would happen." Vivianna moved around the room like a woman possessed. Vivianna knew she wouldn't be able to take a third of what she wanted to take. "That bitch was yelling her demands at me, threatening me, and all Daddy did was sit there and let her have her way. She fucking hit and pulled my hair again, Cora."

"I know you're mad, I know Momma's mad but don't go. Please stay. I don't want you to go. If you leave, I'll be here alone with Momma. Stay, Anna it can't be that bad. Maybe Momma Mae can smooth things over. Get Momma to see things differently. You know Momma Mae can fix anything."

"It's worse than bad, Cora. Momma Mae can't fix this. I have to leave. I have to get as far away from here as I can." Vivianna snapped her bag shut. "Momma is determined to make my life hell."

"Anna, think this through. Where are you going? And wherever you go you're going to need money. We have time to make Momma change her mind about things. Eight months is a long time."

"I don't have eight months, Cora. I have twenty-four hours. And there's a better chance of Momma eating a pile of shit in the next twenty-four hours than her changing her mind. Right now, Cora, I don't care where I end up, just as long as it's not here. I'll figure things out after Ray picks me up."

Sadness swept over Cora's face; she knew Emily would blame her for all of this. Emily would demand Cora explain why she hadn't stopped Vivianna from seeing Raymond. Emily would make Cora explain why she hadn't been more involved with her sister. Why she didn't stop Vivianna from getting pregnant. Cora also knew if Vivianna left there would be no one left to deflect Emily's rage off of her. As much as Vivianna needed to go Cora needed her to stay. "You really can't stay?"

"Vivianna!" The roar of Raymond's voice made Vivianna jump.

"Vivianna! Now!"

"No, Cora, I can't stay." Vivianna threw her purse over her shoulder and snatched her suitcase off of the bed. Raymond's yell grew every time he said her name. Vivianna touched the top of Cora's hand. "I'm sorry. I can't stay."

"Get out now. I told you never to come back here."

"Not without Vivianna, Emily. Once I have her, you will never see us again." Raymond had barreled through the back door.

"Quincy! Quincy! She's not going anywhere with you. You have destroyed my family with your presence in her life. Quincy, where are you? I want you out of my house now. You disgusting lowly waste of flesh, you are nothing more than gutter trash, and I will not allow that thing my daughter is carrying to enter the world."

Raymond faced Emily in the foyer. "Lady, I have never hit a woman. But you call my baby a thing again, and tonight will be the night I punch one in the face."

Raymond caught Emily's raised hand in midair. The sheer strength of his grasp startled her. Emily felt Raymond's anger as they glared at each other. "Lady, keep your damn hands to yourself."

"Get out of my house."

"After I get my woman."

"Raymond?" Vivianna's voice broke the tension in the room. Emily snatched her hand back with a vengeance. Emily rubbed at her wrist as if Raymond's dark skin had rubbed off on her. "Disgusting. Don't ever touch me again."

"Trust me, Lady, I got nothing out of it." Raymond kept his eyes locked on Emily as he spoke. "Vivianna, go wait in the truck. I have something to say, and you don't need to hear it."

"Vivianna, don't you move."

"Vivianna, the truck, now."

Vivianna froze in place, trapped between two worlds.

"What in the hell is going on in here?"

"Daddy." Vivianna made her way down the stairs. "Do something to make her stop."

"Vivianna, where do you think you're going?" Quincy stood next to Emily. He voice was too calm for the situation. Quincy paused for a moment the rage emanating off of Emily was suffocating. "Vivianna, I asked you a question. Vivianna, answer me."

"Sir, I am taking the mother of my child, and I'm leaving. Vivianna told me everything over the phone, and we're leaving tonight." Raymond glanced over at Vivianna. "Baby, go get in the truck."

"I think you need to think this through, son."

"I'm not your son, and there's nothing to think through. You and your wife made things very clear to me the night I came over for dinner."

"You stupid bitch, you're going to throw your entire life away to be with common trash. He's worthless. Look at him. He has no money, no lineage, no stature, no nothing. Standing there in flea market clothes. Add to that he's blacker than tar, and that makes him less than nothing." Emily smacked Quincy in the arm. "Quincy, you do something to stop this idiot from leaving with this thing. I will not have my family shamed. There are too many wagging tongues around here that are far too eager to recite her stupid decisions over and over. Shoot him. Shoot both of them if you have to. I will not be embarrassed." Emily hit the side of Quincy's arm with greater force. "Quincy, do something. Right now you had better do something. Besides stand there looking half dead." Emily stomped her foot on the floor.

"Emily, I've had enough of your tantrums for today. Hell, for the rest of my life. I'm not one of your kids so watch how you talk to me and don't hit me again. Vivianna is grown. If Vivianna wants to leave let her go. Stop fighting and let her go. You and I both know you don't want her here. Stop acting like you're a mother trying to do the right thing. Just let the child go. The only reason you're fighting is because she's leaving and you're not throwing her out. Damnit, let her go. I'm too old and too tired to keep doing this back and forth with you two. Let her leave, Emily. It makes it easier for me to deal with you if she leaves."

Emily growled. "I never should have married you."

"Finally, something we're in agreement about."

"Move." Emily shoved Quincy out of her way. "You're just as worthless as her damn father."

"I told you not to hit me again." Quincy dug his hands into Emily's arm as they glared at each other.

"Get your worthless hands off of me." Emily stumbled as she snatched her arm away from Quincy. "Never touch me again." Emily raged.

Vivianna froze mid-stride when she heard her mother's declaration. Vivianna turned to face her mother. Vivianna's ears stung as she searched Emily's eyes for answers.

"That's right, he's not your father. Quincy is not your father, and he's always known. Isn't that right, Quincy? Tell her, Quincy. Tell her now."

Vivianna's eyes darted over the Quincy. "Daddy? Is it true?"

Quincy shoved his hands in his pockets as he took the coward's way out and quietly walked out of the room. He couldn't stand to look at the hurt in Vivianna's eyes.

"Daddy, is this true?" Emily mocked Vivianna's distress. "Don't bother looking at him." Emily smiled at the pain in her daughter's eyes. "Oh, it true. He's not your father. See how easily he walked out on you. It's because you're not his and now that you know he doesn't have to pretend anymore. You're nothing but a sorry bastard child who ruined my life. Just like the one you're carrying. My mother was right, I should have gotten rid of you. I should have drunk the juice I got from Mae's Momma in the bottoms. You are my biggest mistake. Just like the thing you're carrying is going to be yours."

"Who's my father then?" Vivianna's lips quivered as she spoke.

"Doesn't matter. All you need to know is he didn't want you either. He gave me fifty dollars to make you go away."

"That's it, we're done." Raymond grabbed the suitcase out of Vivianna's hand and led her out the door. Vivianna could hear her mother's rants as she left Lakeland.

"I hope you have a miserable life, you worthless whore. You are nothing without my family or me. You will never be anything but a whore. I never want to see you again. Don't you ever come back." Emily clung to the front door. "You're a whore, Vivianna. A worthless whore."

Vivianna wiped her steady stream of silent tears. She watched as the tears she couldn't catch dampened her blue shirt. Vivianna took one final look at her mother as Raymond tore off down the driveway. Vivianna studied the revulsion on her mother's face until she could no longer see her. Broken-hearted, Vivianna didn't make a sound as her head fell back on to the headrest. Her whole life had been a lie.

Raymond rubbed Vivianna's leg. "I'm going to fix this baby. I'm going to fix all of it. You hear me? I don't want you to think about anything she said to you. I got you. Everything is going to be fine. I'm here, and I'm going to fix everything."

How Ray, how.

~ * ~

"Here baby." Mae handed Vivianna the flowered teacup. "Drink this. I know you've been through a lot tonight. It will help you feel better. Take slow slips." Vivianna pulled her leg under her as she inhaled the smell of black tea and honey. Raymond sat as close as he could to Vivianna on the brown-striped fabric sofa. Raymond rubbed her shoulder in a vain attempt to comfort her.

"Why would she say Daddy's not my father?" Vivianna paused. The popular commercial brand tea tasted better than anything she had drunk while at Lakeland. "Why would she keep something like that from me? What type of mother does something like that? Momma Mae, you should have seen the way Daddy turned his back and walked out. He wouldn't even look at me. His daughter." Vivianna huffed under her breath. "Well, I guess I'm not his daughter."

Mae looked over at her youngest daughter, Brenda, who sat in her rocking chair more than prepared to drink in all the details. "It's time for you to go in the other room. Grown folks are talking."

"I'm seventeen, Momma. That's grown." Brenda was the mirror image of her mother in looks and attitude.

"Girl, I'll take a switch to the behind you're sitting on if you don't take yourself out of here. Telling me you're grown. What kinda mess is that? You're grown when I say you're grown. Besides, this doesn't concern you anyway. None of it's your business. Now get gone."

Vivianna smiled at Brenda as she walked her out.

"Move faster."

"Yes, ma'am."

"You're going to cut all that mumbling out too. And close the door all the way and I'd better not find out you were trying to listen at the door." Mae waited until she heard the click of the bedroom door before she softened her tone. "Raymond, you're gonna rub the sweater right off the poor girl's arm."

"Sorry, Auntie Mae. I don't know what else to do."

"Be still, that's what you do. You can't fix everything that's broken. This stuff has been broken for a long, long time."

Raymond folded his arms across his chest while his foot shook. Mae twisted her face in a grimace. "Aunt Mae you know I've been doing this with my foot since childhood."

"Boy, you are not a child anymore, you about to have one of your own. Now stop. Back to you, young lady." Mae leaned back in her worn imitation leather chair. Mae played with the tear in the armrest as she spoke. Her eyes shifted to the water stain on the tired wallpaper. Mae filled her lungs with the stagnant air and released it slowly before she spoke. "I shouldn't be the one telling you all of this, but the ones who should speak have chosen to leave it all unsaid. Probably why you are in this mess now. But it is what it's going to be now. This story starts long before either one of you was a thought, but it involves both of you." Mae gazed over at Raymond. "Your Momma used to mess with Quincy, Raymond. They were both sweet on each other, but when it comes to skin tone down here light ones go out of their way to stick to their own kind. Quincy's mother, Miss Emma, wasn't having any parts of my sister sitting at her table. Quincy wasn't stuck up about his color the way most blacks are around here. He didn't see black people that way. He fell for your Momma hard. He loved the way my sister could challenge him intellectually. They would spend hours disusing life, politics, books, black rights, women rights, even black women's rights. In a lot of ways, they were both born before their time. But like I said, Miss Emma wasn't having it. Miss Emma paid our mother off to get rid of the child Doreen was carrying and get your Momma a bus ticket out of town. That's how your Momma ended up in Chicago. Miss Emma told my sister she was to never step foot back here or she would make sure none of us who lived here could find work. Miss Emma even said she would make sure our babies starved. To people who have nothing and no way out that's a scary thing, the thought of not being able to feed your babies." Mae let out an exhausted sigh as she thought about things she hadn't thought about in decades.

"Miss Emma was a mean woman, and always looking for wrong in somebody and always going out of her way to wrong somebody. There were any times I thought that woman was void of a soul. Oh, how she kept a scowl on her face even in the casket. I think her meanness was a cover for her sadness. That woman had some hard times laid on her. Her husband died in a terrible accident, and her eldest ran off with a half Indian, and she never heard from him again. Her daughter suffered from fits as we called them back then. Anyway, Quincy was the one who seemed undamaged. Miss Emma leaned on him to be the one to hold things together. Growing up and even now Quincy was known for being smart, hardworking, and fair. That's how he was able to keep his family's money intact. He loved my sister, but he was always fair to your mother, Vivianna. Miss Emma and Miss Delphine saw Quincy as a way for two dysfunctional families to lean on each other, one for societal redemption and one for financial redemption."

"Mom never told me any of this. She always told us she came to Chicago because she was tired of the country living."

"My sister is a proud woman. She never wanted any of her children to think less of her. Doreen didn't want any of you carrying her baggage on your shoulders. Talking about this makes me miss her even more. You know I went to see you all once when you were just a little thing. But all that city noise is not for me. Everything moved too fast up there. I wasn't there a whole day before a car almost took my foot clean off. I knew then a phone was going to be the most important thing I would ever own."

"Mom should have told us. It wouldn't have changed the way we feel about her. If anything, it would have made us raise the pedestal we put her on."

"I know." Mae rocked softly back and forth. "I know. But you have to understand your Momma and I come from the generation that keeps secrets. From the time were little we were raised to know there are some things you don't talk about, not to people inside the family and especially not outside the family." Mae grabbed the faded blue plastic cup from the water-stained oak-colored side table. The coolness of the tap water soothed her. Mae took several large swallows before she spoke again.

"Vivianna, I don't want what I'm about to tell you to define you. You are more than the story I'm going to tell you. Never forget that. It's your choice whether or not you let the story consume you." Vivianna nervously nodded her head. "Your Great-grandfather, Cairo Chastian, was a hard man in looks and spirit. Cairo did everything to extremes: drink, cuss, gamble, and women. That man blew through money like most people drink water. And I don't think he knew the word fidelity existed. Cairo made a lot of poor choices, and almost lost his family's land on countless occasions. Trust me when I say poverty knocked on the front door a couple of times. Your Grand-Mère and Papa were losing everything trying to dig Lakeland out of the hole Cairo had put Lakeland in before he died. Appearances are expensive, so with Doreen run out of town Miss Delphine quickly offered Emily up as an acceptable mate. Your parents married and your Daddy salvaged Lakeland and the business. But the reality was your parents weren't in love with each other, and your mother, like you, has a little bit of a wild streak."

Vivianna blushed and nervously pushed her hair behind her ear. Raymond slid even closer and rubbed her stomach.

"After Cora and Jack were born your mother got bored, and when you have a spirited personality boredom can get you in a lot of trouble. Quincy is not real exciting, he's what we call steady. He'll never have you on the edge of your seat trying to figure what his next move is. But the seat he provides for you will always be sturdy and comfortable. Emily wanted exciting; in a lot of ways your Mother craved it. So, when she could no longer control her itch, she started sneaking around with several different men. Your Momma went out of her way to keep her indiscretions out of the local gossip circles. She didn't want to end up like her grandfather. But gossip always finds its way onto the tongue of those who are all too eager to spread it. The last man your mother got involved with was this white man who was a judge in the next town. Waller, Judge

94

Edward Waller was his name. Your Momma fell in love with that man, and he told her all the things she wanted to hear to keep her coming to see him. Dropped Cora and Jack off here a few times, so she didn't have to rush back home. Your Daddy thought the three of them were visiting your Aunt Jacqueline. And how your Aunt lorded that over your Momma. Your Momma might have been wrong, but there was no reason for Jacqueline to do your mother the way she did. But she always did anything to be the favorite child. That child is going to get her due one day for all the mess she has caused." Mae huffed under her breath.

Vivianna leaned back on Raymond. The warmth of his body and the smell of him comforted her raging thoughts. Vivianna's heart shattered into million jagged pieces. The possibility of picking up just one piece overwhelmed Vivianna.

"But now ain't the time to discuss that child's skeletons. Anyway, baby, that Waller man even went so far as to convince your momma he was gonna leave his wife, which he wasn't. He was never going to leave his wife for your Momma. Ain't no white man in these parts gonna leave his white wife for a black mistress, doesn't matter how light she is. Besides any man with a working dick and half sense know the only thing he needs to do is tell his mistress she's the better woman and mix that with the empty promise to leave his wife. And he'll have a more than happy mistress, damn the wife. Excuse my language. Every time I try to give up cussing shit goes sideways, and I'm back to swearing."

Vivianna wiped more of her endless tears as Raymond kissed the side of her head.

"I'm gonna fix everything. I promise. I'm going to make everything better. Better than before." Raymond whispered.

"Your Momma found out she was having you, and never heard from Edward Waller again. Your Grand-Mère put your Momma through hell. I think that's why Emily was always hard on you because you reminded her of the past. Quincy without hesitation accepted you as his. He never yelled at your mother or threw her misstep in her face that I saw. Not once did I see him treat you any different. You were never Waller's daughter, always his. And somehow Emily resented Quincy for it. It's like she wanted him to yell, scream, get mad or punch a wall. But that's not

Quincy. It was as if she wanted him to hate you. This is a pot that has been on the verge of boiling over for a long time. You, Raymond, and your baby were all that was needed to make the scalding water splash onto the stove. Now, I'm not making excuses for anything your Momma said or did. Wasn't nothing done without Emily having a choice in it. When it came to her affairs and how she treated you, wrong is wrong. She chose to do wrong. I'll also say this, you can't pretend your demons away, you have to deal with them. All of them before they deal with you."

"Well, that explains why Daddy turned and left the room when Momma was going psych ward crazy on me. Why he always gave into her by saying nothing. Where is Edward Waller now?"

"Oh, he's long gone, baby. Cancer claimed him years ago."

"So, I'm alone."

"Hey." Raymond squeezed her shoulder. "You're not alone. I'm right here, and I'm not going anywhere. You'll always have me, baby."

"I know." Vivianna mustered up a weak smile.

"Listen, baby. A family isn't always the one we're born into, sometimes it's the one we make. Don't forget that. Remember, you, like your mother, have a choice. Do with it what you feel is right." Mae stared at the lace curtains. "Lakeland," Mae mumbled under her breath. "Sometimes I think that land is cursed."

~ * ~

"Baby, you need to eat."

Vivianna continued to play with the burger wrapper. "I know but I can't. I mean I physically can't. It's beyond losing my appetite." Vivianna folded her legs under her and pulled the blue throw on the back of Raymond's sofa over her.

"Is it the baby? Do you need to go to the hospital? I can take you right now."

Vivianna giggled. "Ray I'm fine. Everything is fine. I hope you're not going to do that the entire time."

"Do what?"

"Go into a total panic."

"I won't if you eat."

"I know I should but I can't. I know what's going to happen if I eat this so I would rather not. I don't feel like spending the rest of the evening with my face in the toilet."

"Okay, you don't have to eat." Raymond slid beside Vivianna. "But you do have to tell me what's wrong."

"Everything and nothing, that's what's wrong." Vivianna played with the tassels on the throw. "I know I'm probably not making any sense right now. It's just that it's been a long and crazy night. And I don't know what to do next. I'm just glad we're back at your place. Right now I just want to crawl into bed next to you, fall asleep, and hope the everything I can't explain will get better, and the nothing will make sense."

"We can definitely go lay down if that's what you want. And I want you to relax and let the nothing go and trust me when I say I'm going to fix everything."

Chapter Eight

The conversation Mae had with Vivianna and Raymond made Raymond even more determined to get Vivianna far away from Lakeland. Raymond sold everything he could in two weeks' time to put together the necessary funds to leave. Raymond even parted with the majority of his cherished book collection.

Clarence helped Raymond secure the tarp on his and Vivianna's remaining belongings. "So, this is really it, man?"

"Yep. We gotta get the hell out of here, man. I don't want either of my babies anywhere near these people. My Mom said we could stay with her until we get on our feet. And trust me, I've already got a plan to get us in our own place. That's the difference between a real family and that up-stuck bullshit Vivi grew up in. Real families come through for each other and support each other."

"I hear ya." Clarence double-knotted the twine through the loop of the truck. "Man, people with money are always more fucked up than us flat broke mutha fuckers."

"Say that shit again."

Bernice leaned in the passenger side window. "It will be okay, sweetheart. I know we don't know each other well, but I know Raymond, and he's really good people. Clarence might be crazy, but he doesn't run with trifling men. He's gonna take really good care of you. I know he is. All you have to do is let him. You feel what I'm saying?"

Vivianna pulled the blanket tighter under her chin. "Okay. I will. I'm just nervous about things. Meeting his family, and everything. What if they don't like me? Considering I'm not showing up under the best circumstances."

"No, it's just not okay. It's better than okay. Raymond loves you, which means they are going to love you. It doesn't matter the circumstances, baby. When the love is real, I mean, really real, that love is going to get you through the rough patches. They are going to welcome you. I have no doubt about it. Everything is going to be just fine as long as you two have each other. Never forget that."

"Thank you."

"Alright woman, stop all that mouth running so these two can get on the road. They got a long drive, and they don't need you making the trip any longer."

Bernice swatted Clarence away. "Don't pay him any mind. Clarence loves showing out for folks. But he's a good man, so I keep him." Bernice's gap-filled smile rained over her plump face.

The squeak of the tired truck door opening broke the conversation.

"Take care of her."

"You know I will."

Bernice's smile warmed Vivianna.

Vivianna watched Clarence and Bernice through the side mirror until they disappeared. Raymond rubbed Vivianna's leg in between shifting gears. "Baby, we're going to be just fine. I'm going to fix everything. I don't want you to worry about anything. I've got it all under control. Trust me. You trust me?"

"Yes, baby, I trust you."

"Good. That's what I want to hear. Now try to get some sleep. We've got a long drive."

Vivianna readjusted and rested her head on Raymond's shoulder, and drifted off within five minutes.

~ * ~

Raymond drove straight through. He only stopped for gas, snacks, and coffee. Vivianna slept the majority of the way, which relieved Raymond. He thought back to what his aunt said as he turned down the familiar streets to his old neighborhood. *Take her and keep her away from Lakeland. If you two are ever going to have a chance, she can't be there, not even for a visit. That place does something to people. Keep her and your baby away, Raymond.* Raymond shifted into park and rubbed the side of Vivianna's cheek. "Baby, wake up. We're here."

The sight of Chicago reinforced her new reality in Vivianna. The various noises that marched through Vivianna's ears created a city symphony unique as the city itself. Vivianna focused on the massive apartment building in front of her. It was three times as high as Raymond's apartment. Vivianna took a long hard stretch, still tired from the journey as she tried to look less worn. Vivianna rubbed the sleepiness out of her eyes and slid on her shoes.

"Come on, sleepy. I know you're probably still tired." Raymond brushed his lips across Vivianna's. "But if I don't take you upstairs someone's going to come down and get you. Because if I know my nosey sister, she's been sitting in the window all day waiting for us to show up." Raymond grabbed as much of their stuff as he could before ushering Vivianna up to his mother's ninth floor apartment.

"Boy, what took you so long to get up here?" Raymond's younger sister Regina yelled as she opened the door. "I saw you pull up. I've been at the window all day."

"See, I told you so." Raymond whispered from behind Vivianna.

"Ray, stop playing. You just got here. And why do you have her standing out in the hall like a guest?"

"Because you won't move your big behind out the way so Vivianna can get through the door. Always staying in the way. Now move your load to the left so she can come in." Raymond chuckled through his words.

"Don't start showing out for your woman." Regina playfully pushed Raymond in the chest. "Don't make me tell Momma on you. You know I'll tell what you said and how you let her linger in the hallway because you were running your mouth."

"I know full well you'll tell Momma. You're the family snitch, always have been, always will be. You tell everyone's business but your own."

"Ohhhh, you make me so sick." Regina sucked her teeth as she moved out the way.

The people, sounds, and laughter overwhelmed Vivianna as she made her way through the door. The apartment was more significant than

Raymond's, but with the number of people in it, you couldn't tell. People covered every inch of the living room, and there were ore pouring out of the kitchen. The excited energy grew in volume: before Vivianna finished one hug, another person grabbed her for a hug and introduction. Everyone introduced himself or herself as aunt, uncle, or cousin someone. There were so many faces and names swirling around the apartment Vivianna got lost in a sea of pleasantness.

"Now, that's enough. You all step back now, give her some space. She doesn't need all of you up in her face. You gonna scare the poor child. Come here baby." Raymond's mother pushed her way to the front of the chaos. Doreen was a short woman with a thick build. She was of the same complexion as Raymond and her skin was flawless. A mother's smile stretched across her face. Doreen wiped her hands on her red apron and pushed her silver-framed glasses up before she embraced Vivianna. Doreen held onto Vivianna until she felt Vivianna relax her posture. "It's okay, baby. You're here now. Everything is going to be okay, baby. We're family now and family takes care of family. Now, you come over here and sit down next to me."

"Okay." Vivianna's voice barely fluttered above a whisper.

The room fell silent as Doreen guided Vivianna to the sofa. Everyone waited to take the next cue from Doreen. The level of instant love and warmth Vivianna felt from Doreen overwhelmed her. Doreen stared into Vivianna's eyes. "You are so pretty." Doreen leaned past Vivianna to speak to Raymond. "Real pretty, Ray. That means you're gonna have a pretty baby."

Vivianna couldn't contain her smile.

"Well, we damn sure don't want the baby looking like Ray's ugly ass. No child should have to carry that on them." The entire room broke out into laughter.

"Harold, act right. Showing out for no good reason." Doreen's warm smile overwhelmed Vivianna.

"That's your Uncle Harold, my late husband's brother. He may talk foolishness but like the rest, he has a heart of gold and he'll do anything for you, baby." Harold's chest swelled with pride. Doreen patted Vivianna's hand. "You and I are gonna talk later. Just the two of us, okay.

After everything calms down. I want us to get to know each other."
Vivianna nodded her response. "The rest of you listen to me. I'm going
back in the kitchen to finish cooking. Don't any of you crowd her when I
leave out of here. I mean it. Give her a chance to get comfortable. You
will all have plenty of time to talk to Vivianna later."

Regina quickly took her mother's spot next to Vivianna. "You all
hear what Momma said. I wish one of you would come over here with that
mess. And that means you too, Raymond. She doesn't need you hovering
over her. Ain't nothing going to happen to her. Go over there with your
uncles." Regina folded her arms across her ample chest hidden under her
grey sweatshirt. Regina looked over at Vivianna. "Trust me, Momma and
I got them under control."

Vivianna felt the small hand tugging at her arm. The little girl
couldn't have been more than seven years old. Her jet-black ponytails
brushed the sides of her chubby cheeks. Her bright black eyes stared at
Vivianna with amazement. Her voice was soft and a little unsure as she
spoke. "You have really pretty hair."

Vivianna smiled softly at the little girl. "Thank you. You have
pretty hair too."

"Can I brush your hair?"

Vivianna nodded, and the little girl's chocolate face lit up.

~ * ~

Even though Vivianna had slept the entire way, tiredness lingered
over her. The dinner and lively evening, everyone trying to get to know
her, left her energy depleted. Vivianna found peace in the fact that no one
asked her too many questions about what had happened at Lakeland.
Vivianna quietly unpacked her bags in Raymond's old room. It looked as
if a teenage boy still lived in it. Raymond quietly walked past Vivianna.
He noticed the old tape on the window as he pulled the curtains shut. His
boom box still sat on his dresser next to old basketball trophies.
Raymond's favorite Bruce Lee poster adorned the wall. The wrinkles
weren't from age but water when Regina threw a cup at him and missed.
Raymond pulled back the green-and-red plaid bedspread for Vivianna as

she pulled out her nightclothes. Vivianna exhaled hard when she realized she didn't have her slippers and robe. For several minutes they moved in silence. It was the first time neither one of them had something to say. Raymond leaned against his dresser and studied Vivianna's movements. Raymond felt obligated to start a conversation. He knew he would be able to tell by her voice how she was really feeling. Vivianna could never mask those slight inflections that let him know her true feelings.

"I hope they didn't frighten you. My people can be a little overwhelming when they are excited. They mean well, even my sister in her crazy way. They really like you; Momma told me they do. And she doesn't lie for anyone." Raymond shoved his hands in his jeans. "Vivi, I know this place is nothing like Lakeland, but I am going to make you happy here. We are going to make our version of happiness. I mean that. We're only going to be here for a little while. I promise. I've never been without a job long, and once I get things saved, up we'll be in our own place. And you can decorate it the way you like." Raymond wrapped his arms around Vivianna and kissed the side of her neck. "I'm going to get us a two bedroom. So, you and I always have our private time." Raymond left a trail of kisses on her neck.

Vivianna looked around at the worn band posters and shabby furniture. Vivianna didn't know how to process her spectrum of emotions when it came to the drastic downgrade in her lifestyle. "It's fine, Ray, really, it's fine." The tone in Vivianna's voice told Raymond the truth he dreaded to hear.

~ * ~

Raymond kissed Vivianna and whispered more endless promises in her ear before he migrated back into the living room, and Vivianna went to shower. "Momma, who are you making the sofa up for?"

Raymond's perplexed tone collided with Doreen's matter-of-fact response. "You." Doreen smoothed the pink fleece blanket over the yellow flowered sheets.

"Momma, I'm going to sleep in the room with Vivianna. It's a full bed, but we'll make it work."

"Oh no, you won't, Raymond Anthony. I don't know how you've been living, but we don't do that here." Doreen curled the corner of her lips.

"Really, Momma?"

"Son, don't you *really Momma* me. Vivianna, while she's a lovely girl, and I have nothing against her, is not your wife. You know full well how you were raised. You know in this house, husbands and wives sleep in beds together. If you wanna shack, you are going to have to get your own place." Doreen placed the pillows at the top of the sofa bed. "No sir, we don't do that here."

"I know, Momma, your house, your rules. It's been that way since I was a boy, but can't you make an exception this time? I mean, she's having my baby and everything. It's not like we don't—" Raymond paused and a sheepish grin spread his face.

"All that talk means is you did things in the wrong order, Raymond Anthony. That's all it means."

"Momma, can we please leave my middle name out of this. This isn't a middle name situation. All I'm saying is, it's, it's just that Vivianna's, she's in a new place with new people. And—"

"And that's supposed to mean what to me? Vivianna seems fine. She got on with everyone well enough. She is a woman about to have a baby; I think she can handle sleeping alone. And from everything you have told me about her people, her Momma didn't allow you or any other boy to stay in her room in the bed with her. So, sleeping separately shouldn't be anything new for the two of you. If you two are grown enough to make a baby you're grown enough to sleep without each other. And if Vivianna needs anything I'm right down the hall. Now, Raymond Anthony, you keep acting like you don't remember how you were raised and I'm going to use your full name. And you know full well a pop to the back of the head will come after that."

Raymond knew it was pointless to argue with his mother. Doreen redefined the word stubborn. "Can I at least say good night when she gets out the shower?"

"With the door open you can. And don't worry, Raymond, I'm going to leave my bedroom door open tonight just in case you forget how to get from the bathroom back to the sofa in the middle of the night."

Raymond's chuckled at his mother. It didn't matter how old he got Doreen would always see him as a mischievous sixteen-year-old boy too smart for his own good.

"Uhmmm, exactly. I know you two haven't been together long, but I also know Vivianna better have a different last name before the next baby comes along. We don't do that either. Babies, Mommas, and Daddies running around with different last names. Do you hear me, son?"

"Yes, Momma. I promise, Momma. I would marry her tonight if I thought Vivi would say yes, but she's not there yet." Raymond closed the distance between Doreen and himself as he lowered his voice to speak. "Momma, Aunt Mae told me everything."

Doreen busied herself straightening up things that were already in place. "I know she called and told me. I'm not mad she told you. My sister said what needed to be said." Doreen kept her back to Raymond in a vain attempt to hide the shame on her face. "I'm surprised she didn't tell you before, before all this." Doreen picked up the flowered vase and repositioned it along with the other knick-knacks on the end table.

"Momma."

The sound of Raymond's voice made her move faster. "Momma." Raymond stepped forward and placed his hand on Doreen's shoulder. "Momma."

Doreen kept her eyes focused on her preschool teacher hands. "I'm a good woman Ray. I'm not proud of everything I've done, but I stand by everything I've done. I don't know anyone without a past. Mine is just a little more colorful than some. My heart got broken, and I survived it. I did what I had to do back then. Not just for myself but also for the people I love. I never told you kids because I didn't want my mess to become your mess. I told your Daddy everything, he never judged me, and loved me until the day he passed."

"Momma, I know. I'm not accusing you of anything. I know you don't have a malicious bone in your body. I wish you had told us. Maybe I could have made things better for you. Or at least have been a less tenacious child. Maybe Regina would have mastered the art of shut up if we had all known."

"You leave your sister be." Doreen popped Raymond playfully on the arm. "There is no more wrong with her than that is wrong with you. I swear you two have been at each other since she could hold her head up."

"If she would just admit I'm your favorite, and you love me more, we would get along just fine. We fight because she won't accept it."

Doreen threw her head back with laughter. Doreen had the type of laugh that came from the gut and filled the room. "You are all my favorites. I love you all equally. You are a mess, boy, I swear. You must get that messiness from your Daddy's side." Doreen softened her smile as she rubbed the side of Raymond's face. "I am so glad you're home, Raymond. I felt like there was a part of me missing when you were gone. I know you're grown and like doing your own thing, but I like having my children close. Makes me feel good when I can see my children on a regular basis."

"So, that confirms it, I am your favorite because Regina didn't have the ability to fill my void."

"You are a mess. Listen to me. I need you to accept that everything that happened to me, it's all in the past. There is no need to keep dwelling on it. What you need to do is focus on the present, which means your woman and your baby. That's your family now, and I want you to make sure everything you do makes them better."

"I don't have any choice. It's the way you and Dad raised me."

~ * ~

Vivianna sobbed as the warm water rushed over her entire body. The more she tried to control the tears the harder they flowed. The shower was the first time since leaving Lakeland Vivianna had been alone. The twenty minutes of solitude forced her to deal with the mess her life had become. Vivianna, consumed with her thoughts, didn't realize how hard she was rubbing her body with the washcloth. *Everything, all my things gone. No more Paris, no more shopping sprees. My father is gone. No more life. I'm Vivianna Harrow. I'm supposed to have everything, and everyone is supposed to want to be me. My life is supposed to be perfect.* Vivianna's reddened as she pushed and shoved the cloth up and down her *arm. How could Quincy look at me every day and pretend I belonged to him? He's just like Momma only his evil is a quiet evil. Momma treats me like it's my fault she got knocked up by a man that didn't want her. I'll never forget the joy on her face when she told me the truth. That sick twisted bitch loved every minute of it. What about me, why didn't anyone care about me?*

Now, I'm here, and I don't even know what here means. How am I going to take care of this baby when I can't take care of myself? I've never had to care for myself. She'll never have the things I had. She'll never know what it's like to have people wait on you. She's going to be stuck. Like me stuck. I had everything, now I'm a pregnant, broke bastard child. Vivianna let the cloth slip from her hands. Vivianna studied the worn white tile and noted all of the small imperfections. Vivianna noticed how at a distance the tiles looked fine but up close there were tiny hairline cracks in some of them. *Distance doesn't give you perspective, it takes it away. All of my wonderful, beautiful things gone. This isn't marble, it's tile. Tile. I have never showered on dingy tiles. I can't breathe. I really can't breathe. What am I going to do? How do I live now? I can't do this.* Vivianna gulped back her sobs when she felt her stomach tighten, the last thing she needed was to vomit. Vivianna knew the sound would send Raymond rushing into the bathroom. Vivianna knew he would pledge to fix the unfixable and that would make her vomit more. *I just don't want to feel right now.*

~ * ~

"You were in there for a while. You okay?"

Vivianna jumped when Raymond put his hands on her shoulders. "Yeah. I was in need of a long shower. I'm just tired, it's been a long day and I needed my muscles to relax, that's all."

Raymond could feel the tension in her shoulders. "You sure that's all? You seem like there's something more? You need me to do something? If you're hungry, I can't make you a plate or go get you something. Just tell me what you need, and I'll get it."

"No, I'm fine. I'm fine." Vivianna snapped. "I don't need you to do anything. I just wanna sleep." Vivianna turned around to face Raymond. "Really, Ray, I'm fine."

"Okay, as long as you're okay. Because you don't look okay."

"Then tell me what I need to do to make you believe I'm okay. Do you want me to smile? If I do that will you let me go to sleep?"

Raymond wrapped her arms around Vivianna as he pulled her into his chest. "Listen I'm sorry. I don't mean to bother you. I just want you to be happy, baby. That's all I want." Vivianna reluctantly wrapped her arms around Raymond. "As long as you're happy I'm happy. Everything is going to be fine, I promise you. I'm going to make you so happy. Our life with our baby is going to be perfect."

Please don't say the word perfect again. Nothing is perfect, nothing is going to ever be perfect for me. My life is over.

~ * ~

It only took Raymond a few minutes to fall into a hard sleep. It had been over twenty-four hours since he stretched his long body out. The sleeper sofa felt like bliss to his tired frame. Vivianna's warm body shattered his slumber. Vivianna slid close to him and placed her head on his chest. "I can't sleep. I don't like being in there alone." Vivianna mumbled in a half whisper. Raymond kissed the top of Vivianna's head as he wrapped his arms around her. Vivianna inhaled Raymond's scent as she listened to the sound of his heartbeat. Raymond could feel the tension that flowed through Vivianna as he rubbed her arm.

"What's wrong?"

"I'm scared I'm not going to do things right. When this baby gets here, she is going to need me to do everything. And she's going to be so tiny. My experience with babies is holding them for a moment at a family gathering. I've never changed a diaper. I've never done everything for anyone not even myself. Some women don't take to their babies. I have a cousin who didn't hold her son for the first three months. My Aunt Lorraine had to move in and do everything for her daughter and grandson. What if I end up being like my cousin? What if I don't have enough to give?"

"What your cousin went through, it's real and happens sometimes. I'm sure I've got a cousin who had a similar experience. But that's not going to be you. So, relax. It's going to be okay, Vivianna, stop worrying. I've got you. Everything is going to be fine. All those things will come. Your instincts will take over and you'll be fine. And I'll be there to help you. Everything you need to give our baby is inside of you."

"But what if my instincts don't show up? What if you're gone and she needs something, and I don't know what to do? Then what do I do with her?"

"You'll know what to do. And, if by the one in billion chance you don't know what to do, call Momma. She will be more than willing to help. Hell, you'll probably have to tell her to stop helping. Baby, you're going to be fine. I don't have any more experience being a father than you have being a mother. But we will figure it out the two of us. And just think, it doesn't matter if we do a great job or an okay job as parents, when the kid becomes a teenager the hate for us will be equally shared." Raymond chuckled as he spoke. "I notice you keep calling our baby she. Never he, always she."

Vivianna hunched her shoulders. "I don't know. Saying she just feels right."

"Then it must be right." Raymond kissed the top of Vivianna's head as she snuggled closer to him. Raymond listened to Vivianna's breathing change as she drifted through the different stages of sleep. Any subtle shift in Raymond's body made Vivianna cling tighter to him. Raymond had no fears about becoming a father. He smiled every time he thought about it. His concerns centered around how Raymond was going to make Vivianna forget about the material things she left behind at Lakeland and focus on what they were building together. Raymond wasn't a fool, he knew he could never provide anything close to Lakeland, but Raymond also knew he had the drive to carve out a life for them that centered around family and love. Something Lakeland was never able to provide. Vivianna positioned her body halfway over Raymond's as she moaned softly. The way her body rubbed against his inner thigh made Raymond want to do anything but sleep.

Yeah, we gotta get our own place.

~ * ~

"There's no need to hover. Come in and sit down."

Vivianna sheepishly followed Doreen's command. Vivianna had put on one of Raymond's old sweatshirts with a pair of his old gym shorts. Everything Vivianna packed suddenly seemed too dressy. The high ponytail gave her face an adolescent like quality. "I'm sorry about last night. I know you wanted us in separate rooms, but I couldn't sleep. I tried to sleep, but the noise and then I started feeling lonely. I have to get used to the all the streetlights and everything. Lakeland is quiet at night. Everything comes to a halt until morning." Vivianna sat at the kitchen table. "But nothing happened; I wouldn't disrespect your rules. Sorry." Vivianna's voice oozed insecurity. Doreen quietly placed a plate filled with bacon, eggs, and potatoes in front of Vivianna.

"It smells good. I hope I can keep it down. I have never had an appetite like this before. This must be how Cora feels, and she's never been pregnant. Just f—" Vivianna felt a twinge of guilt talking about her sister. "Never mind."

"It will all stay down. I put some spices in it that are known for calming a pregnant woman's stomach. Make sure you drink all of this too."

"Thank you, but I don't like milk."

"It's calcium. You have to drink it. What you don't provide the baby will take from you." Doreen's matter-of-fact tone stopped Vivianna from pushing the issue.

"Yes, Ma'am."

"So, you dated my father. Not my real father but the one who raised me."

Doreen didn't answer right away.

"I'm sorry. I was rude to bring it up. I shouldn't have said anything. I don't always think things through before I dive headfirst, as you can tell. I was just trying to have a conversation."

"Facts are never rude. Sometimes unpleasant because they are true, but never rude. Yes, Quincy, your *real father* and I had a thing going.

You don't get to cast him off because there's no biology there. It takes more than blood relation to be a child's father. I'm sure Quincy did the best he could. All things considered." Doreen nodded her head slowly. "Quincy and I were together before he got with your Momma. But I'm assuming you know that already."

Vivianna nodded as she ate. "I'm sorry about everything. I wish it could have been different."

"I don't."

Shocked littered Vivianna's face. "You don't."

"If things had been different, I wouldn't have Raymond and my other kids. You wouldn't be here, and I wouldn't have my first grandchild on the way. Quincy's path is his, and my path is mine. Everything moved the way it was supposed to. The time we had was just the right amount of time for us." Doreen scraped the chair across the floor as she sat across from Vivianna. "You should never wish for the past to be different. Instead, learn from it. And work to make the present and future better. Looking back keeps you stuck, and causes you to rhapsodize the past to the point of forgetting why that part of your life needed to end. You'll see. Here is different, but here can be good as long as you let go of all the things you left."

"I know you said don't look back, but can I ask you a question?"

Doreen nodded her response.

"What were they like? I mean Quincy and Momma. Were they different from what I know them as?"

"I don't wanna hear you call Quincy by his first name again. He's your father, like I said, takes more than blood." Doreen leaned back in the chair as she remembered things she hadn't thought about in decades. "Your father was funny."

Vivianna's eyes grew in amazement.

"Yes, funny. Quincy could have the room in stitches with the stories he would tell. Quincy had this larger-than-life personality that drew people into him. His laugh could overfill a room. Your father could make you laugh so hard and for so long you would forget why you were laughing, and that would make you laugh harder. He could be at home anywhere. You know your father wasn't for the high drama stuff. It was never really his thing. At every event, he would make his way into the kitchen and hang out. He preferred simple over lavish. That's how we met. I was helping out in the kitchen at one of his mother's countless gatherings. My cousin had the flu, so I filled in for her. He came in, fixed a plate, sat down and started talking to everyone like they were old friends. It's strange, the only time I saw him quiet or curt is when he had to interact with the people in his circle. His genuineness made it hard for Quincy to be around phony people."

"What about my mother?"

"Your mother, well, I didn't know Emily. I knew of her. I was removed from Quincy's life almost as soon as your mother entered. But I'm sure you knew that as well. But what I noticed is your mother always seemed like she was trying to figure out who she was. Always trying to mold herself into what others wanted, especially your grandmother. I'm sure it was hard on Quincy and Emily. They were two people pushed into a marriage where love need not apply."

"I know that feeling." Vivianna retorted as she inhaled the last of her eggs.

"Family cycles are hard to break. Your mother learned to mother by the way she was mothered. Your mother is a woman who is always searching, and from what little I saw she was never content with still. She always seemed to surround herself with things to make herself seem important and fulfilled. Your mother put a lot of stock into things. Nothing was ever too big, too grand. There was always room for more even if there wasn't any room. Living a life that always has you wanting more is a very destructive way to live. It will leave you in a place where your things own you instead of you owning them." Doreen placed her hand on Vivianna's. "This isn't going to be easy for you. I would be lying my whole ass off if I told you it would. But if you're willing to fight for it, and give up the material stuff, it can be good, really good. I know my son, and I know he loves you. Not your family name, but you. He can't give you Lakeland, but he will always take care of you. Now eat before it gets cold. Cold food doesn't always settle well on a pregnant woman's stomach."

Chapter Nine

Vivianna slammed the dish in the sink and unleashed another wave of tears. Lately, crying endlessly had become a daily ritual for Vivianna. Vivianna wailed like a wounded animal. Vivianna's sobs grew in volume as she slid down onto the kitchen floor as the smell of overcooked meat and burnt pasta lingered in the air. *I can't do this. I can't do this. I can't, I can't. I hate all of this. I'm not meant for any of this. I don't want any of this. I want to go home. I just want to go home. I hate it here. I'm not supposed to cook. I'm not supposed to take buses. I don't walk. I can't. I can't do any of this. This is not supposed to be my life. How am I going to care for this baby? I'm supposed to have a Momma Mae in my house whose job it is to care for my baby. I can't. I can't. I can't.*

"Hey, hey, hey baby, what's wrong? Is there something wrong with the baby?" Raymond rushed to Vivianna when he heard her cries as he left the bathroom.

The baby. The baby. He always asks about the baby. Well, what about me? Ask about me for once, damnit.

Raymond tried to pick Vivianna up, but she refused. Raymond tried to lift her head, but she buried it deeper in her arm, "Vivi, you're scaring me. I can't help you if you don't tell me what's wrong. Are you hurt? Is the baby hurt?" Vivianna shook her head no as she screamed. "Baby?" Anxiety grew in Raymond's voice. Raymond felt helpless and confused because he didn't know what had changed while he was in the shower. Raymond slid his hands under Vivianna and lifted her off the ground. Raymond cradled Vivianna in his arms as he moved to the living room. Raymond allowed her tears to fill the silence as he rocked her back and forth. He could feel her body tighten as she soaked his bare chest with her tears. Raymond pressed his lips to the side of her face. "Baby, please tell me what's wrong." Raymond whispered over her tears. "Tell me. I

113

can't fix it if you don't tell me."

"I can't tell you, and you can't fix it."

"Yes, you can. And yes, I can."

Vivianna shook her head in defiance.

Raymond lifted her chin and stared into her eyes. "Yes, you can. Now tell me."

"No, I mean I can't. I can't do any of this. I can't cook. I burnt another pan, and it wasn't on the stove long. It was mac and cheese out of the box, which we both hate, but I don't know how to make the stuff that comes out of the oven. The beef is brick hard. And it probably tastes a hundred times worse than it looks. Your mother can't keep coming over here to cook for us. I'm terrible at cleaning. Your white socks are every shade of off-white you can imagine because the smell of bleach makes me sick. Grocery shopping stresses me out. I can't do anything I'm supposed to do. I'm a failure. This baby is going to need me to do everything, and I can't cook without burning a pan. Ray, I can't." Vivianna gulped. "There is still so much stuff she needs, and we don't have it. I have a crib, no bassinet. I know I don't have enough clothes. She's going to need more than two weeks of clothes. We can't afford to have professional newborn pictures done. She only has a couple of stuffed animals. I don't have a high chair or playpen. She's going to need so much more than just those things, and the thought of breastfeeding scares me. It's too much, Ray, it's all too much. I'm not ready. I need more time. Four or five months would be better, almost perfect."

Raymond smothered his laughter. Vivianna pleading for more time amused him considering last month Vivianna declared her pregnancy over. "You don't have months, baby. You have days, a week at most." Raymond rubbed Vivianna's arm as he swallowed the last of his amusement. "Listen to me." Raymond repositioned Vivianna on his lap and cupped her face in his hands. "Vivi, our daughter has everything thing she needs. Does she have a closet full of clothes? No, but she has clothes, and she'll never be cold. We'll do laundry once a week. Hell, twice a week if we have to, if that's what it takes to make sure she always has something clean to wear. The day our daughter is born, Mom, my brothers, sister, aunts, uncles, and cousins are going to take so many pictures there isn't going to be a need for a photographer. If one were there, believe me when I say he or she would get pushed out the way. We have a crib. She doesn't need a bassinet. But if you really feel one is necessary, I'll make one out of the top dresser drawer. Hell, my Momma used a dresser drawer as a bassinet with us, and we all turned out fine. What our baby needs is you, and me, and not a bunch of things. Things can't teach her how to walk and talk. Things can't change her and feed her. Things can't hug her and hold her. Things can't teach her to be a woman. Things can't be an example of what a good man is. Things are just stuff, and they don't make good parents. I need you to let the things go, Vivianna. Half the time stuff just gets in the way of living because people hold onto stuff so tight, they obsess about their stuff. Where it's at, what happens if someone tries to take their stuff, how do I get more stuff, that they stop living and enjoying life. And just live for their stuff. "Vivianna lowered her eyes, and Raymond pulled her gaze back up. "I mean it, Vivianna. I need you to let the things go. It's not good for our baby girl or us. Everything we need we have. Everything."

Vivianna laid her head of Raymond's chest. "You always find a way to calm things down and make me feel better about our life together."

"I'm your man: that's my job. I'm supposed to make my baby feel better." Raymond placed a soft kiss on top of Vivianna's forehead. "Our life may not be perfect but it's ours and right for us. Our family is going to be just fine. Better than fine, you'll see. We are where we are supposed to be."

Vivianna jolted up and stared at Raymond. Her cheeks turned deep red. "I think my water broke."

Raymond let out a hearty laugh as the warm fluid soaked through his jeans. "I hope so because if it didn't then you just peed on me, which means we have a lot more to discuss."

~ * ~

"Do you think she likes me?" Vivianna stared into Grayson's week-old ebony-colored eyes. Vivianna found amazement in every yawn, every sound, and every movement Grayson made. As flawless and smooth as Grayson's baby skin glowed, the opaque complexion of Grayson's skin blocked her from being genuinely overjoyed and completely in love with motherhood. Vivianna studied her daughter's nose and full baby lips and wondered in vain if they would change and look more like her features. Grayson's full-bodied yawn exaggerated the fullness of her cheeks. Through no choice of her own Grayson fully embraced her father's looks and his family's traits.

"I think—" Raymond slid next to Vivianna on the sofa, "no, I know Grayson doesn't like you. Grayson is in love with you." Raymond tested the bottle a second time before he passed it to Vivianna. Raymond wrapped his arm around Vivianna as she fed their daughter. "You know, I wasn't sure about the name considering it's your mother's middle name. But in a strange way it fits. I look at Grayson and I couldn't imagine calling her anything else."

"My mother didn't like her middle name. Momma said it sounded like a boy's name. I always thought it was beautiful. Do you think she'll change?" Vivianna listened to Grayson grunt as she drank her formula.

"Your mother, I don't know, maybe? Babies have a way of softening a person's heart. But I would be lying to you if I said I wanted my daughter around your mother. She would have to come here if you really wanted her to see Grayson. There is no way I'm taking Grayson to Lakeland. Sorry, baby, I can't allow that."

"No, Ray, I mean Grayson."

"Change how? What do you mean?"

Vivianna studied Grayson. "She's just so. I don't know. I mean her skin tone and her hair. Her curls are so tight. I expected her hair to be more like mine. I don't know she's going to look. I just thought she would be more—"

Raymond took a moment to gather his words. He knew where Vivianna was going with the conversation and he wasn't pleased. "Vivianna, our daughter is adorable and she's going to grow even more beautiful as she gets older. It doesn't matter that she favors my side of the family over yours. She's still our daughter no matter who she looks like. Does she need to look like you to be yours?"

"No, but I figured she would look just like me. She would have my advantages. It's different in life when a woman looks like me. There are places I can go and organizations I can join because of my skin, my looks, and I want her to have those opportunities. I want certain doors to be open to her, and now I just don't know."

"Grayson doesn't need to be around anyone who is only going to see her as her skin color. If they can't get over her skin then they aren't worthy of being around her. She doesn't need those so-called opportunities. Our daughter is going to be able to do anything she wants to do in life. Her skin color is not going to hold her back because I'm not going to let her think of herself as anything less than wonderful and limitless. And anyone who thinks dark-skinned women can't succeed clearly needs to have a conversation with my sister. She would be more than happy to set them straight. Regina may get on my last nerve, but she is also a successful business owner twice over. Our job is to love her and teach her that her skin tone is not in any way a liability. We have an obligation to fill her mind with a positive image of herself. As long as Grayson knows her mother doesn't see her as less than she'll be fast on her way to overcoming the light skin dark skin good hair bullshit. Grayson is Grayson."

Vivianna knew she had better leave the conversation alone. It wasn't worth the argument to try and explain to Raymond how people treated dark-skinned women back home. She knew Raymond didn't give a damn about back home. Vivianna immediately felt a little lost when she thought about Lakeland and all the things she could provide Grayson if they were there. Vivianna also thought about all of the things she would get back if they were there as she cradled her daughter in her arms and looked around her apartment. Vivianna knew a windfall for Grayson meant a windfall for her as well. Vivianna could smell the crêpes that were always served for Sunday brunch and taste the mimosas she hadn't had since leaving Lakeland. Vivianna romanticized the private fittings at clothing stores and the endless gifts that appeared every birthday and poured from under the Christmas tree. Vivianna tried to shake her growing need for those things, but the need etched itself in her DNA. Vivianna blocked out the misery that plagued her at Lakeland. *When is it going to stop being so ordinary?*

Chapter Ten

Vivianna made a habit of window-shopping with Grayson at least twice a week, it broke up her domestic life. She explained all of the different designers in the display windows to her and talked about the different fabrics, patterns, and colors used. Vivianna explained the differences between couture, retro, chic, and vintage. In a strange way, the window walks gave Vivianna comfort. The high-end dresses and shoes reminded her of the things she used to wear. Vivianna's desire for material things allowed her to sentimentalize her past and fault the good in her present life. Vivianna paused mid-sentence when she heard her name called. It had been a long time since she heard her name said with such a strong Southern accent. The familiar voice made Vivianna's body tense, and a chill ran down her spine. Vivianna quickly maneuvered her stroller through the endless people in front of her. Vivianna quickened her pace as the voice grew louder. Vivianna's heart vied like a racehorse headed towards the finish line, and her palms sweated as she gripped the thrift store stroller. Vivianna barely uttered a sorry as she cut off another mother with her stroller, desperate to lose the voice.

"Vivianna!" the winded well-dressed woman said as she rushed in front of Vivianna and stopped in her path. "Damn, you walk fast. I thought for sure you heard me call your name but then you just took off. Deer don't even move as fast you were during hunting season. My word, I'm going to need a latte after all that cardio." The woman tightened the belt on her winter white Chanel oat. The woman pushed her endless wind-thrown raven-colored hair out of her face. "Look at us. I knew the world was small, but bumping into you right now makes it feel downright tiny. Never in several lifetimes did I think I would cross paths with you and in Chicago of all places. How are you? Tell me everything. I want all the details." The woman gave Vivianna a once-over pity glance. "I love this whole modest chic thing you're doing. It's so earthy. It's very first apartment vintage." The woman, same age as Vivianna, causally rubbed the side of Vivianna's arm. "I can't believe the rumors are true; you really did escape to the North. People told me, but I never really believed it until now. I always said not Vivianna, she would never leave her heritage. I always thought you did something romantic like run off to Paris with a lover. But here you are. Just blending in with your surroundings. So, tell what's really going on with you."

First apartment vintage, really, bitch. Yeah, I bet you do want all the details so you can run back and tell everyone. Vivianna found the strength to muster up her best fake smile. Vivianna felt her stomach constrict as she spoke. "I'm doing fine, Michelle. As for the great escape, there was no great escape. Just life. Life having its way is how I ended up here in Chicago in the cold weather." Vivianna forced a saccharine giggle past her teeth. "That and my terrible sense of direction sent me in the opposite direction of Paris. Now that we have discussed me, how did a girl who hates to leave the house in anything below fifty-degree weather end up in Chicago of all places?" Vivianna forced another fake smile.

"I'm getting married." Michelle squealed as she flashed her three-carat emerald-cut diamond ring. "To Brad Lafayette. I know you remember him. Brad was two grades ahead of us in school, captain of the football team."

Remember him? Child, please, I fucked him so hard he screamed my full name out. I'm the reason why you're having mind-blowing sex. You're welcome, you dizzy bitch. "I vaguely remember a Brad. But I was more into the soccer players." Thirty degrees outside plus the wind chill and Vivianna's demeanor could make it even colder.

"Well, every woman wanted him, and I got him. He's all mine. Forever and ever." Michelle pushed her narrow rectangular glasses up on her round face. Michelle's words oozed of insecurity. "Three months and he popped the question. Just like." Michelle snapped her fingers. "But I guess when you know, you know."

So you say. Vivianna matched Michelle bogus smile for bogus smile. "Three months, that's awfully fast. Is that gunpowder I smell? Never mind."

Michelle took a long guilty pause. "Well, anyway, Momma's been driving me crazy with all her grand plans. But I guess when you're the only girl in the family it's nothing but best for the princess. I'm here interviewing potential photographers. Momma said she wanted to use someone no one in town had ever used before, you know really give them something to talk about, and with my dress coming from Paris there will be plenty of envy gossip. The flowers are being flown in from St. Croix. Momma is having my cake made by one of the most exclusive bakers in New York. Her client list is a who's who among actors and politicians." Michelle squealed. "I've lost count of the number of cases of champagne ordered. Daddy even got me a horse-drawn carriage, all white horses. It's going to make Olivia Ellington's wedding look absolutely department store clearance. She got married right after you left, to Richard Weston." Michelle studied Grayson in her stroller. "Now who is this little one?" Michelle stooped down to admire Grayson.

"Her name is Grayson."

"She has such an interesting look, and that hair. It's so urban and wild. Who's her mother do I know her?"

"I'm her mother."

"Oh, that's interesting. She's so, colored. Is her father from the West Indies or maybe Senegal? Her hair has a Senegal type of texture." Michelle ran her hand over Grayson's hair and face.

"Yes, Senegal." Vivianna weak smile mirrored her self-loathing. Vivianna couldn't stand the thought of Michelle knowing her daughter's father was just a working-class average dark-skinned man. "He's a med student. Neurosurgery is going to be his specialty. His father is in politics in Senegal, and his mother has a royal lineage. You know, pre-colonization and all."

"Good choice. There is a lot of money in neurosurgery. Ear, nose, and throat doctors are so boring and common. And I heard it doesn't pay well either. I guess royal lineage is royal lineage even if it is pre-colonization and all." Michelle took a long dramatic pause before she spoke again. "Well, at least you can play up her being an exotic dark skinned and being of a royal line. It will be far better for her, in the long run, to play up being royal and exotic. Ordinary dark skin doesn't do well

120

among our kind. Her father being a doctor, and grandfather in politics will help too. And who knows? With the right cream she could be a better hue in no time." Michelle lowered her voice. "Especially if you keep her out of the sun."

Vivianna felt her shallowness take hold. "Oh absolutely. Everything is more than possible with the right creams."

"Well as much as I would love to chat. I've got to meet with the photographer. Please let me know the next time you're home. We'll have to get together."

"Of course. I wouldn't have it any other way." Vivianna gritted her teeth as she watched Michelle bounce down the sidewalk. Vivianna screamed on the inside. Vivianna felt she had suffered an undue humiliation. *This shit stops today.*

"Thirty-five dollars. Shit." Vivianna mumbled her disappointment under her breath as she eyed the box. The overtly despairing slogan on the box meant nothing to Vivianna. She focused on the phrase "guaranteed to be lighter and brighter in three weeks." Vivianna shifted her stare from the box to Grayson who was too pre-occupied with her plastic, primary-colored keys and Zwieback biscuit to notice her mother's disapproving gaze.

"Ma'am, are you finding everything okay?"

Vivianna studied the face of the chocolate skinned drug store worker with the braces and round-rimmed glasses. Vivianna couldn't get past how dark the saleswoman's skin was. Vivianna completely overlooked the woman's pleasant expression and how her skin was unblemished, she ignored the natural beauty and retro style the saleswoman possessed. Vivianna refused to see the confidence the young woman had. All Vivianna saw was the darkness that was similar to Grayson's complexion.

"Ma'am?"

"I'm sorry. Yes, I'm fine."

"Okay. If you need anything just let me know."

Vivianna returned an equally pleasant smile. The small exchange with the saleswoman was the reinforcement Vivianna needed. Vivianna made her way to the front register. She waited patiently as the same saleswoman oooed and ahhhed over Grayson as Grayson squirmed in her stroller.

"She's tired." Vivianna placed her small bag in the stroller. "We have had a long day."

"I understand. My husband and I have two little ones. They keep us busy but I can't see my life without them." She smiled and waved at Grayson. "Bye, bye, sweet baby."

Vivianna walked a couple of blocks before she paused. Vivianna quietly pulled the box of lightening cream from behind Grayson's back. A sense of accomplishment washed over Vivianna. *Haven't lost my touch.*

~ * ~

"Vivianna."

"Yes."

"Vivianna." Raymond's voice increased in frustration. "Look at me when I'm talking to you."

Vivianna peeled the magazine she bought earlier away from her face. The frustrated silence echoed between them. "I'm looking. What do you want, Raymond?"

"Stop. I'm serious. I'm not in the mood for the attitude. I've had a really long day and I'm tired. Just answer my question. And then you can go back to being in one of your passive aggressive moods."

"Fine. What do you want to know?"

"I want to know what the hell is this shit?" Raymond snapped as he slammed the jar on the coffee table.

"It's cream. It's for the face and body. It says it right there on the jar." Vivianna's tone was flat and dismissive. "Is there anything else I can explain to you?"

"I know what the hell it is. I want to know what's it doing in my house."

"We don't have a house, remember that promise fell through? 'Oh, wait and see, Vivi, in a year we'll have our own house. You can decorate it any way you want. I promise. At least three bedrooms and a big bathroom for you to get ready in the morning.' Remember saying that to me, Raymond?"

"I told you I'm working on it. I haven't forgotten, it's just taking me longer than expected. But it still doesn't excuse this. Why would you bring this into our apartment?"

Vivianna paused as she thought back to the conversation she had earlier in the day. "I'm just trying to give our daughter the best chance in life, Raymond."

Raymond's voice echoed off the walls as snatched the jar off the table. "Best chance? Bullshit! Grayson doesn't need anything in this jar. Hell, Vivianna do you even know what's in this stuff? One of the main ingredients is mercury. Mercury is poisonous, Vivianna. How is rubbing poison on our daughter good for her? How is poisoning Grayson going to give her a better chance in life? When did poison become a step up?"

Vivianna slammed her magazine on the sofa. "First off stop being so dramatic. If it were really bad, they wouldn't sell it, okay. A little bit of mercury never hurt anyone. You act like I'm feeding it to her."

"Putting it on her skin is just as bad as feeding it to her. That's why they sell it; because they don't care about the people they are selling it to. The makers of this crap don't give a damn about what this does to people of color just as long as they assimilate."

"So what else was I supposed to do? I don't know if you've noticed but our daughter is a poor, dark-skinned black girl from Chicago. Grayson's going to have to find a way to stand out; it's not going to matter how smart she is if she can't get in the door. Beauty is how you get in the door. And as much as you don't like hearing it, lighter and assimilated is how you advance. It's a truth you need to understand and accept. Raymond, she is not going to advance in life looking the way she does. So, I have two options: keeping telling people her father is from Senegal or some other country that sounds exotic, so it makes it more acceptable she's so dark or change her color so she can become more pleasing to mainstream's eye."

Raymond's stomach soured at the words pouring from Vivianna's mouth. She had never openly spoken about their daughter with such disgust before. It stunned Raymond to hear how easily Vivianna could deny he was Grayson's father.

"Are you going to say something or keep staring at me? Geez. I'm going back to my magazine if you don't have anything to say."

"How could you tell someone I'm not Grayson's father?"

Vivianna crossed her arms over her chest. "I didn't say *you* weren't her father. I said her father was a med student from Senegal because it sounds exotic and interesting. But I never mentioned you by name. I never said Raymond is not Grayson's father. I ran into someone I used to go to school with, and she got under my skin. Michelle was showing off her diamond ring, and bragging about who was making her wedding cake, the flowers being flown in and it really pissed me off. And when she looked at Grayson with that *look*, and trust me, I know *the look* because I've given it, I had to do something. So, I created a story she could take back to those nosey bitches back home that was a little better than the truth. You don't understand, Raymond. I had to. I can't have her and those other bitches laughing at me. I just can't."

"I get up every day and work with my hands, but I'm not a damn doctor and never will be. I put in—"

Vivianna threw her hands in the air. "I know, Raymond, I know." Her tone was mocking and cold. "You put in an honest day's work. You don't take anything that doesn't belong to you. I know. But let's deal in reality, there's no place for regular dark-skin girls with regular fathers."

"Every place is a place for our daughter." Raymond paced around the petite living room clutching the jar in his hand. "Everyplace."

"And again, that's where you're wrong. There are without a doubt places I can go, clubs I can join simply because of the way I look. There are people who will listen to me, be kind to me simply because I'm the right skin color for the situation. Men will always open the door for me. Monetary mobility is easier when you look like me."

"I don't know how to tell you this, but there are economically strapped light-skinned people in this world, too. We have a bathroom mirror for you to look in if you don't believe me."

Vivianna glared at Raymond. "You're fucking rude."

Raymond threw the jar against the wall. His eyes oozed with indignation as he stared Vivianna down. Raymond's actions shook Vivianna she had never seen him so enraged. "And you're out of your fucking mind telling someone my daughter is not mine. I would never tell anyone you're not Grayson's mother. I'm proud you're her mother, and it has nothing to do with you being light skinned. It has everything to do with you giving her life. Grayson is you. She's us. My daughter could be the darkest person on the planet and I would love her, care for her, and do everything in my power to give her the best life I could. I don't give a damn about what shade of brown she is, I care about her mind, her heart. Those are the things you should be focused on when it comes to our daughter. Not her fucking skin color."

"It's so easy for you to spout the glass is half full bullshit because you have never had a glass that was overflowing. I'm not like you, Raymond, I can't just worry about her heart." Vivianna's tone turned harsh and cold. "I want her to have nice things. And the darker you are, the harder it is to attract a man with the wealth to give her those things. I don't want her to have to settle."

"This isn't about Grayson. This is about you, Vivianna. You feel like you settled. You feel like you're missing out because I can't buy you all the things you had at Lakeland. It's doesn't matter Lakeland was a cesspool of dysfunction and you were miserable there. All that matters to you is you had a lot of expensive stuff. I told you from day one I would never be able to give you *that life*. I told you I would love you like you had never been loved, and I would always make sure you and our daughter had what you both needed. But I also knew my limitations. You and Grayson have never gone without. I make sure all the bills are paid, never been late on the rent, and there is always plenty of food in the house and clothes for both of you. I'm a good man, but I will never be able to give you or Grayson anything close to Lakeland. Not now, not ever. I need you to understand that and understand we don't need anything like Lakeland to be happy. And our daughter will be great in spite of not being raised in that environment. When are you going to let the lust for material things go?"

"It's not lust. You have no idea what it's like to walk down the street and see women wearing everything you used to have. To ask me not to miss those things is to ask me not to be human. I know it's hard for you to understand because you've never lived the life I have. But this is not easy for me, Ray,"

"You're right I've never lived your life. But, from the little bit I experienced, I would never want to. Nothing I saw was real, it was all a well-manufactured illusion. And if you don't fit the illusion, or better yet delusion, you don't get to play in the deteriorated sandbox. I would rather be from where I'm from and have my daughter be from here, and have her grow up to be a real person versus growing up in anything like Lakeland. I want her to see people as people, and not stepping-stones to something better. I want her to grow up knowing status doesn't mean shit if you're a fucked-up person. Broken little girls grow up to be broken women when no one invests in telling them how important and valuable they are as they are. It doesn't matter how light or dark a woman is, broken is broken. My daughter will not be *broken*."

Vivianna closed the gap between herself and Raymond. Vivianna held his hands as she spoke. She could feel the hurt in his eyes and she knew she had crossed a major line with Raymond but her insecurities couldn't let him be mad at her. "I'm sorry. I'm sorry. I promise it was just one person I told the Senegal thing too. She's someone I never thought I would see again. It bothered me the way she looked Grayson over. She looked at Grayson like our daughter wasn't human, and it got to me. I just wanted her to think of Grayson as more than average, so I told her you were from Senegal. When I said it, Michelle looked at our daughter differently. Not the way she would have acknowledged her if she looked like me, but the little lie gave Grayson an instant edge. That look gave me the idea for the cream. I thought if we could lighten her just a few shades than she would have even more of an advantage." Vivianna put on her best bashful smile as she stepped in closer.

"Stop." Raymond increased the space between them, "Just stop. I'm not in the mood for the pouty girl act. This is not a game, Vivianna. This is serious. Our daughter is a bright and beautiful chocolate-skinned baby who is going to grow into an intelligent and even more beautiful woman. Her beauty is going to go deeper than her looks. Grayson is going to excel at everything she does because she can. I will not allow my daughter's world or potential to be limited by skin color. Grayson is more than worthy the way she is and if anyone doesn't want to deal with her because of the richness of her skin then it's his or her loss. Don't ever limit my daughter and don't ever define her by the ass-backward standard you were defined by. I don't ever want to see that cream or anything like it again in my house." The sternness in Raymond's demand shocked Vivianna. "Love our daughter as she is. Don't love the version you want her to become. I'm gonna take a walk. Don't bother holding dinner for me."

~ * ~

Raymond walked block after block. The heat from his anger kept him from feeling the blustering cold. He shoved his right hand in his pocket and death gripped the jar of bleaching cream with his left. Raymond continued his journey until he ended up in the one place where he could find clarity about the situation.

"Raymond." Doreen's eyes lit up when she opened the door. "You should have told me you were coming over. I would have cooked something. And how dare you show up and not bring my grandbaby with you."

"Momma, I need to talk."

Doreen let out a long sigh when she heard the disappointed tone in Raymond's voice. "Come on in the kitchen. We'll work it out. Whatever it is."

Raymond followed quietly behind Doreen. He collapsed into the closest kitchen chair. "Momma, I don't even know where to bring."

"Start at the beginning." Doreen turned on the kettle. "The easiest way to get to the problem is to start at the beginning of all the confusions."

"It's Vivianna, Momma, she starting that Grayson is too dark thing again and this time I found this damn cream in the house, lightening cream." Raymond slammed the jar on the table.

"Boy, watch my table."

"Sorry, Momma, I just mad."

"I know, but no need to tear up my stuff in the process." Doreen sat across from her son. "Raymond, slavery may have ended generations back, but there are some of us, light and dark, who are still shackled by the institution. It's the chains of mental slavery that still bind all of us to some degree." Doreen took a long sip of hot lemon tea. She traced the design on the tablecloth as she spoke. Doreen always calmed the storms in her children's lives. She studied the jar Raymond brought to her before she released a long exaggerated huff as she quietly placed the jar on the table. "You have to understand, Raymond, Vivianna's people have always considered themselves better because they were lighter than us. It didn't matter that the same people who owned her people owned our people. Her family prides themselves on being able to blur the line between white and non-white because it made it possible for them to inherit and own certain things." Doreen softly held her hand up to Raymond. "Let me finish. I'm not excusing the behavior, or taking sides. I'm also not placing blame, just stating the facts for you. Vivianna is a product of her environment. From the time she was born, Vivianna was raised to hate anyone who wasn't light. She was also raised to worship all things white. Like I said, I'm not excusing the behavior, but this is a lot for Vivianna. It takes a lot of mental strength to resist Vivianna's type of upbringing. We don't walk onto the planet hating each other: we're taught it. Hatred is a powerful thing. It seeps into our DNA and it controls our every thought. It makes us reject the things we should embrace. It makes us not only turn on others, but also ourselves, and in some cases, it can drive a person to madness."

"Momma, it's been over a year. If I hadn't found the jar in the cabinet who knows what effects the cream would have had on Grayson." Raymond expelled an aggravated groan as he folded his arms across his chest. "It's not supposed to be this hard, Momma."

"Son, relationships aren't just hard, but they are also hard work. For you, a year is a long time. But for her, a year isn't long enough to change deep-seated hatred for one's people. You're not dealing with just Vivianna, you're dealing with her entire family tree. What did I tell you before the two of you got your own place? What did I ask you?"

"You told me to be patient with Vivianna, to give her space to make missteps. To understand that in a lot of ways Vivianna was immature when it came to the realities of life. Then you asked me was I sure about moving out so soon?"

"Because?"

"Because while she may appear okay on the inside, she's still pretty broken, and her new life is going to be a hard adjustment for her."

"You were so focused on sleeping in the same bed again you didn't give her the necessary time to really adjust to her new reality."

A wide grin flew across Raymond's face.

"Uhm hum. Exactly."

"So, what do I do?"

"You've got to talk to her and keep talking to her. Be firm when it comes to Grayson. Don't attack her. If you attack her, she'll shut down and lash out. And do the one thing you're not good at, Raymond Anthony, be patient. I have grown to love Vivianna like she was my own. When people ask how many children I have, I always include her in my number. But it doesn't matter how much we all love Vivianna. She has to want to change. It's going to be a long process, but it's all fixable. But you can lose it this way because this is not going to help solve anything. Remember, you jumped in this all quick and fast: now you have to take the lead and work to making it better."

~ * ~

Raymond returned to an unusually quiet apartment for nine at night. Vivianna never went to bed before ten thirty. Raymond loved the fact Vivianna enjoyed staying up late. Raymond used the moonlight that peered through the blinds to guide him to the bedroom. He studied Vivianna while he undressed and wished the peace on her face while she slept would be there in the morning. For a moment Raymond felt a twinge of guilt for bringing Vivianna into his world. Raymond remembered the first time he noticed her in the bar and the smile stretched across her face when he said hello. Raymond wanted that woman back, the woman he taught to cook eggs back. He wanted his Vivi back, and he wanted Vivianna to leave. Raymond slid into bed and molded his body to hers as he kissed her shoulder.

"You're home."

"Go back to sleep, baby. It's late. We'll talk in the morning."

"I wasn't sleep."

Raymond pulled Vivianna into him more.

"I didn't mean to upset you. I just ran into someone I never thought I'd see again. It was just the way she looked at Grayson. I've given it enough times you would have thought I invented it. She just made me so mad looking at Grayson that way. I never want her to be seen as inferior and—"

"I know. I know." Raymond kissed the top of Vivianna's shoulder.

"I know how I obsess about having things sometimes. And how it gets on your nerves. It's just sometimes I miss those things. I had them, and Grayson never will. It's not just about me wanting things it's about Grayson too, I just want our daughter to be whole, and treated like she's special."

"Grayson was born whole. There is no one else in the world like her and that makes her more than special. Bleaching her skin isn't going to do anything but break her and leave her open to a lifetime of mistreatment. Grayson is fine. It's you that has to believe it. You've got to let go of this hold your upbringing has on you. You and our daughter are more than your skin tones. Come here." Raymond turned Vivianna so she faced him. "I know this is hard for you. Living the way we do. My life is not what you dreamed of when you were growing up. I should have found a better way to say things. I was concerned about Grayson. I know some women who turned out to be real train wrecks because of shit like this and I don't want our daughter to end up like them, and you too. I'm concerned about you never really being happy. I want you to be happy, and I want you to love yourself the way I love you. You're more than a face. I know you are. You have talents and gifts you haven't even discovered."

"I know, I'm just scared. Everything I've done has been about my looks. If I'm not the pretty light-skinned girl then who am I?"

"You're whoever Vivianna decides she is." Raymond placed his lips on hers. Raymond pulled back slightly. "Give Vivianna the opportunity to be more than the definition you were given. And let our daughter develop into who she's supposed to be in life."

Vivianna tilted her up and brushed her lips against Raymond's. She pushed her body against Raymond's. Raymond slid his hand down Vivianna's back and under his thin white t-shirt that clung to Vivianna's body. Raymond's calloused hands grabbed Vivianna's behind while he used his tongue to part Vivianna's lips and slid his tongue inside. Raymond and Vivianna found themselves entangled in each other. Her hair tickled the side of his face as she rolled on top of him. Raymond wished the speechless connection they found in the bed would translate to their everyday life.

Chapter Eleven

Three years since Grayson came into the world and Raymond and Vivianna still possessed the same stressors between them. They were still in the same ordinary apartment with the paper-thin walls. Except for the 'new to them' sofa Raymond bought from his boss, the same second-hand furniture stood in the same place, no-name posters taped to the boring walls. Raymond saw the glass as half full because the bills stayed paid, Grayson had everything she needed, Raymond had a good job, and there was plenty of food in the refrigerator. But to Vivianna the glass wasn't half full; it was shattered on the floor in a million pieces. Vivianna desired more and more of the things Raymond would never be able to buy her. Vivianna's desperate need for things caused her to romanticize her life at Lakeland as she spent her days dreaming about the parties, balls, clothes, and vacations. She blocked out her mother's verbal assaults, endless drinking, and her father's benevolent yet distant attitude. Vivianna willfully stayed shackled to the definition of herself Emily had forced on her. Every year Raymond promised to buy Vivianna a house, and every year something wiped out their house down payment savings. The truck repairs, the emergency room bill when Grayson ran a fever, baby clothes, toys, the truck repairs again, the list of saving drainers seemed to grow every year. Raymond did everything he could to keep Vivianna believing in the dream, but she silently abandoned it two years ago.

Through all the unexpected setbacks in their life, Raymond always managed to find extra money for a date night, flowers, or a bottle of wine and chocolates. "I'll ask Mr. and Mrs. Borjarski if they would watch Grayson tonight, and we can go see a movie. I'm not scheduled to work overtime tonight. Look Vivi, I know it's been a rough couple of months around here. I think we need to get out just the two of us." Raymond shoveled his scrambled eggs into his mouth. The extra shifts for extra cash left him with little sleep and sporadic meals. But for him, Vivianna and Grayson were worth all the hard work. He would have worked a hundred hours a week with no complaints for his woman and his daughter. Raymond vowed to work three jobs before Vivianna worked one.

Vivianna studied the crack in the kitchen wall while Raymond spoke. She had become a master at halfway listening to his endless stories and explanations. She always nodded or smiled at the right time, never letting on how she didn't give a damn about the words flowing from his mouth. "Sure, whatever you want to do." Vivianna's voice possessed a dreary tone. Vivianna didn't dare express her misery to Raymond. How every year left Vivianna feeling empty and longing for the things she left at Lakeland. Vivianna's new routine of caring for their daughter, cooking, and cleaning overwhelmed her senses with boredom. Vivianna wiped the pancake syrup off of Grayson's chubby smiling face. Grayson had grown into a clever toddler who possessed Raymond's love of learning and exploring and Vivianna's stubbornness. Vivianna envied Grayson's confidence. She also envied how Raymond lavished love onto Grayson and how Raymond worshiped the ground Grayson toddled on. Grayson could do no wrong in Raymond's eyes; even when Grayson wrote on the wall Raymond explained it away as Grayson having a creative mind. On more than one occasion Vivianna found her jealousy kick in because Grayson could pull Raymond's attention away from her with such ease.

Vivianna finished her coffee as Raymond spoke in between mouthfuls. "Vivi, I know things have been hard on you lately. Grayson is so active, and it's been all on you for the past few months. I know you need a break, but we need the extra money. Once I get a few more things paid off and put a little padding in the saving account again I'll cut back, and I'll be here to help with Grayson more. We will be on our way to saving for our house again in no time." Vivianna forced a smile. Raymond wiped his face as he stood. He kissed Grayson. "Love you, baby girl." Grayson's chubby cheeks jiggled as she giggled. Raymond kissed Vivianna twice. "Love you more and always."

"I know." Vivianna whispered.

Raymond grabbed his bag lunch. "I put a twenty in the emergency money mug if you want to buy a new sweater or something for tonight."

"Okay."

Vivianna listened for Raymond's footsteps to disappear before she moved. Vivianna reached under the kitchen sink and removed a white envelope. Over the past year, she had taken little bits of money out of Raymond's wallet while he slept. Nothing he would ever notice. She also hoarded all of the change she got from grocery shopping as well as collecting all of the spare change she could find around the apartment. Vivianna turned the change into the bank for bills every time she reached ten dollars. Vivianna counted the worn bills twice. It wasn't a lot, but it would cover two bus tickets and maybe a couple of meals. Vivianna glanced over at Grayson who occupied herself with the last of her breakfast. *Vending machine food will have to do.*

Vivianna had reached the end of her ordinary life. Her run-in with Michelle had triggered something in her she could not escape. Vivianna tried to make it about Grayson in the beginning, but when she stopped lying to herself and admitted her truth to herself, she started hiding money to leave. Vivianna would bring Grayson along because she knew her father wouldn't deny her if she had Grayson with her. And, deep down inside, Vivianna's jealousy over the way Raymond fawned over his daughter pissed her off. The little girl inside of Vivianna who never really experienced a father's love ruled her emotions when it came to Grayson. The thought of Grayson living the perfect life without her, and Raymond not giving a damn about her absence because he had Grayson ate at her soul. *Why should she get what I never had? She's not better than me. If anything, she owes me. Her being here is why I had to suffer through life here. The least she can do is be cute, and get me back in the house. Who gives a damn how Raymond will feel? I get to keep her. Fuck him. She's mine.* Vivianna placed the letter it took her a week to write on the table. Vivianna grabbed the twenty out of the coffee mug and put it with the rest.

Grayson stared at her mother. She could sense a change in the mood in the room. Even at three years old Grayson knew when her mother's mood became sour the best thing she could do is make herself small and be as quiet as possible. For a moment Vivianna debated whether or not to wash the dishes. *Let him deal with the mess. It will be the first time in three years he has cleaned something up.* Vivianna scooped

Grayson out of the high chair. "Let's get you ready, Grayson. You and I are going to take a trip. A nice long trip." Vivianna grabbed the pre-packed bag she had hid in the closet weeks ago. "Grayson, stop. Stop it. We're leaving." Vivianna snapped at Grayson as she struggled to get Grayson's hat and gloves on. Vivianna sensed Grayson knew the truth, but Vivianna didn't care. Vivianna was a woman who wanted the luxury of her old life back, and she wasn't going to allow Grayson to stop her from getting it. Vivianna took one last look at the apartment she vowed to never return to as she gathered her daughter and bag. Grayson clung to her panda bear teddy. *We're done with this place. No more winters. No more having to save. No more promises of it will get better. No more dreaming of the house that's never coming. I'm not made for this life.* Vivianna stared into her daughter's eyes. *I'm going to give you a father who can buy us everything.*

~ * ~

Vivianna's body ached from the uncomfortable Greyhound bus seat. Her patience worn from the endless conversations Vivianna endured about Grayson cuteness and smarts. Vivianna nearly lost it when Grayson spent over an hour asking for Raymond. The *Where's daddy?* question over and over shredded Vivianna's nerves down to almost nothing. If the elderly black woman across the aisle hadn't agreed to hold Grayson for a little while Vivianna would have shaken her daughter.

"Finally." Vivianna listened to the sound of the pebble stones under her feet as she dragged her exhausted body up Lakeland's drive. The heel on her bargain basement heels buckled a couple of times as she moved closer to the house. Vivianna almost broke under the weight of carrying Grayson and the bag. *This girl needs to lose weight.* Vivianna marched with aching determination up the long drive. "Baby, do you want to walk for Momma?" Grayson shook her head and squeezed Vivianna tighter. "Of course not. Why would you make anything easier on me?" Vivianna huffed her annoyance under her stale breath. Vivianna's feet burned with exhaustion with every step as she shifted Grayson from side to side trying desperately to find some relief from the weight of Grayson's equally tired body. Vivianna knocked softly on the back door. Vivianna held her breath as she waited for the door to open. She prayed Momma Ma still kept her same schedule. Vivianna's palms pooled with sweat as she watched the knob turn. Vivianna realized as the door made its familiar squeak she had no more money, and no plan B if the door slammed in her face.

"Hi." Vivianna's tired voice echoed her physical appearance and mental state.

"Vivianna?" Brenda gasped as she opened the door wider. Brenda may have only encountered Vivianna a handful of times, but she could never forget those green eyes.

Vivianna nodded her head.

"Come in. Come in." Brenda took the bag off of Vivianna's shoulder. "Let me help you." There was an obdurate silence that lingered between the two of them before Vivianna spoke.

"How are you?"

"No, how are you?" Brenda placed her hand on Vivianna's shoulder. Vivianna struggled to contain her tears. A feeling of failure washed over her because at that moment Vivianna realized she was everything Emily declared three years prior.

"I'm fine." Vivianna's lie didn't convince herself or Brenda. Vivianna gulped back her tears as she forced air down her lungs. "Where's Momma Mae?" Vivianna cleared her throat hard. "Did she go home for the night already?" Vivianna apprehensively asked as she sat Grayson at the head of the kitchen table before resting in the adjacent chair. Vivianna counted on Momma Mae to plead her case to Emily. "I would really like to talk to her."

"Momma doesn't work here anymore. Momma had to slow down last year after doctor's orders. We needed the money, with Momma's medicine and doctor visits so I replaced her here. I've gotta make sure my Momma has everything she needs." Brenda didn't ask she just made two plates. Grayson zealously took the fork from Brenda. "She's beautiful, Vivianna, absolutely beautiful."

Vivianna tried to pretend she wasn't ravenous, but the smell emanating from the plate made her mouth water and stomach growl.

Vivianna savored the taste of macaroni and cheese as Brenda bombarded her with questions she didn't want to answer.

"How did you get here? Where's Ray? How long are you staying?"

Vivianna swallowed hard. "We took the bus. I don't want to talk about Raymond. We're here for good. Where's Momma?" Vivianna knew her foot wasn't fully in the door until her mother said so.

"She and your father are in the den, probably."

"Father, that's a strange word now." Vivianna mumbled under her breath.

"You said you didn't want to talk about Ray, why? Did something happen to him? Momma and Aunt Doreen haven't spoken in a couple of weeks. Is everything okay?"

"I'm sure he's fine." Vivianna's snappish tone made Brenda recoil a bit. "Sorry, I just don't want to talk about him." Vivianna looked up from her plate. "Where did you say Momma was, again?"

Brenda kept her tone controlled. After years of being exposed to the Harrows she knew better than to push the conversation. "In the den. You want me to let her know you're here?"

"Please." Vivianna bit her bottom lip. She couldn't take up permanent residency in the kitchen. Vivianna tried to smooth Grayson's kinky curly Afro down. Grayson pulled her head away as she ate. "Baby, please be good, and smile when you see your grandmother. Show her your pretty teeth. We really need her to like you." Grayson briefly looked at Vivianna as if she spoke a foreign language before she returned to her plate. "And don't eat too much, Momma doesn't like big eaters." Vivianna wiped Grayson's mouth. Grayson protested in the same way she did when they were at the apartment. Vivianna adjusted her worn blouse and pushed her loose hair behind her ears. Vivianna tried to look less ordinary. Vivianna wiped her mouth and corrected her posture. Her heart raced as she heard two sets of footsteps echo closer. Vivianna jumped to full attention when Emily entered the room. Grayson paused at the sound of the chair hitting the floor, shoulders back, feet together, and hands clasped together in front of her. Vivianna glanced over at Grayson to encourage a smile out of her.

Vivianna felt the disgust smeared on Emily's face as Emily looked

Grayson over. Vivianna knew her mother was making a mental list of things wrong with Grayson. Vivianna swallowed her motherly instinct to protect Grayson when Emily commanded Vivianna not to speak. Vivianna looked on in shame as Emily inspected the texture of Grayson's hair. Emily only showed true contentment when Grayson told Emily her name.

"Brenda take my granddaughter upstairs, and get her a proper bath, and put her in whatever nightwear she has until I can buy her proper clothing."

"Yes, Miss Emily."

Grayson struggled with Brenda for a moment. Brenda whispered words of comfort in Grayson's ears to soothe her anxiety.

Emily glared at Vivianna. "The tarnished debutante has come home to roost, I see. I will say I didn't expect you to last in the real world as long as you have. You don't look like complete shit but still shit nonetheless." Emily waved her hand at Vivianna. "You are exuding vomitus in a way only you can." Emily savored the broken look in her daughter's eyes. Emily inhaled the scent of defeat that seeped from Vivianna's pores. "I would say I'm happy you're home but that would be a lie, and I only lie to people I give a damn about." Vivianna didn't make a sound. "No snide remark. I figured poverty had humbled you, I didn't realize it had broken you." A devilish grin ran across Emily's face. "So, am I to assume you want your seat back at this uppity light-skinned house nigger who's living off of massa's money table? That is what you called me before you stormed out with that big-lipped beast. Isn't it?"

"I'm sorry." Vivianna mumbled.

"You're what?"

"Sorry."

"Yes, you are. I'm just glad you finally realize how sorry you are, along with being worthless, pointless and an endless source of disappointment."

Vivianna rolled her eyes as she bit the inside of her cheek.

"Don't you dare roll your eyes at me. You don't have the right to roll your eyes at me. If you find my words so offensive then go upstairs, get your darkie and leave. Let me be very clear, the three years you were gone I never once thought about looking for you. I didn't lose one night's sleep worrying about where you were and if you were okay. You could have been a stripper in a shitty club or a dead tramp in a dumpster. I wouldn't have cared. I didn't ask you back, you showed up. So, don't you dare give me attitude. I don't need you for anything but you need me for everything.

"So, that means I can be as mean and callous with my words as I want to be, as it pertains to you and that child whenever I want, for as long as I want. I will never offer you a kind word. I will never show you compassion. This is going to be a real mommy dearest vibe between the two of us. I just don't care anymore, Vivianna. But because you are a representation of me, I will clean you and her up. Now that you know the terms of staying here, which one is it? Are you going to take your darkie and leave or are you and the darkie staying?"

Vivianna stood silent and studied her hands. Vivianna looked at her chipped nail polish and her grown-out-of-control cuticles. Her eyes moved to her worn skirt and pleather shoes. *I can't go back. I can't go back.* "I'm staying."

"Enough with the humble act. Look at me when you speak to me."

"I said I'm going to stay."

"And the darkie too."

Vivianna crinkled her skirt in her hands. "Yes."

"Say it." Emily folded her arms across her chest and waited for Vivianna to say the word she needed to let her know her daughter was truly broken.

Vivianna swallowed hard before she spoke. "And the darkie too." With those words Vivianna had traded her daughter for material things.

"Then let all your ideas about love and character dissolved, you are a pathetic pretty face and nothing more." Emily pushed herself away from the table. "Make sure you never again forget who owns you. Your decontamination begins tomorrow."

~ * ~

"Get up." Emily violently flung the drapes open. "This isn't a resort. I told you last night your decontamination starts today. You have no idea the number of endless hours I am going to have to put in repairing your image. And that doesn't include the time it's going to take me on that child of yours. It's absolutely ridiculous what you have allowed yourself to become."

Vivianna squinted as the early morning light filled the room. The sixteen hundred-thread count and plush bedspread had put Vivianna in almost a coma-like sleep. She tried to clear the fog from her head. Vivianna's body fought moving out of her warm bed. She wanted nothing more than to pull the covers overhead and sleep from the morning into early afternoon.

Any ounce of dignity Vivianna went to bed was stripped away with Emily's morning rant. "Now." Emily screeched in her all-too-familiar annoyed voice. "You are under my roof, and not where you were. We don't sleep our mornings away here. We don't lay in the bed like common people all day. We get up and get focused. We have appearances to maintain.

"What time is it?" Vivianna sat on the end of the bed and tried to get her thoughts together.

"It's eight, and your daughter has been up. She's downstairs with Brenda eating as if she just discovered she has opposable thumbs, absolutely ridiculous. Get the hell up, Vivianna. Don't you dare make me regret not throwing you both out last night. "

"She's three, Momma, three, she eats like any other three-year-old."

"If she eats like a three-year-old who was raised with etiquette she would chew with her mouth closed. She has no class. By three you were speaking French and drinking out of glasses with ease. You have twenty minutes to shower and get downstairs. I'm having clothes delivered for you to try on. I refuse to allow you to be seen in anything you brought with you. It will all be put in the burn pile."

Vivianna's eyes lit up at the thought of new clothes. "Don't get too excited. This is an investment, nothing more. Hopefully I will be able to clean you and her up. And then maybe, just maybe, I will be able to find the right man who's willing to overlook your flaws and definitely that child's flaws. Marrying you off will net me a return on the decades of money I've spent on you."

~ * ~

Doreen's living room overflowed with family the way it did when Vivianna first arrived.

"We were nothing but nice to her how could she do us like this?" Doreen rarely spoke so openly in front of the entire family, but her heart ached.

"I should go down there and whip her ass. That's what I should do."

"Regina, calm down. Nobody is whipping anybody's behind. Fighting isn't going to solve anything."

Regina rolled her eyes hard.

"Girl, I know you're not rolling your eyes at me like I'm not your Uncle. You might be catching a foot in yours if you roll your eyes at me again. Do you understand me, young lady? You ain't too old. I swear to God you ain't too old."

"Harold, too much yelling at each other isn't going to help either. I'm talking to you too, Regina."

"Sorry, Doreen. I'm just on edge. We all are."

"Yes, ma'am." Regina softened her posture as she mumbled under her breath.

Doreen looked over at Raymond who, still in his work clothes, hadn't uttered more than a few sentences to her since Vivianna had left with Grayson. Raymond looked like a man who had aged ten years in a few hours. Raymond took a deep breath as he stood.

"I gotta go." Raymond kissed Doreen on the cheek. "Momma, I'll see you later."

"Where are you going, baby? We still need to discuss this." Doreen's voice oozed with anxiety laced with concern.

"Listen to your Momma."

"No, Momma, I'm done talking. I gotta go, Momma, I just gotta go. I'm sitting here doing nothing. I don't know what I'm going to do, but I can't just sit here. I don't know what I'm going to do, but I can't do that.

I can't just be still like you want me to be, Momma. My baby girl is gone. My heart doesn't beat the same right now because my baby girl is gone."

"Ray, don't do anything in haste. Haste can make this bad situation much worse. Please, son, I have lost my grandbaby, I can't lose my son too."

"I gotta go, Momma."

"Ray... Raymond... Raymond Anthony."

Raymond waived Doreen off before shutting the door.

~ * ~

Brenda softly hummed as she finished the last braid in Grayson's hair. Brenda had found that her own daughter's hair was easier to comb when you occupied her with breakfast. The six cornrows Brenda put in Grayson's had made her face look even fuller and her resemblance to Raymond undeniable. "There you go. Now let's see if we can find your mommy." Brenda hadn't told Momma Mae yet about Vivianna's arrival. Her mother had been under enough stress in the last few weeks. Momma Mae's in and out of the hospital took a toll on everyone and Brenda couldn't handle another relapse. Brenda smiled at how easily Grayson had taken to her. Brenda wiped the crumbs off of Grayson's face as she carried her down the hallway. "You look so much like you your daddy." Just the sound of the word daddy made Grayson's eyes light up.

"And where are you taking her?"

The sound of Emily's voice made Grayson uneasy.

"We were going to find Vivianna."

Emily eyed Grayson. "No need, she has fittings today. Take the child outside to play."

"Yes, Miss Emily."

"Also please refrain from putting those ghetto braids in my granddaughter's hair. And make sure she has on a hat. She's already too dark."

"Yes, Ma'am."

Chapter Twelve

Emily spent seven months and incalculable hours shopping Vivianna around to several different men looking to settle down, but no amount of family lineage allowed men who hailed from color-stuck families to overlook Grayson. Emily had underestimated the complexity of her *Grayson* situation. Emily poured tea as she spoke with one of her closest, and honestly only real friend, Orinda Williams.

"Emily, you know I have always thought the world of you and your family. We've been friends since we were assigned seats next to each other in second grade." Orinda was like Emily, a woman manufactured by Southern colonialism who prided herself on the number of dead Anglo-Saxon slave-owning relatives in her bloodline. "I value you like a sister."

"Thank you, Orinda. And I think the same of you."

Orinda sipped her ice tea with the large lemon wedge pushed halfway down. "No thank you is needed. I've always known you felt the same way about me."

"No, I need to say thank you. You have no idea how much your words mean to me especially with everything I have endured over the past months. But—" Emily smoothed the pleats in her navy blue skirt which fell a few inches below the knee. Emily kept her legs crossed at the ankles. Her white blouse was pressed to perfection and her hair was in its usual bun that made her look tired even when well rested. "I think my family has finally turned the corner. Jackson has pulled himself together. Cora has found a suitor to overlook her weight problems. Vivianna and your Anthony are really hitting it off, well." Emily gazed out the den window as she spoke. "I couldn't ask for a better son-in-law."

"And that's what I wanted to talk to you about, Emily. Like I said earlier, I adore you like a sister. In some respects, you're closer to me than my own blood sister. And I am so thrilled Vivianna has returned home and is getting herself together. You deserve that peace. Hell, you've earned it." Emily felt tightness in her stomach as Orinda carefully formed her sentences. "So, it pains my heart deeply to say this. While I think Vivianna is developing into a lovely adult despite all the bumps and hurdles." The sound of Orinda's glass hitting the table echoed through the silence.

Emily cut Orinda off. "Orry, if there is anything she's lacking I can fix it. Give me four more months, six at the absolute maximum. I will mold Vivianna into whatever type of daughter-in-law you desire. Vivianna speaks fluent French. She will learn another language of your choosing, maybe Italian, so they can travel to Italy on their honeymoon or maybe German, whatever your preference. I will make sure she puts in the time to learn it. You have my word. If it's her weight, I can have her twenty pounds lighter if you prefer. Whatever you want, Orry, I'm willing to have anything done. And I do mean anything, Orry. Nothing is off limits. Please Orry, don't shut me out." Orinda knew the exact anything Emily offered to have done.

Orinda made no attempt to hide the disappointment she felt watching her best friend beg her for the impossible. "Emily, I'm going to save us both the discomfort of a lengthy dialogue about this issue. Like I said earlier, Vivianna has done a huge transformation. She's now refined, and well put-together. She is now the young woman she was meant to be before her descent into her wild child phase, which leads to the whole incident per se. As great as her progress is her indiscretion comes with a glaring reminder." Orinda motioned for Emily to pause. "Please let me finish. It won't matter how much you straighten her hair, or how mannered she is. You can't overlook her physical appearance. The child is not going to be able to move in certain circles and you know this, Emily. As Anthony's mother, I have an obligation to put him first. He's considering a career in politics, and the child is not a good look for Anthony or my family. Now, while I respect your decision to keep the child, I just don't understand it. A child like that would be better off with people more like her. Did you really consider the social implications of having her around? I'm not judging you, Emily, so please don't take it that way, because all things considered you're definitely a better woman than me for taking on such a daunting task. You are a saint, Emily, a true saint. But as your friend, I must say I will never understand why you didn't send her back with her father when he showed up. From the looks of her, she would fit in better with them. It would have solved all of your problems if you had. Grayson's just not made for our circles. I'm so sorry, Emily, I can't. I just can't. Maybe you should consider other ethnicities or lowering your standards a bit. I'm not saying bottom of the barrel by any means, but maybe a nice successful gentleman with a slight infidelity problem might be a better fit. You know, kind of speaking of one who's not reckless, knows better than to create outside children. He simply keeps a steady on the side, and the steady knows her place. Those type of men are more willing to overlook such flaws."

Emily sighed deeply. "I didn't want to keep her I had to keep her. Keeping Grayson keeps Vivianna under control, Orry."

~ * ~

Grayson yelled hysterically. Her earth-shattering screams violently bounced off the wall and traveled down the stairs and muted the sound of the piano as they assaulted Cora's ears. Cora's heart jumped as she flew to what was now Grayson's room. Grayson's room possessed the typical cliché princess-pink look. The white canopy bed with the matching white lace skirt and lace fabric for the canopy. The bed which had been Vivianna's adorned one wall; it also had an ultra frilly pink and white comforter with white lace trim. There were pink curtains, a pink rug, a giant stuffed teddy bear adorned the corner, and dolls that looked nothing like Grayson lay on the bed.

"Hold still." Vivianna gripped Grayson's hair tight with one hand as she violently dragged the comb through Grayson's thick and heavily-textured black hair. "Damnit, hold the hell still," Vivianna shrieked. "Hold still, I said." Vivianna jerked Grayson's head back and forth.

"Ouch, ouch." Tears mixed with snot ran down Grayson's face as she struggled against Vivianna's heavy hand. Grayson's scream turned to an ear-piercing shrill on the last tug.

"Hold still, or I'll rip your nigger hair out of your head." Vivianna jerked Grayson's head back. "I swear to God, I'll rip it all out, all of it. You make me sick with this hair. I can't stand it. You make me sick. Damnit, I said hold still."

"Vivianna, what the hell is wrong with you. I can hear Grayson screaming downstairs." Cora stormed through the bedroom door.

"So what? Why are you here anyway?" Vivianna glared at Cora.

"Don't worry about why I'm here. Why is Grayson screaming? She sounds terrified and like she's in severe pain. What in the hell are you doing to her?"

"Well maybe if you were at your house instead of always here you wouldn't hear anything. If you must mind my business instead of your own, I'm sick and tired of fighting with this head of hers. Every day it gets harder to comb through. I'm sick of it. This girl isn't in pain she is a pain. And she gets on my last nerve too with all this damn hard-to-comb hair."

Grayson gulped and gasped as she tried to calm herself down. Grayson wiped her nose on the arm of her sweater. Her tiny hands trembled at the sight of the comb Vivianna waved around while she ranted. "No one's head should be this nappy. I have better things to do than to spend all day combing through her nappy hair. It's pissing me off."

"She's a child, you dumb bitch. You don't pull on a child's hair the way you are. You're going to hurt her jerking her head back and forth the way you are." Cora grabbed onto the comb. "Let go." Vivianna stared Cora down before relinquishing the wide tooth comb. Cora picked Grayson up and pulled her into her. Cora decorated Grayson's face with kisses. "It's okay, baby; Aunt Cora is here." The warmth of Cora's whispered words helped Grayson calm her breath. Grayson balled parts of Cora's shirt into her fist as she pushed her body into Cora's. Grayson clung to Cora as a drowning person clings to a lifeguard for survival.

Cora glared at Vivianna. Cora's light eyes oozed revolution for her younger sister. "What the hell is wrong with you?" Cora gritted through her capped teeth. Cora wasn't the meek, frail, and unsure-of-herself woman Vivianna had been accustomed to engaging in arguments. Gone were the days of Cora being the easy mark. Cora still had the same full face as well as her full curves, but the gym had allowed her to tone it all. Cora traded in her middle of the back length hair which always hid her face for a sleek top of the shoulder length bob dyed dark brown with blond highlights. Cora rubbed Grayson's back in a circular motion. "I asked you a question. What in the hell is wrong with you? She's just a baby."

"She's not a baby."

"You know what I mean. You shouldn't treat Grayson the way you do. Every day it gets worse. You treat her like she's nothing."

"I'm tired of dealing with her nappy hair. I'm tired of dealing with her."

"Vivianna, she can hear you."

"I don't care." Vivianna flung her body onto Grayson's bed. "I don't care. I'm sick of trying with her. Everything I do, and she still looks so, so *black*. I'm tired of everyone looking at me funny because she so dark. She's ruining my life."

"Vivianna, this is your daughter." Cora said in a loud whisper as she rocked Grayson. "Your *daughter*. You carried her nine months, gave birth to her. She is you. Or did moving back here cause you to forget that? Grayson didn't ask for any of this. Just because a couple of color-struck fools turned down a second date doesn't mean you take it out on your daughter."

"A couple? Try everyone, Cora. Anthony was beyond perfect. We got along great. He checked all the boxes on my list. But one look at *her*, and he would rather be a friend. Orinda told Mother Grayson was the problem. Because of her Orinda doesn't want me anywhere near her family."

"Oh please, Orinda is a dried-up old fool. You should be glad she doesn't want you in her family. You don't want to be anywhere near the fallout when Anthony comes out of the closet."

"You mean?" Vivianna's face lit up when she thought of hot gossip.

"Yes, I could tell you stories but I won't. He doesn't need any more people gossiping about him."

"Well, that explains why he made eye contact with me, and totally ignored my fabulous cleavage. And here I thought it was because he was into legs. I mean I have those too, but my tits have always held a man's attention."

Cora rolled her eyes. "Whatever the reason. Still doesn't excuse your treatment of Grayson. You knew from the beginning she wasn't going to look like us. You chose her father, and you knew what he looked like. Don't act like his blackness was a surprise. You knew damn well Grayson wasn't going to look like your half-white ass."

"Why is everybody blaming me for this, for her? This is not my fault. I didn't want any of this either. You and momma are always blaming me like I had a choice."

"What do you mean no choice? Everything you did here was your choice. You want to talk about no choice? Do you, Vivianna? Because I know firsthand what it's like to have no choice. I had no choice but to live cautious because you were always reckless. I had no choice but to take the blame for every bullshit blunder you made. Because every mistake you made Momma always blamed me. Your wrongs were always my faults. I had no choice but to clean up behind you. But you, you, Vivianna, you always had a choice."

"Traded in your cape for a cross I see."

"Whatever."

"No, don't whatever me. How come you don't care how I feel? Why don't you care how having her has affected my life? Not once have you, or anyone asked about me. Am I happy? I'm your sister, and all you're worried about is her. When is somebody going to worry about me?" Vivianna slammed her fist down on the bed. "When. When is it my turn to be happy?"

"Wow, are you serious right now? You always make it about you. When hasn't it been your turn to be happy? You're a mother, Vivianna. A mother, which means your child comes first. And I did worry about you. I worry about you when I found you on the bathroom floor, I worry about you when you left that night, and I worried every night you were gone. And now I worry about this little one. It's sad that being a mother has done nothing to change your self-centeredness. Hell, I think it may have made it worse. She's a child, Vivianna, that's why I'm concerned. You are going to destroy her if you keep treating Grayson the way you do. And it's not right. Hell, it would be nice to have one generation in this family that isn't damaged beyond repair."

"Too bad your fat ass isn't as invested in your life as you are in what happens to Grayson."

"Fuck you. I'm fifty pounds lighter."

"More like thirty, and you definitely didn't lose any around the chin."

"You're lucky I'm holding your daughter."

"Or what, you'd run to the kitchen and cry over a plate of food."

"No, I'd beat the shit out your sorry ass. I'm not the Cora you remember, Vivianna. Under the right circumstance, you could find yourself counting the number of teeth left in your head. I have no problem knocking you out."

"If you were trying to put fear in me, you failed."

"The look in your eyes tells me I succeeded." Cora shifted Grayson to her other side. Grayson held onto Cora even tighter. Grayson wrapped her legs around Cora's waist. "Vivianna, you need to stop this. You are no better than Momma with the crap that comes out of your mouth to Grayson. You go out of your way to hate this precious little girl. It breaks my heart to see you treat her the way you do. You would think you would be different considering you know firsthand what it feels like to be ridiculed and belittled by a woman who's supposed to love and raise you."

"If it's so bad, Cora, then why are you here instead of at home with your lawyer husband. Aren't you supposed to be living your happy-ever-after right now? Creating your two-point-five perfect kids to splatter on the Christmas cards. And don't you dare tell me you come here to use the piano. I'm sure Terry would buy you a piano."

"Beating up on me isn't going to stop you from having to deal with your reality. You know I could ask you the same question about being here. If memory serves, you flew out of here vowing never to return. You said you had found something better. You left here all in love with being in love. But here you are three years later, back at Lakeland and treating your daughter the way Momma treated us. Maybe we keep coming back here because the dysfunction is familiar and familiar makes it comfortable. Or maybe on a subconscious level, the allure of things and status has forced us to forgo our happiness and well-being."

"Speak for yourself. I lived in the real world, and it sucked.

There's nothing happy out there, just thrift-store furniture, thin apartment walls, and cheap wine. No, thank you. I'll take affluent dysfunction over poverty any day. I need a life that's more than what I had." Vivianna sat up with her legs pretzel style. Vivianna toyed with one of the dolls on Grayson's bed. "I mean, Grayson needs a life void of poverty. Trust me when I say there is nothing pretty about poverty. Grayson needs comforts and opportunity."

"No, Vivianna, you said it right, you needed more because I'm pretty sure Grayson was fine with what she had. Grayson probably loved everything about her life. I still don't understand how you could take her from her father. Don't you feel any guilt considering your own situation?"

Vivianna scoffed. "She's mine, that's why I took her. He doesn't get to keep my doll. Damnit, Cora, you've got my nerves on edge. I meant to say, daughter. And I don't have a situation, Cora. As for that thing I was dumb enough to deal with I sure he'll find some other thing to spawn a litter with, and live happily-ever-broke."

Cora kept rocking Grayson in her arms. "You know Grayson isn't the doll we fought over as kids. You know the one you only wanted when I wanted it. She's a person, and she deserves a mother who wants her always. Not a mother who uses her to get things or just when someone else does or keeps her as a way to get back at her father. You don't really want to be her mother, and it's not fair to Grayson. He didn't mess your life up. You made choices. You can't erase the fact that Raymond is her father. Vivianna, you keep acting the way you are, and you are going to end up being a miserable mirror image of our mother. A woman determined to make her children just as unhappy as she is, a woman who pushes away anyone who tried to love her. And if you do get married, a woman who drags her husband to an early grave with her countless antics. You weren't back here six months before daddy died. I'm not blaming you for his heart attack, but the mass destruction you and Mother rain down on each other didn't help things."

"Like I said you're still here. Sitting at the dinner table every Sunday. Never missing any of Momma's events. Fat Cora always near." Vivianna snapped back.

"No one knows better than me I'm still here. I'm not proud of it.

That's why I don't have two-point-five kids for the Christmas cards. I refuse to do to a child what was done to me. I refuse to drag them into my mess. I may never have children if I can't figure out what this thing is that keeps me stuck here. Sitting at the dinner table every Sunday like Pavlov's experiment."

Vivianna scrunched her face. "Who the hell is Pavlov? A cousin I don't know."

"Damn Vivianna, read something besides a romance novel once in a while. I'll finish Grayson's hair." Cora closed the door behind her.

Vivianna lay on Grayson's bed staring at the ceiling. Vivianna thought back to the night Raymond took her on the roof to watch the movie. Vivianna remembered how good it felt to be free and living in the moment. Vivianna had tried to remember her time with Raymond in a different way, but the good always outweighed the lies she tried to tell herself. Vivianna rejected Grayson because she was a constant reminder of what was good. Vivianna felt if she found fault in Grayson then the fault was a product of her father. Vivianna engaged in a despise the child and eventually, you'll hate the father game.

Why couldn't he have been rich?

Chapter Thirteen

After a quick engagement and a small wedding under one of Lakeland's grand willow trees, Vivianna upgraded to the title of wife, a title she welcomed as a means to her ends. Courtland watched the last of the burnt-orange evening sky fade into the darker blue-black cosmos as he held Grayson's limp body on his chest. "Beautiful. Beautiful. Beautiful. My beautiful." Grayson nuzzled her four-year-old head in Courtland's neck as he held her. Courtland turned out to be the husband Vivianna didn't deserve and the father Grayson needed for her situation. Courtland opened his heart and welcomed Grayson into the place a man reserves for his daughter. Something in Grayson's eyes told him he needed to be there even if the story Vivianna told him didn't make any sense.

Vivianna rolled her eyes. "Really Courtland, enough with all the beautiful stuff. I swear you call her that more than you call her Grayson." Vivianna swatted the evening bugs out of the air as they sat under the giant weeping willow tree. The sound of the katydids filled in the silence between exchanges.

"Why does it bother you so much to hear me refer to Grayson as beautiful? My beautiful."

"I don't want you filling Grayson's head with foolishness. She needs to learn her limitations while she young." Vivianna rubbed her seven-months-pregnant belly. "She's almost five years old. Don't you think she's getting too old for you to rock like that? She's must be heavy as hell." Vivianna hated the nightly ritual Courtland had requested after they married. Courtland made it clear from the beginning he didn't enjoy living at Lakeland, but he would tolerate it as long as Vivianna agreed to certain things, and sitting under the tree at night and talking was one. Vivianna married Courtland to appease Emily. Vivianna got pregnant soon after to get back in good standing with Emily. Vivianna resented the way Courtland actually believed in their marriage.

"Enough. She's as light as air." Courtland kissed Grayson on her shoulder. "And beyond beautiful."

"You should never lie and tell a woman she's small when she's not. It gives her a false sense of self. Look at Cora, her husband is constantly telling her how she looks good and she believes him. Grayson can't afford to see the world through rose-colored glasses. Grayson needs to be rooted in reality. Grayson is not going to be like this one." Vivianna patted her stomach. "Grayson is never going to be able to wow the room the way I do, or the way this one will. Grayson is going to have to focus on being smart and leave pretty to the rest of us. She's not going to have the luxury of being catered to by a man."

"The only limits Grayson will have are the ones you put on her. Stop thinking of her as flawed. Grayson is going to focus on her education because little girls need to know they are just as smart as little boys. Grayson is my beautiful little girl, and the one you're carrying is going to be my gorgeous little girl. They are also going to be my smart girls as well."

Courtland rubbed Grayson's back. "Vivianna, there is nothing wrong with the way Grayson looks. I want our daughters to wow the room because the room is in awe of their brilliance. Looks fade, and hair turns grey, but their intelligence will always be with them. This beautiful little girl has done nothing to deserve the limits you place on her. What is your issue with her? You take such a heavy-handed approach to Grayson. You always see her through a very narrow lens."

"She too, too, Courtland, she's just too—"

A grimace soured Courtland's face. "Don't you dare say dark, Vivianna. Don't you dare let the word come out of your mouth. You know how I feel about that. I told you from the beginning to never look at Grayson like that again." Courtland's voice grew to a loud whisper. "I don't know what happened between you and her father. I wish you would tell me, but I've learned to leave it alone. But it's clear your issue with him is blocking you from seeing Grayson."

"So, you're saying I don't know the difference between him and here? Well, you're wrong because I do. I do, Courtland."

"No, that's not what I'm saying. All I'm saying is you don't have the right to put whatever it is on Grayson. Grayson is part of her father, but not her father. She should not have to pay for whatever scars he left on you." Grayson slept peacefully as Courtland rubbed her back. "It's not right, and you know it."

"Tell that to Momma." Vivianna mumbled under her breath.

"You tell Emily. Stand up to her. The more you make those comments about Emily, the more I feel you are not telling me everything about this thing between the two of you."

Vivianna scoffed. "You don't even know. I would need three lifetimes to fill you in on the half of it." Vivianna stared off and focused on the woods that met the crisp line of newly cut grass.

"Or you could cut the bullshit, and give me the twenty-minute version."

"Can we not do this, Court? My hormones are all over the place. I don't want to argue tonight. Or any other night for that matter."

"I don't want to argue either. I also don't want Grayson hurt, in any way, by anyone. And I mean anyone, Vivianna." Courtland reached over and held Vivianna's hand. "Listen, I love you." Courtland's blue eyes stared deep into Vivianna's. "And I love this little girl too. When I look at Grayson all I see is endless potential. I want you to see her the way I do. And not through that messed-up lens you keep looking at her through." Courtland grabbed Vivianna's hand. "I love her with all of my heart. I want her to be my daughter. I mean not just in my heart, but also in name. I want Grayson to have my last name. I want us all to have the same last name." Courtland took a deep breath before he spoke again. "And I want us to leave here. I want us to have our own place where it's just the four of us, and we can make our own rules. We can be us instead of being part of Lakeland.

Vivianna didn't have the backbone to tell Courtland about signing custody of Grayson over to Emily. Vivianna knew Courtland would lose it if he knew the truth and the reasons behind it. "I'm tired of telling you, Courtland. I'm not leaving my family home. I'm not leaving." Vivianna snatched her hand away.

"Vivianna, I'm your family now. Me."

"No. I said I'm not leaving." Vivianna's voice filled with rage. "I'm not leaving, Grayson's not leaving. No one's leaving." Vivianna struggled to stand. "If you don't like staying here you can go."

"Wait a minute." Courtland juggled Grayson in his arms and blocked Vivianna from storming off. "How in the hell did I become the bad guy? I'm not asking you to cut your family out of our lives. I'm asking for our own home. I want to walk in the door after work and just see you and the kids. Hell, I want to walk around the house in my damn drawers. What in the hell is wrong with me wanting us to live on our own?" Courtland's loud whisper grew in volume.

Vivianna stared into Courtland's eyes. She didn't possess the courage to tell him the truth. "I don't know what you want from me." Vivianna tried to side set Courtland but he blocked her.

"I want you to tell me why you're so afraid to pack your bags and leave."

"I'm not answering your bullshit question."

"It's only bullshit because you're afraid to answer it."

Vivianna shoved Courtland in the arm as she thundered past him. "Go to hell."

"Why did you marry me?"

Vivianna pivoted back to face Courtland. "What did you say?"

"I said, why did you marry me?"

Vivianna looked ridiculous squaring her shoulders up to face Courtland. Her posture only reinforced their height difference. Courtland looked down at his wife. He tried to find something in her glare that would lead him to the truth.

"I could ask you the same bullshit question. Why did you marry me? How does it feel to have me ask you?"

Courtland kept his tone even. "I married you because I love you, and I love Grayson, and I want to spend the rest of my life spoiling the two of you, and our baby. I married you because when you're not pretending to be a pretentious debutante, you're a beautiful person. And I don't mean looks. You are so much more than a pretty face. I married you because your laugh, not the fake giggle, but your loud 'I'm happy' laugh is infectious. Hell, I even fell in love with the way you snore. I live here, a place I have no desire to live, with your mother monitoring our every move, because I love you. I don't know what else I can say or do to prove to you how much I love you." The silence between them surpassed anything played out in a romantic movie. "You don't have anything to say?"

"If you're looking for me to have this soap opera moment with you it's not going to happen."

"Damnit Vivianna, I just gave you my heart, and you think I'm looking for a movie moment with you."

"What do you want from me? What the hell do want me to say? Tell me what to say, and I'll say it."

Courtland grabbed Vivianna's hand. "All I want is the truth. That's all. Why did you marry me, Vivianna?"

"Because." Shame sweep over Vivianna. Vivianna wished he had rejected her from the moment he met her. It would have made things easier for Vivianna if Courtland had. Vivianna had no idea how to tell her husband her secrets had secrets.

"Get up and get dressed." The girdle smacked Vivianna in the face. Vivianna laid still in the bed and squinted at the bright light. "I said get up." Emily flung the covers onto the floor.

"The doctor said I should take it easy for the rest of the day."

"I don't give a damn what he said. You have a date tonight. Now get out of the damn bed before I drag your ass out of the bed. I don't care how much discomfort you're in. You remember one thing, you came back here. I didn't go and get you. Therefore, you do things my way. Vivianna, up! You are not on vacation."

Vivianna dragged herself to a seated position. Vivianna watched as Emily tore through her closet. "You'll wear this."

"That doesn't fit."

"If the girdle doesn't make it fit. You'll put a corset on top of it."

"You don't care about me?"

Emily stood in front of Vivianna as she spoke. "What did you say?"

"I said you don't care about me. You honestly don't care about

me. You don't hate me you just don't care."

"*I care your womb was successfully vacuumed out. I care another ill-produced child will not make its way into this family. I care that you get your sorry ass out of the bed and get dressed. I care you present well tonight, and with any luck, he'll overlook your bullshit and marry your sorry ass. I care about wealth. Those are the things I care about. I have told you several times over I wasn't sorry when you left, and I'm not thrilled you're back. But your father insisted."*

"*Edward Waller can't insist. Edward Waller is dead."*

Emily's hand made a loud pop sound against Vivianna's face. "Never mention that man to me. He's an unfortunate poor choice I am reminded of every damn day."

"Vivianna, answer me."

"Court, I think the world of you but the last time I left things didn't go well for me. Lakeland is safe for me right now. I know Momma can be overbearing, but we'll find a way to make it work. Right now I'm tired, and I want to go to bed, Okay?"

Courtland knew he wasn't getting the answers he wanted, but he also knew he could stand there all night with Vivianna and she wouldn't break and tell him the truth. "Fine, we'll go in, it's getting dark and we need to put Beautiful to bed anyway."

Chapter Fourteen

Lakeland buzzed from its annual winter party. The Lakeland winter celebration took months of preparation, was the highlight of the year, and it had to ooze perfection. Emily spared no expense: every year topped the last in price and décor. Every year Emily made it a point to have her party on the lips of everyone in town. Emily had one large white Christmas tree with custom ornaments placed in the foyer and its twin situated in the formal sitting room next to the fireplace. Large oversized Christmas bulbs hung from the ceiling. Two giant nutcrackers flanked the bottom of the grand staircase. There were wreaths on the front door and all the windows and lights adorned everything. Family and people of importance mingled all over the downstairs. The wait staff moved effortlessly in between people offering them champagne and tiny hors d'oeurves. The multiple endless conversations overlapped each other and created a buzzing sound.

Cora hovered next to the bar with a plate packed with hors d'oeurves. Cora glared at Vivianna and Emily. Cora couldn't hear the conversation but she could tell Emily playing up Vivianna's perfect looks for the mayor. *Bullshit. Absolute bullshit. Look at them playing the perfect mother daughter combination. I hate—*

"Momma wants me to tell you she noticed this was your second plate. And if she noticed that means others have as well." Jackson unbuttoned his tuxedo and rested his arms on the bar. Jackson Harrow in looks was the mirror image of his father Quincy, but in personality and appetite for women, he was identical to his great-grandfather Cairo.

"Don't you have a half-drunk socialite to drag into the bathroom and molest?"

"I'm just the messenger Cora."

"That just gives me another reason to shoot you, Jack."

Jackson motioned for another scotch. "Whatever. Keep eating your feelings and I'm sure momma will be over here to tell you what she thinks about your food consumption herself. You know how reckless Momma's mouth can be when she feels we didn't represent her well at one of her parties."

"Jaaaaack," The twenty-something woman with ample cleavage said as she grazed her fingers across Jackson's back. "You haven't taken time to talk to me all night. I wore this dress just for you because I know it's your favorite color." She pouted. "I'm very upset with you, Jackson Harrow. I don't go the extra mile for just anyone."

"Well, let me offer you a dance to make up for it."

"Cora," Jackson smirked at her, "you don't mind if we end our conversation, do you?"

"Goodbye, Jack."

Cora nursed her plate of food while making momentary eye contact with Vivianna. Cora loathed the way Vivianna could wow the room, how men gathered around her to listen to her spew nonsense. Cora noted the men's lust-filled glances, all of them desperate to see more than they should. Cora saw how Courtland pretended not to notice. *She doesn't deserve him. If those men only knew half of what I know about her. God, I can't stand her. Why couldn't she just stay gone?* Cora shoved a miniature crab cake in her mouth and washed it down with a glass of champagne. *I hate—*

"Hey, sexy."

Cora jumped at the sound of the familiar voice behind her. The tickle of his beard broke her internal rant and made Cora giggle. "Terry, stop. You're going to mess up my makeup."

Terry wrapped his arms around Cora.

"And wrinkle my dress."

"Well, if you let me take you home, I would really mess up your makeup and wrinkle your dress. And completely destroy your up-do." Terry Connors was a man of average height. He had a round face and a slender build to him. Terry wore his jet black hair cut low, and his equally black eyes had an old-man quality to them. Terry was crazy about Cora, and he was obsessed with her curves.

Cora rolled her eyes. "Terry, stop. Why are you messing with me?"

"I'm messing with you because I don't like it when I look over and see a frown on my wife's face. There is no reason for you to have a sour look on your face."

"I'm fine. I'm just tired of the way Momma parades Vivianna around in public. It's all for show, you know. She won't be able to stand Vivianna after everyone leaves. I have done everything Momma has ever asked of me and still she ignores me. She never shows me off to her friends. She never brags on me. But Vivianna is the pretty one, so she always makes sure she's center at her events. Mother makes sure everyone sees how perfect she looks. Just look at the way Vivianna stands there in a group of men and how they all hang on her every word. I swear she could fart and they would all inhale deeply."

"Well, I don't see her because I'm too busy looking at you." Terry left a trail of tiny kisses on Cora's cheek. "You are the only woman I see in the room right now." Terry planted more kisses as a louder giggle escaped from Cora's lips. "You shouldn't let things get to you. You know you don't want your sister's life. No one should want that life. You should be happy Emily ignores you. Your life is easier when she does. Trust me, baby, you don't need or want the drama. Let me take you home and I'll give you so much attention I'll have you making that breathy moaning sound that drives me wild."

Cora rested her body against Terry. "You are so bad." Cora giggled. "And poking me too."

"And nasty. Don't forget nasty. We could go upstairs to your old bedroom and I could poke you in a different way. I'll poke you and you'll have to bite the pillow to keep quiet."

Cora couldn't control the redness that spread over her face.

"But seriously, Cora, you don't want any of your mother's bullshit fake love. You know it all ends when everyone goes home."

"I know. Everything you're saying is true. I can't argue the point, but I still hate it."

"If you're this unhappy then why don't we go home? It's not like either one of us wants to be here." He whispered. "We could discreetly walk out, and no one would notice. We could pick up a pizza on the way. I don't know about you, but I can't take much more of this stuck-up food. When we get home, we can get out of these bougie ass outfits and throw on some sweats. Or we could say to hell with the sweats and just get butt naked, my personal choice. Make love, eat pizza, watch TV, and repeat. Until we fall into a deep sleep. What do you think? Sound good?"

Cora turned to face Terry. "That's my point, Terry, I could walk out of here and no one would notice. It's not fair. After all the dirt Vivianna has done and all the drama she has caused, and she still gets to play princess at Momma's events."

Terry let out a long exhausted sight "Enough Cora, let it go, leave it alone, and let's get the hell out of here. I'm serious, no one is forcing us to stay." Terry scoffed. "It's not worth it getting into it with your sister or your mother. You know how it ends if you do and I don't like seeing you like that." Terry's eyes pleaded with Cora. Cora caressed the side of Terry's face. "Please."

"You're right, again, you're right. I'm not being held hostage here. We should go, but I want to say a proper good-bye to Courtland before I go. Give me ten minutes and I promise we'll leave."

"I'll give you five, and not a minute more. That's enough for a quick good-bye. I'll be waiting by the door."

"Okay."

"I mean it, Cora, five minutes, and if I have to come and find you, I'm going to pick you up and toss you over my shoulder caveman style." Terry playfully swatted Cora on her backside.

"You wouldn't. Momma would have your hide if you caused a scene."

"Yeah, but I would have yours when we got home so it would be worth it."

Cora kissed Terry and quickly made her way across the room. Cora linked her arm through Courtland's. "Court, darling if I could steal your ear for a moment. I'm sure Jack won't mind. If you have heard one of Jack's conquest stories you have heard them all. The details never change; Jack meets girl, Jack and girl get sloppy drunk, Jack and girl end up in a car, bathroom, or in a pew at church. Isn't that right, Jack? Oh, don't give me that look, Jack. I only need a couple of minutes and then Courtland will be all yours again. Besides, it will give you time to play the prodigal son for Momma."

Cora tugged on Courtland's arm.

"You don't mind do you, Jack?"

"Take all the time you need, brother-in-law. I see a gorgeous-looking filly I'm going to chat up."

"Look at that, Court, Jackson will have another story to tell you when back. Or should I say when Jackson gets out of the bathroom with her."

Cora pulled Courtland into the one quiet corner she could find and quickly spilled one of her sister's secrets to him. Cora actions went beyond sibling rivalry. Cora had reached her limit with being ignored and passed over and with the way her mother and sister pretended in public. So, she decided tonight she would make an unforgettable splash.

Cora left Courtland standing shell-shocked as she rushed towards Terry who eyed his watch as she approached.

"You had twenty seconds to spare."

A wide grin washed across Cora's face. "Fuck the pizza, I want burgers and fries."

~ * ~

"What the fuck is wrong with you? How in the hell could you do any of it, let alone all of it?" The etched frown line on Courtland's forehead mirrored the utter revulsion he had for Lakeland and everything it embodied. Courtland slammed his clothes down on the bed.

"You don't understand." Vivianna placed her body between Courtland and his suitcase. "Trust me, you don't understand."

"I'm far from stupid, Vivianna. I understood everything Cora said to me. I digested every disgusting detail. I don't understand how you could do half the things she said. Look at yourself. You're not sorry you did it, you just sorry I found out about your bullshit." Courtland jerked his arm away. "You are the worst form of human."

Vivianna shoved Courtland in the chest. "I had to survive,

Courtland. I had to survive, so I did what I had to do." Vivianna's gold bracelets echoed as they slammed against each other.

"No, you did what you wanted to do. You did what fucking made you happy without any regard for anyone else, typical fucking Vivianna. You don't love the girls or me. And after the shit Cora said, I doubt you ever did. I now know I was just something you did to soothe your mother's bruised ego. Every damn time you told me you love me you lied. You lied when you said you wanted us to be a family. You lied to me that night we were sitting under the willow tree. You knew the truth, and you lied about everything. Vivianna, I don't think you have the ability to speak the truth." Courtland rushed back into the closet to get more clothes.

"Why are you putting so much stock into what fat ass Cora says? You know she pops pills, Court. She says it's for weight loss. Weight loss my ass, she's still as wide as outside. Valium isn't for weight loss anyway. Cora's never met a pill she didn't thoroughly enjoy. Did she tell you that while she was emptying my closet of secrets?"

Courtland slammed more clothes into the already stuffed suitcase. "That right there. The bullshit flying out of your mouth is how I know Cora is telling me the truth. You're not denying what she said you're just attacking her. I could care less about what pills fucking Cora takes. Cora could choke down a bottle of Valium and chase it with a bottle of wine and it would make her a junkie, not a fucking liar, Vivianna. Her habit isn't my problem, but your fucking lies are."

"Don't leave me, Court, please." Tears flooded her eyes. "Please, Court don't leave me. I'll do anything you want me to. I'll get on my knees, and beg if that's what you need from me." Vivianna crinkled the front of her gown in her hands. "Tell me, and I'll do it. Right here. I swear I'll do it." Tears streamed. "Tell me, Court. Tell me to do it."

"Vivianna, stop. This isn't one of your soap operas. I don't need you to beg. Humiliation has never been my thing."

"Then tell me what to do. Please Court, I'll do anything."

Courtland studied the river of mascara that mapped the desperation on Vivianna's face. Courtland searched her eyes for something profound from her, in her. Pity infused his anger as he spoke. Courtland hoped he would get the remorse he needed from her. "If you want to salvage any of this then I need you to tell me the fucking truth. Not Vivianna's truth, but the fucking unfiltered truth. Starting from the moment you met him, and include the day you left. I also want to know everything about Chicago and every fucking thing that happened when you returned before we met. And I swear on the heads of my daughters you have better not omit one damn detail or I'll show you a level of rage you never thought existed. Then, and only when I'm satisfied with your explanation, you will pack bags for you and the girls and leave with me. And we are going to get as far away from this fucking place as possible. You will also agree to never bring my girls here or come here by yourself ever again. And I mean never again. I don't care if it's Emily's funeral. *Never.* That's the only way I can even think about possibly starting to forgive you. What are you going to do?"

Vivianna smoothed the front of her dress down. She knew Courtland was asking her to do the impossible. "I'll tell you everything. Every raw detail on our daughters' lives I will. But I can't leave, Court. I just can't leave." Vivianna sat back on the edge of the bed.

"You mean you won't leave. You're so attached to the bullshit things in this house and the twisted perception of status your family owns that you won't leave."

"No, I can't leave." Vivianna twisted her dress in her hands the same way she always did when she had to explain herself to Quincy and Emily. "You don't understand, Courtland. When I came back here with Grayson." Vivianna kept her voice controlled and her eyes focused on her hands. "Mother wasn't pleased with my decision to have a relationship with Grayson's father, and she especially wasn't happy with the way Grayson turned out. What you refer to as a twisted perception of status we call lineage in our family. We are to always look like our lineage. Grayson—"

"Vivianna, you're going to make me put my fist through the fucking wall if you start with the dark-skinned bullshit again." Courtland folded his arms across his chest. "This shit needs to stop, right now. If you think for one minute that white people like you better because you're light, let me let you and the rest of your family in on a secret: we don't. Asshole white people who don't like Black people don't like Black people of all shades. That light skin shit is just something white people started to get you all to envy each other and keep control even after slavery. There, secret out now, move on from our daughter being dark skinned, quickly."

Vivianna glared at Courtland. "Easy for a white man to say. You have no idea what it's like on this side of the table. I know what it's like to walk into spaces and get a different level of service because people think I'm white. I know what it's like to be given a pass because I'm light and what it's like to be called a nigger because I'm not white. Skin is everything. And when my mother took one look at Grayson's father, she was livid. Because I single-handedly destroyed our lineage and there is no covering up what Grayson's father is. What my family is. Mother was thrilled when I ran out of the house with him. When I left that meant the Harrows could keep pretending, we're different from those who can't pass the paper bag and the comb test. Why do you think we all speak French? It was a requirement in this family because one French slave owner took his chattel property as his concubine. When I returned three years later Mother made sure I would never leave here again. Never make another lapse in judgment. So, in order to get my life back, I had to agree to certain things. Sign permanent custody of Grayson over to her and daddy. Keeping control of Grayson keeps control of me, as Momma so rudely put it. I also agreed to let Mother pick my husband. She decided I didn't have the judgment and lacked the ability to choose for myself. Mother also made me agree that any children born in our marriage would be raised here so she could make sure they were raised the right way, meaning the Harrow way."

"So, you sold Grayson, our daughter, into your twisted form of slavery so your closet could be filled full with high-end heels and handbags. Is that what you're telling me, Vivianna? As long as you have a bunch of stuff, fuck your daughter."

"Fuck you, Courtland. I lived in poverty for three fucking years. Wearing off the rack clothes from no-name designers. Eating in restaurants with trays. An apartment littered with second-hand furniture. You have no idea how awful it was for me. Judge me all you want, I don't give a fuck, but don't you dare pull that slavery shit with me. I did what I had to do. I had to fucking survive, Courtland. I had to take care of me. I deserve to be happy too."

Courtland clinched his jaw. "Listen to yourself, all you keep saying is I. 'I' this, 'I' that. No we. No us. No Grayson. Just I. When does it stop being about just you? You're a mother, for fuck's sake, Vivianna. How in the hell can you put your happiness before your daughter's wholeness? How could you give her away?" Courtland stepped around Vivianna. He jerked a handful of socks and underwear from the tall solid honey-colored wood dresser. "And let me tell you something else. I didn't agree to have my daughter raised under your mother's twisted thumb. But I guess our lawyers will deal with that in the divorce."

Vivianna twisted her hands tighter around the ruby red material of her evening gown. Vivianna clenched her fists so tight her nails dug into her palms. "Courtland, remember when you had to have surgery on your knee?"

Courtland turned to face Vivianna. Courtland's stomach tightened as the grimace lines on his face deepened. "Yes." Courtland's response had a slight growl to it.

"Remember how you said everything was going to be fine, but you gave me a power of attorney just in case. So, I could make any decisions just in case anything happened, medical and otherwise, just as a precaution. But nothing happened."

"Yes." Courtland growled harder at his wife.

"Well, Momma insisted."

"What." Courtland's voice pierced Vivianna's ears. "What did you do?"

"I agreed that Gigi would be raised here. To make sure things stayed on the right path. I signed both of our names that day. I didn't think you would care. I thought eventually you would be happy here. I thought—"

"No, you didn't think." Courtland snatched Vivianna off the bed. Vivianna winched as his fingers dug into her arms. Courtland's breath splashed across her face. "You didn't think." The smell of the wine from the party still lingered on Courtland's breath as his words assaulted her ears. "While I was lying on an operating table with my knee cracked open you sold Gigi the way you sold Grayson. How much did you get for our daughter? How expensive was the trinket you sold her for? Let me guess. You get Lakeland when that hag of a mother of your drops dead. That's it, isn't it? I can tell by the look in your eyes that's it. Everything you have told me tonight makes me question if your evil, parasitic, narcissistic ass is even human." Courtland squeezed her arm tighter. Vivianna winched under the searing pain. "When I was twenty, I fucked a whore in a Louisiana cathouse. I can't remember her name but she charged me two hundred dollars, and she was worth every damn dime. She told me she loved it. I knew she was lying. She loved the money I gave her and nothing else. She was a money-loving whore who I could respect. You are a selfish money-grubbing bitch I can't stand."

Vivianna spit her saliva as well as her hatred for Courtland in his face because he called her out on her shit. Courtland seized Vivianna by her neck. Vivianna clawed at Courtland's hand. Vivianna locked eyes with Courtland. *Just kill me. Just fucking kill me.* "I'm not going to kill you. Death would be too merciful. I want you to live because I want you to suffer. I want you to live a long and miserable life." Revulsion oozed from Courtland's eyes. "And because my Daddy raised me to never hit a woman, I'm going to refrain from knocking your teeth out for spitting on me." Courtland flung Vivianna onto the bed, and her head knocked against the baroque headboard. Vivianna knew better than to speak. She lay motionless on the bed afraid the sound of her dress would trigger Courtland and he would go back on his word and beat her senseless. Vivianna's heartbeat pounded in her ears and sweat pooled on her hands. The tremors started at the top of her and raced to her toes. Vivianna felt a level of fear she thought only existed in near-death experiences. Courtland threw a couple of things off the dresser in his suitcase before he slammed it shut and stormed out. The pictures crashed to the floor from the force of the door.

~ * ~

Emily watched as Courtland flew through the foyer and raced out the front door. Courtland gave no regard to the vase that shattered to the floor under the force of his movements. Emily curled her mouth in a wicked smile. Emily enjoyed watching Vivianna's world crumble, again.

"Courtland! Courtland! Please, I'm sorry. I'll fix everything." Vivianna screamed from the top of the stairs. Vivianna reverted back to the little girl who always wanted what she couldn't have. Vivianna only wanted him because she knew he was through with her. Vivianna's shrieks grew as she repeatedly chanted Courtland's name.

"Enough. I'm not going to listen to your howling all night." Emily glided out of the sitting room and leaned triumphantly against the front door. Emily looked at the shattered pieces of the crystal vase. The yellow tulips and water splayed on the floor like abstract art.

"He left me." Vivianna stood at the top of the stairs her fists curled into white-knuckled balls. "Courtland left me, Momma. A man left me."

Emily casually played with the ice floating in her scotch. "He owes me a new vase." Emily drained her glass.

"Did you hear what I said, Momma, I said Courtland left me and he's not coming back."

"Yes, I heard you, and he broke my vase on the way out."

"Fuck your vase. My husband just walked out on me because of Cora. Did you tell Cora to tell him about Grayson? She had no reason to say anything unless you commanded her to." Vivianna stumped her foot.

"My floors are not for stomping on, little girl. I said a lot of things to a lot of people tonight. I can't recall everything I said to everyone. You can't blame Cora for your husband walking out on you. He was going to leave you eventually anyway. He just did it before I could get a grandson to name after my daddy. Shame, Courtland was good breeding stock too. Just look at Gigi, she's exquisite. That skin and those doll-like features. A little boy to match would have been perfect. What a shame my last chance to be a grandmother again just walked out the door. Because I'm still not convinced anything Cora would have wouldn't have some sort of weight problem. And since it's obvious Jack is never going to settle down that left you." Emily's ball gown made a rustling noise as moved towards the center of the foyer.

"You, you." Vivianna stomped her foot, again. "You ruined my life."

"Bullshit. You ruined my life, and I still did everything I could to make your life wonderful. You were never smart enough to see it so you fought me every step of the way. If you have just listened to me instead of your twat your life would be flawless right now."

"Twat listening, isn't that how I came into existence, Momma? I bet you want me to apologize for being the product of your affair. And I'm the one they call self-absorbed. God, I hate you."

"Said the grown woman who acts like a ten-year-old child."

"I hate you. I hate you. I hate you." Vivianna slammed her fist on her thighs. Vivianna's cleavage heaved as she stared at Emily.

"If you don't like it here leave my granddaughters and go. You're free to go."

"You are so evil. Why are you so evil?"

Emily rolled her eyes. "Enough with the dramatic bullshit." Emily's voice mocked Vivianna's. "Why are you so evil? Please. This is how life works. There are no happy endings unless it involves a hand and a dick. Problems don't have a cute resolution. There is no hero coming to save you. Life gives you two choices: to be treated like shit or treat others like shit. You have two choices, little girl, pick one."

Chapter Fifteen

As the seasons faded into each other and the years carried on, Vivianna embraced her mother's get treated like shit or treat others like shit aphorism with flawless ease and no shame. Unfortunately, Grayson became the casualty of Vivianna's newfound pleasure. Vivianna resigned herself to the falsehood that Grayson was the reason Courtland left her, the reason why Emily and she never got along. Grayson became the reason for everything wrong in Vivianna's life. Vivianna even blamed Grayson for shitty weather, flat hair, and engine trouble. "Stop running in the house. Stop it. Stop it. Stop it." Vivianna slammed her magazine on the coffee table. Vivianna hated childish laughter and children's noise more than she hated her own self-inflicted situation. "You two sound like a herd of savages running around. You two are terrorizing my peace of mind. Grayson, where do you think you're going?" Vivianna glared down at Grayson.

"I'm going outside with Gigi to play." Grayson had grown into a beautiful brown-skinned girl. Even after Vivianna chopped her hair off for malevolence. Grayson possessed a prettiness that Vivianna refused to let her see. Her perfect white teeth always glistened against her chocolate complexion.

"Not without a hat, you're not. Where's the hat?" Vivianna sneered. "You know better than to even think about outside without the hat on."

Gigi giggled at the thought of the hat. Grayson hated the hat. Vivianna forced her to wear the hat every time she ventured outside and the sun was in full bloom. The hat defined awful. Bulky and ill-fitting, the hat also reeked of childhood sweat and hair oil. The hat covered almost all of Grayson's face. Grayson couldn't take three steps without having to push the floppy paper-bag-brown hat off of her eyes. The hat impeded every game she and Gigi played and every bike ride they took.

"I don't want to wear it. It's ugly, and I don't like it. It gets in the way when I'm outside. Besides, Gigi doesn't have to wear one. Why do I have to?" Grayson's eight-year-old voice sounded more mature than her age. "I want to go play. I don't need a hat to play. It's just the sun. It doesn't hurt."

Vivianna bent down to Grayson's level and dug her nails into the sides of Grayson's chin. Grayson winched as Vivianna's newly-acquired French manicure dug into her tender flesh. "You'll wear the goddamn hat because you can't afford to get any darker than you already are. Why do I have to keep reminding you of this? You're not blessed with a fair and delicate complexion like Gigi and I have. You can't play in the sun and come back in with a beautiful sun-kissed tone. You'll just get darker and darker, you're already too dark as it is. There is nothing attractive about the color of coal. It's going to be a struggle for you to find a man as dark as you. I am not going to allow you to go out of your way to make it any harder. You're not special like Gigi and me." Grayson's eyes pooled with tears. "Don't you fucking cry. I'm so sick of seeing your pointless tears. If you think I'm going to allow your black ass to run around here acting light skinned by going out without a hat you have lost your cotton-picking mind." Vivianna straightened her posture. "Gigi, go outside right now and play like a good girl. And you Grayson, you, can keep your bubbled-lipped black ass in the house for the rest of the weekend. Since you don't like the hat." Vivianna relished in the misery she rained down on Grayson.

"It's okay Gray. We can play inside. I don't mind." Nervousness and uncertainty laced the words Gigi spoke. Gigi's nerves always flared up when Vivianna yelled at Grayson in front of her. In her own way, the abuse made Gigi feel helpless and small as well. Gigi slid her hand inside of Grayson's. "We can color together. You like to color, Gray."

Vivianna stared down Grayson. "No, it's not okay. Gigi, go outside and ride your bike, now. Don't make me tell you twice." Gigi quickly released Grayson's hand. As bad as Gigi felt for Grayson, she didn't want Vivianna's anger turned on her. "And you had better find something to do besides standing there and looking dumb for days."

~ * ~

Too sad to read, also too wound up for a nap, and disinterested in toys Grayson wandered to her second-favorite place at Lakeland. The kitchen gave Grayson the same comfort the willow tree she hid behind did. The kitchen allowed Grayson to be free. Grayson could express herself, speak her mind, and dream when she was in the kitchen.

"What's got you in a fit, baby girl?" Brenda could feel the depressed energy coming off of Grayson. Grayson crossed her legs in the chair.

Grayson folded her arms on the kitchen table and rested her head on top.

"I asked you a question, beautiful."

Grayson shook her head no.

"What did I tell you about shaking your head, baby girl?"

"Not to." Grayson's quiet mumble barely resonated over the running faucet. Grayson bit the corner of her lip as she stared at the textured kitchen wall.

Brenda paused and studied the despondent look on Grayson's face. Brenda had a pretty strong intuition about who placed the look on Grayson's face. Brenda quieted the running water and calmly wiped her hands off. "Hey," Brenda sat down next to Grayson and lifted her head. "Look at me. What's wrong? You can tell me. You can always tell Brenda anything." Brenda rubbed her hand over Grayson's cheek. "There isn't anything you can't talk to Brenda about, sweetheart."

Brenda's soothing touch and empathy-laced words were all Grayson needed to open up. "Momma said I was too dark to go outside. I wasn't special like her and Gigi. She called me names too. Why doesn't Momma like me, Brenda? She always so mean to me. It's bad enough she cut my hair but does she have to not like me too? I wish Daddy was still here. Momma was nicer when Daddy lived here."

Brenda's heart broke and crumbled into tiny pieces for Grayson. Brenda wanted to tell Grayson everything but knew she couldn't tell her anything. Brenda couldn't risk termination. Lakeland did more than keep Brenda close to Grayson; it kept food on her family's table. Brenda promised herself if she ever got enough money to be financially independent of Lakeland not only would she tell Grayson the truth but she would strangle the hell out of Vivianna as well. "Baby, you are special and unique beyond words. It doesn't matter if your hair is long or short, you are still beautiful. Always make sure your mind and spirit are just as beautiful, if not more beautiful, than your outside. I know you miss your daddy, baby. Trust me, I know he misses you. You're his baby girl."

"Baby girl? No, I'm Daddy's Beautiful and Gigi is his Gorgeous. That's what he calls us."

"You're right, baby. My apologies, Beautiful."

"Brenda, can I ask you something?"

"Anything, sweetheart."

"Did I do something to make Momma mad? Am I the reason Daddy went away?"

"No, baby, you didn't do anything. Listen, adults can be messy, really messy and sometimes unkind to not only each other but also children as well. I know there is a lot you don't understand. But, the one thing I want you to understand and never forget is, it's not you, baby. It was never you and will never be you. There is nothing wrong with you. You are P and P. You know what that means? It means perfect and priceless. Understand?"

"Yes."

"No, I want you to say it like you believe you're perfect and priceless."

"Yes." A small smile crept across Grayson's face.

"You want to help me in the kitchen for a little while? I know you want to." Brenda's wink brought a giggle out of Grayson. "Don't nod, baby, use your words."

Grayson's eyes lit up at the thought of spending time with Brenda. "Yes."

"Go grab your step stool, and meet me at the sink." Brenda filled the sink with warm water and poured the blackberries into the sink. Brenda placed the bowl next to Grayson and stood behind her. "I want you to go through the pile, and pick out the darkest berries. And put them in this bowl." Grayson loved the smell of lavender that always lingered on Brenda's skin. Grayson relished love she always felt when she was with Brenda. Brenda slid her hands around Grayson's and picked through the berries. Grayson grabbed as many of the purplish-black colored berries.

"Did you get them all?"

"Ahh uh. I think so."

"Good girl."

"Brenda?" Grayson stared up at Brenda.

"Yes, baby."

"Are these the bad ones?"

"Oh, no baby." Brenda kissed the side of Grayson's cheek. "These are the ones for the pie. You have to use the darkest berries because they are the ripest ones. They are the sweetest, richest, and have the best flavor. And when we add the sugar, butter, and vanilla they will mix smoothly and bake into a beautiful pie."

"So, the other ones are bad?"

"No, they're not bad either. They're just not ripe enough to make a delicious pie. I can do other things with them. I can put them in a fruit salad or sprinkle them over vanilla ice cream. See, neither one is bad, and neither one is better than the other. Neither one is a mistake. They are both beautiful, and both have value. I just use them for different things. Dark is just as beautiful as light."

Vivianna fumed as she listened to words Brenda spoke to Grayson. Vivianna refused to give Grayson the self-esteem she had stripped. Vivianna's happiness depended on Grayson's misery.

Grayson grabbed the bowl and headed to the table. "Look, Momma, I'm making a pie."

"Cute. You need as many life skills as you can acquire. Considering the margins you have to work within in life."

Grayson softened her joy.

"I tell you what, I'll finish the pie, and you can have the first piece. After you finish your dinner of course."

"A small piece." Vivianna folded her arms across her chest. "A very small piece, Brenda. We don't want her to end up like her Aunt Cora. Remember, Grayson, no man likes a bigin. Now go read or play with something so you're not tempted to eat before dinner. Brenda, am I to assume since you have pie-baking time dinner won't be late like it was last night?"

"I'll have dinner ready on time."

"Very good."

Brenda kept her eyes focused on the movements of her hands as she slowly pinched the edges of the pie around the glass pan. "I know I have no right to ask. I'm not really even asking for me." Brenda continued to construct the top crust of the bakery-quality pie. Brenda used a knife and fork to construct her signature design. "The last few years have been rough on Momma and with her health being the way it is and all. And I was thinking, well," Brenda moved deliberately to the oven, "I was wondering if," the sweat pooled on Brenda's hands as she locked eyes with Vivianna. Vivianna stood with her arms folded more consumed with her own thoughts than Brenda's conversation. Vivianna huffed as Brenda's stammering dragged on.

"I know you are not about to ask me for money."

"No, absolutely not. Nothing like that at all."

"Good. I can't stand panhandlers. It degrades everyone involved. I'm not going to be responsible for the bad decisions you people have made with money."

Brenda bit down on the inside of her cheek. The pain reminded her to stay calm. "What I wanted to ask you was...I mean for Momma's sake, if she could...I mean, if you would permit me to take—"

"Oh, I don't have time for all your babble. If you're trying to ask me if Grayson can go see Momma Mae, I don't care. Hell, it will get her away from me for a while. Take her for the weekend if you want. It will give Courtland, Gigi and I some space to have quality family time." Vivianna defiantly shoved her finger in Brenda's face. "And I'm warning you right now you had better make sure momma Mae and the rest of your family never say anything to her about that thing. Do you understand me? Or I promise you I'll make sure you're selling oranges on the road in a piss-poor attempt to feed those kids of yours."

"When you say 'thing' am I to assume you mean Raymond?"

"Yes, that 'thing.'" Vivianna gritted her teeth.

"We wouldn't bring Raymond up to her. Momma hasn't heard from him in years. I just thought it would be nice for Momma and Grayson to meet."

"Good. I'm glad no one from around here has heard from him. With any luck hopefully he's dead."

Brenda swallowed her anger hard. Brenda had grown to despise everything about Vivianna. Brenda still couldn't reconcile how the woman who sat in her mother's living room desperate for belonging and looking for answers turned out to be the rude and unscrupulous woman who stood before her.

"And make sure you or one your cousins does something with her head of hair. I'm fed up with the extra work I have to put in on her head."

"Is there anything else?"

"Make sure the pie is perfect. I want Courtland to be happy when he comes for a visit."

~ * ~

Vivianna triumphantly journeyed to her bedroom. There was something about psychologically and verbally destroying others that always put Vivianna in a good mood. Vivianna flung her heels in the corner and casually tossed her body across her bed. Vivianna hummed as she dialed and then listened to the phone ring.

"Hello."

Vivianna couldn't contain her smile. "Courtland, darling."

"Vivianna." Courtland's tone turned flat and emotionless. "What do you want, Vivianna?"

"I want to know how my husband is doing? Is it wrong for a wife to check in on her husband?"

Courtland forced himself to break the long awkward pause. "How are Beautiful and Gorgeous doing, Vivianna? Do they need anything?"

"They only need what I need. For you to come home."

"You know I can't do that, Vivianna."

"You can at least come and visit."

"I always visit my girls, Vivianna. Don't make it seem like I don't.

I was there last weekend. And if you would let me take them with me, I would see them more."

"And me. Don't forget you visit me as well." Vivianna sounded more like a jealous child instead of a grown woman.

"I visit you because you're the mother of my daughters. I will always engage with the mother of my children. Is there anything else, Vivianna? I've really got to get back to things."

"Listen, I didn't call to argue, Courtland. I just thought it would be nice for us to see you."

"This conversation has dragged on long enough. What do you want from me, Vivianna?" Annoyance grew in Courtland's voice.

Vivianna changed schemes. "Momma won't be here while you're here. Cora is out of town and Jack as well. You know Jack. It will be cozy."

"And by cozy you mean the girls will be there?"

"I mean family, Courtland. Just immediate family."

"I've got things I have to do before coming out to see the girls. But let them know I'll be there later on today."

"Fabulous, Courtland, this is going to be wonderful." Vivianna hurled the phone on the bed and rushed out of the room. "Gigi, Gigi." Vivianna bellowed down the hall. "Gigi."

"I'm in Grayson's room, Momma."

Vivianna burst through Grayson's bedroom door. "Gigi, I need you to come with me right now. You have to come with me. Momma needs you to be perfect."

"But Grayson and I are playing a game."

Vivianna scowled at the sight of the board game. "Gigi, we don't have time for games. Come with me now."

Gigi shoved her excessively-flowing hair out of her petite face.

"What about me, Momma?" Grayson's large eyes pleaded for inclusion and acceptance.

"Grayson, you're going with Brenda. And pack a bag. Come on, Gigi, let's go. Quick, quick, quick, we don't have a lot of time. Grayson can clean this mess up before she leaves."

Grayson sat quietly on her bedroom floor. She hugged her knees tightly into her chest. Grayson rested her chin on her knees. Grayson stared at the half played game. "I want to be perfect, too." Grayson mumbled as the tears she tried to hold back drenched her cheeks.

Chapter Sixteen

"Brenda, where are we going?" Grayson looked out of the window in amazement. Grayson had never seen anything like the low lands. The low lands got its name because everything from bad weather to oppression, to shitty pay, rolled down to the low lands and settled there. The people of the low lands were generational working-poor people who were making their way through life the best way they could. People in the low lands came in all shades and backgrounds. The people in the low lands were too consumed with surviving from week to week to worry about who was darker, who was light, and who was white. The homes in the low lands came in two sizes: small and smaller. They were the type of homes you couldn't dress up with words like cozy or quaint. The houses made shotgun houses seem spacious. All the homes in the low lands wore their age with withered dignity, but if it had a good roof, a front porch with steps and a small garden on the side you were doing good by low land standards. The clay roads and common areas stayed filled with children playing and a barrel with the smell of charcoal oozing out. On the weekends the smell of barrel barbeque could start an impromptu gathering of loud spades games and horseshoes that would carry on well into the late evening hours.

"We're going to see my people. You can play with my kids and meet my mom."

"Oh, okay." Grayson couldn't tear her eyes away from everything going on outside the window. "Why didn't Gigi come with us?" Grayson couldn't get over all the movement. There was so much life. Lakeland's isolated beauty couldn't compare to the energy in the low lands. Grayson also couldn't process the instant feeling of belonging she had.

"Gigi has her riding lessons and other stuff to do this weekend. So, I thought you and I could spend some time together. Besides, it beats sitting in the house." Brenda playfully nudged Grayson.

Grayson's grin shy of her two front teeth splattered over her face. Brenda parked her time-worn faded blue sedan with the rust spots on the grass. Momma Mae's house was an old three-bedroom ranch style with a tired front porch and a swing that people sat in at their own risk. There were two old kitchen chairs with the faded vinyl that stuck to your legs on humid days and an egg carton with a piece of plywood on top of it that acted as a faux table. Momma Mae had one of the nicer houses in the low lands. Momma Mae's house couldn't have been more than nine hundred and fifty, maybe a thousand square feet front door to back door. No matter the size, Momma Mae's home always had plenty of room and never felt cramped even when it was bursting at the seams with family and friends. The grandma-house smell of gardenias, closed windows and old furniture hit Grayson's nose as she entered. The loud screech of the faded red door cut through the silence. Grayson studied the spots where the paint had chipped off as she entered. A strange feeling of belonging engulfed Grayson as she took in her surroundings.

"Make sure you close the door all the way. It sticks." Brenda whispered.

"Okay." Grayson replied in a loud child whisper.

"No need for all that whispering. I'm not sleeping. It's too early to sleep. I'm just resting my eyes. You all are always whispering and tiptoeing like I'm next to death. Trust me, I'm not dead yet. I'm just an old lady resting her eyes." Momma Mae worn eyes looked over at Brenda. "What are you doing here anyway? I thought you were going over to Shelia's to play cards after work tonight since Billy is out of town on that construction site all month."

"I changed my mind. I thought I'd spend the evening with you instead."

"Girl, you are too young to be hanging around the house with me. I'm fine. The kids are outside playing and you know they are just fine. Get out and go have so fun. I'm going to be here in the chair when you get back."

"Momma, there you go again worrying about me for no reason. I enjoy spending time with you. I can spend time with Shelia anytime.

Besides, it's not just me. I brought someone to spend time with you as well." Brenda stepped to the side.

"Well look you at you precious. You are so beautiful. You bring joy to my tired eyes." Momma Mae gasped as she sat her recliner up. "Come here let me take a good look like at you, baby girl." Momma Mae couldn't get enough of looking at Grayson. She tried to memorize the details of Grayson's face. Every eyelash now had a special place in Momma Mae's heart.

"Hello, Ma'am, my name is Grayson. It is very nice to meet you."

Momma Mae studied Grayson's extended hand. Momma Mae embraced the small hand that greeted her. The softness of her hand warmed Momma Mae's heart. "Well Grayson, it's so nice to meet you too. My name is Mae. I'm Brenda's mother, and everyone around here calls me Momma Mae. You are more than welcome to call me that as well."

"Okay, that sounds nice." Grayson's chubby cheeks glowed as she spoke to Momma Mae. Momma Mae's warm smile invoked a feeling of warmth and acceptance.

"Can I tell you something?"

"Yes." Grayson's eyes lit up.

"Someone who will remain nameless," Momma Mae winked at Brenda, "told me that macaroni and cheese is your favorite food. Is that true?"

"Yes, very true." Grayson couldn't control her smile.

"Well, I have some in the kitchen. How about you and I go in the kitchen and heat some up? We can talk and get to know each other better. I think I might even have some leftover roast beef as well."

"Yes, Ma'am. Yes, please. I would like that a lot."

"Okay then, help an old lady lift her old bones out of this chair so we can eat. We need to put some meat on you."

Grayson blushed at the thought of someone thinking she wasn't big enough.

"Brenda, are you going to eat with us?"

"No baby, you and Momma go and enjoy your meal. I'm going to go and check on your—" Brenda quickly caught her tongue, "my kids.

I'm going to check on my kids playing outside. You'll meet them later. I'm sure you will all get along just fine."

"Okay."

"Come on baby girl, let's go eat. I'm hungry."

"Me too."

~ * ~

"Daddy, Daddy, Daddy." Gigi flew into Courtland's arms. "Momma told me you were coming. I missed you so much. I'm glad you're here."

"My Gorgeous." Courtland spun Gigi in the air and showered her with kisses. Gigi's squeals were uncontrollable.

"Daddy, your face tickles."

"It does."

Gigi giggled grew as she nodded her head. "Yes, your prickles tickle."

"Well then let me do it some more." Courtland spilled more kisses on Gigi's face as her giggle grew into a wild child's laugh.

"Gorgeous, where's Beautiful?" Courtland tossed Gigi on his shoulders.

"I don't know. Momma said it would be the three of us tonight."

"Okay? Well, where is your Momma Gorgeous?"

"In the sitting room. I guess."

"Alright, take me to her."

Gigi fought with her waist-length hair that went everywhere she didn't want it to go.

Vivianna had always saddled Gigi with an overdone look at home, but tonight her look was even more extreme. The big barrel curls, a lacey pink dress with matching pink socks with white lace and white patent leather shoes. Gigi looked more like a pageant princess than a little girl at home. Gigi clasped her tiny arms around Courtland's neck. The familiar scent of Courtland made her smile. Gigi rested her chin on the top of Courtland's head while she took large deep breaths, desperate to fill her lungs with his scent. The lost feeling Gigi felt sometimes when Courtland wasn't around faded within minutes of them being together.

"Courtland." Vivianna jumped to full attention. Vivianna had spent the afternoon making sure everything about her screamed perfection. Vivianna wore a form-fitting, barely above the knee, deep double V-neck dress in Courtland's favorite shade of blue with neutral-colored high heels. Vivianna styled her hair and makeup the way she knew Courtland liked it. She added a fresh French manicure and adorned her plunging neckline with the emerald necklace Courtland gave her after Gigi was born. Vivianna paused to allow Courtland to admire all of her before she strolled over. "Hi, Sweetheart. I swear you get better looking every time I see you." Vivianna rubbed her arm up and down Courtland's arm. "Which isn't enough." Courtland's casual jeans and polo greatly contrasted with Vivianna's excessive look.

"I look the same way I always do, Vivianna." Courtland's voice took on its usual tired edge every time he addressed Vivianna.

"Oh, stop it. You know you're a good-looking man, absolutely delicious." Vivianna's eyes drifted down the front of Courtland's jeans.

Courtland lowered his tone. "Gigi is on my shoulders, Vivianna."

A sly smile ran across Vivianna's face. "Sorry, a girl misses her husband. You know Courtland you haven't given me a compliment yet. I'm wearing your favorite color. How do I look?" Vivianna twirled in a childlike manner.

"You look ignominious, Vivianna. Absolutely ignominious."

"Wow, I love the way ignominious sounds. The way it rolls off the tongue." The dampness in Vivianna's panties made her grateful she decided to wear them. "Ignominious, it sounds extremely sexy, thank you, Court. You know me so well."

"That I do." Courtland couldn't control his smirk.

"Do you want me to fix you a scotch? I can do that, and if you're hungry, I can make you something to eat, or maybe just dessert. I had Brenda make a berry pie for you. I know how you like pie. Whatever you want, Courtland, I'll make it happen. Just ask."

"Vivianna, where's Beautiful?"

"Who?"

Courtland scoffed deeply before she spoke. "Gorgeous, can you be my big girl and get me a glass of water while I talk to your Mother for a moment."

"Uhn hun." Gigi's hair shook out of control as she nodded.

"Use your words, Gorgeous."

"Yes, Daddy. I can get you water."

"Take your time, Gigi. No need for you to rush back."

"Yes, Momma."

"Come sit next to me, Court. We can have a little bit of adult time while Gigi's gone. Are you sure you don't want that scotch?" Vivianna patted the spot next to her on the sofa. Vivianna spoke to Courtland as if he had been on an extended business trip instead of like a woman whose husband had moved out months ago.

"I'll stand. Gorgeous said Beautiful isn't here. Where is she?"

"Who?"

"Dumb, whether actual or pretend, is never attractive on a woman. You know precisely who I'm asking about, Vivianna. Beautiful, Vivianna. My Beautiful. Where is she?"

"Oh, you mean, Grayson. I sent her with Brenda. Brenda asked if she could take her around her people or whatever. I said fine. I told her she could take her for the weekend if she wanted. It's nothing for you to be concerned with, baby. Besides, it gives the three of us the space we need to put in some real family time together. I was just doing something nice for us. It's no big deal. You next to me is all the thanks I need. At least while Gigi is awake." Vivianna splattered a cheap smile on her painted face.

Courtland mulled over what to say before he spoke. Courtland tried his best to be mindful of the fact that no matter how much he despised Vivianna's ways she was still the mother of his girls. "Beautiful is just as much my daughter as Gorgeous. Look, I have nothing against Brenda or even Grayson spending time with Brenda. But, when I come here to visit, I want to spend time with both of my girls. I asked you on the phone earlier about the girls being here, and you were evasive, and now I know why. Beautiful is mine, Vivianna. Mine and I'm tired of reminding you. I don't give a damn about biology or the papers you signed in your half-foolish daze. She's mine, Vivianna. Grayson is mine." Courtland's voice grew.

As much as he tried Vivianna always brought out the worse in him.

"Okay, okay, I don't want to fight with you. Fighting is the last thing I want to do tonight. I get it, you care about Grayson. Trust me, I get it. Come on just come sit next to me."

"Damnit, Vivianna, you don't get it. You really don't get it. I don't care about Grayson. I love her like I love Gigi. I carry her in my heart like I carry Gigi. Whenever anyone asks me how many children I have I say two, two beautiful daughters. I don't hesitate on the number, and I have never used the phrase stepdaughter. Stepdaughter is a dirty word to me."

Vivianna rolled her eyes as she mimicked Courtland. "Beautiful is my daughter. I love them both. Blah, blah, blah. Always with the 'she's my daughter' bit."

The roar in Courtland's voice echoed off the walls. "It's not a bit. It's how I feel. You know some women would do anything to have a man who accepts her child as his own, and you throw it in my face like it's a tacky joke. Why won't you let me love my daughter?"

"Because if you knew how soft you sound when you say it you would stop. Pining over a child that's not your blood child."

"And if you knew what a bitch you sounded like you would shut the hell up. I want both my daughters here the next time I come, Vivianna, both of them. And you'll do it because I said so. Do you understand me?"

"We'll see. It all depends on how I'm feeling when you decided to show up. How you treat me now."

"Don't, Vivianna. Do not fuck with me on this. I told you once, and I'm going to remind you now, you're really lucky I don't hit women. But I swear to God if you keep fucking around, I'll—"

"Daddy." Gigi's tiny hand shook as she held out the glass of water. Gigi's eyes started to tear from the anger she felt Courtland emanate.

"Thank you, baby." Courtland placed the glass on the mantel and scooped Gigi in his arms. Courtland could feel her small heart slam against her chest.

"Are you mad because Grayson's not here? If you are, I'm sorry. I heard you yell."

Courtland kissed the side of her cheek and whispered. "Gorgeous, Daddy is sorry for yelling. Daddy shouldn't have yelled. But I don't want you to worry about anything, Okay. Everything is fine."

Gigi nodded.

"Good girl. Hey, how about you and me go play? You can pick what we play, all right. That sounds like fun doesn't it?"

"Yes, yes, yes." Gigi wrapped her arms around Courtland's neck. "Is Momma going to play with us too, Daddy?"

Courtland planted another kiss on Gigi's cheek. "We'll play something with Momma later. Right now I want some you and me time. I missed my Gorgeous."

"And I missed my Daddy."

Vivianna glared at Courtland as he walked away with Gigi. Jealousy stabbed at Vivianna as she poured herself a double vodka absent of ice. *Bullshit. Absolute bullshit. I look amazing, and all he wants to do is talk about her, worry about her. I allow him to pine over Gigi but I'm not going to allow him to put her before e. I'm who he is supposed to want. I'm who he should be worried about. I should be the only thing on his mind. The whole thing makes me wish I had been able to leave her ass in Chicago. I'm not going to tolerate Courtland looking at her and worshipping her the way that thing did. I've had enough of the 'she's beautiful and special' bullshit. Next time I'll shave her head bald and see how beautiful he thinks she is then.* Vivianna produced an evil smirk. *I bet five inches of my hair if he saw her bald, he would never call her beautiful again. And that little girl better be lucky I won't. I could but I won't.* Vivianna gulped down the last of her vodka and poured a scotch. Vivianna observed herself in the mirror. Vivianna flipped her hair behind her shoulder and adjusted her cleavage. "Courtland needs to get his head out of his ass before he misses out on the best-looking woman to cross his path."

~ * ~

Brenda and Momma Mae sat on the porch fanning away the occasional summertime bug out of the air as the seven o'clock sky started its transition into its usual humid summertime evening appearance. Momma Mae couldn't hide her joy as she watched Grayson play with the kids she had no idea were her family. Brenda smiled, seeing Grayson not just happy but sweating and dirty from playing outside. Hard active childhood play was something that was discouraged at Lakeland. Grayson blended right in and transitioned effortlessly from a game of hide-and-seek to tag.

"This is so much fun." Grayson screamed as she flew by. Her grin, wider than it was in the car, made both Momma Mae and Brenda laugh.

"I'm glad you're having fun, baby. Pay attention he almost got you, baby girl."

"Never, Momma Mae. Neveeeer!"

Momma Mae shifted her posture as she found a dry spot of her well-used tissue to catch her forehead sweat. "If it gets any hotter, I'm going to be using the heat outside instead of the oven to cook."

"Momma, you grew up in this heat. You should be used to it by now."

"Child, close your mouth. No one ever gets used to hell-hot heat, not even the people in hell. Baby, I am so glad you brought the little one by. You have no idea how seeing her has made me feel. If I closed my eyes tonight and they didn't open in the morning, I would be at peace having seen her beautiful face. You don't know how I felt thinking I would never get to see baby girl. I still can't get over how much she favors Doreen when Doreen was her age. Those big stunning black eyes are all Doreen. Look at her, Brenda. Just look at her. Look how she's got her daddy's spirit in her too. Look at how she handles herself. That fire is Raymond through and through, scared of nothing and competitive beyond belief. Doreen used to tell me stories about how that boy would turn a neighborhood stickball game into a blood sport. He never was a sore loser; he just always went down fighting and got back up fighting. I can't stop looking at her. I've been trying to memorize every inch of her. Just in case—well, we're not going to think like that. Like I said, I would be at peace."

Brenda chuckled. "That fight and spirited nature belongs to a lot of people in our family. There's no denying she's one of us."

"I can't argue that truth." Momma Mae fought to contain the puddle of sweat reproducing on her forehead. "Tell me this. How did you ever convince that girl to let Grayson come over here? Short of you selling her your soul, what did you offer her? We all know that girl don't do nothing out of kindness for others."

"Well, Momma, I explained to her how you were getting on in age."

Momma Mae arched her brow.

"*Anyway* Momma, I thought it would be nice for you and Grayson to get the opportunity to meet. I had to endure her usual unpleasantness, but once she finished talking down to me, she said in her usual rudeness Grayson could visit as long as I agreed to not tell Grayson who we are to her, and never mention Raymond. Truthfully, Vivianna was more than happy to let her come. She said I could keep her for the entire weekend if I wanted to. And of course I jumped at the offer, and she didn't even bother to ask what we would be doing this weekend either. Like you said, Momma, Vivianna doesn't do anything out of kindness. It has to benefit her, and when it does, she'll agree to anything. And right now, she's doing anything and everything to get her husband to come back home. Personally, I think it's because her ego won't allow her to accept that a man walked out on her. For whatever reason, she has decided that Grayson is blocking her from having her husband."

"Now Brenda, you know good and well that baby doesn't have the ability to drive her father or any man away. There is no telling what that woman did to push him away."

"I'm not saying I believe her, Momma, I just stating the facts. But it's not just Grayson, Momma. It would break your heart even more if you saw the way she parades the little one around like she's in a show ring. You should see Gigi, Momma, that little one lives under the pressure of having to look perfect all the time. She is always overdressed. You can tell Vivianna is using her to mask her insecurities. The only good thing in all of this is the girls have each other. I just hope Vivianna's ways don't do irreparable damage to their sisterhood. But you know how the women in that family are, Momma. It's like they destroy for the sake of destruction." Brenda scoffed. "But let me stop gossiping. It's not like gossiping about them is going to make things better. I'm just glad Grayson's here with us. Even if it is just for the weekend."

Momma Mae shook her head in disgust. "Lord, that woman. That woman. She better be glad I'm not a woman who cusses a lot or I'd invent trifling names to call her. Just thinking about what that girl did makes my blood boil. She didn't turn out like her mother: she turned out worse than her mother. The word for what she is hasn't been invented yet. That woman would trade her mother for a diamond necklace and her other daughter for the matching earrings. Soulless, that woman is. Just absolutely soulless. If I thought hitting her would change things, I would gladly smack the mess out of her and knock some sense into her. Here there are women out here would want nothing more than to be a mother and she threw away the privilege." Momma Mae slowly rocked back and forth. "It's not right. None of it."

"Momma, you still refuse to call Vivianna by her name."

"And as long as I can take air into my lungs I never will. Can't nothing or nobody make me say her name. I'd rather sit my backside in the front row of hell than say her name. I'm not saying my nephew was all the way right because I told him don't go messing with her. But what she did was all the way wrong. That woman stole an innocent baby away from her people. That little girl never got to experience her father's love the way she should have. Baby probably doesn't even remember her daddy. Now that woman has got her living around her family, and those people don't really care nothing for the baby. My sister still can't shake the sadness from her losing her grandbaby, her first grandbaby at that. And I ain't heard from Raymond since he came down here and tried to get the baby back."

"If it helps, Courtland cares for Grayson. I've seen him with her. He's good people, Momma."

"Still not the same love and care Raymond would have given her. You've got to be a special kind of evil to block a man who wants his child from raising his child."

"I know, Momma. I know."

Momma Mae smoothed the crumpled tissue in her hand out on her lap. "Anybody who tells you men don't love their children the way women do and don't hurt when they're gone is a damn liar. And you can tell them I said so." Momma Mae started to rock her foot softly as she used her hand like an ironing board to dispel the wrinkles in the tissue.

"I never seen that much pain in a person's eyes as I did the night he left for the final time. The scariest thing is to hear someone who lost hope talk about killing himself and know they mean it. You don't know how grateful I was that I got rid of your daddy's gun. He loved the mess out of that precious little girl. And when he saw her outside with you." Momma Mae looked over at Brenda and offered her a withered smile. "You were far enough back he could see you, but you couldn't see him. Raymond said he thought about taking her and running but he knew he would have scared the mess out of Grayson and he also knew he didn't have the means to disappear. Trust me when I say those people would have hunted him down. They only want what they can take from someone else. They kept her and took her to spite him. I know they did. Ain't no other answer that makes sense. He couldn't go to the sheriff. Sheriff Barker wouldn't have listened. Truth being what it is, Raymond would have probably found himself rotting in prison on some made-up crap. So, with no other option he could think of at the time, Ray left her there in the yard playing with you. I think a piece of him died at that moment because he knew he had lost his baby girl. As much as men talk about wanting a boy, there is a place in a man's heart that only a daughter can occupy. And when she gets in there, she becomes his heart. His heart beats because of her. It can make a weak woman jealous when she sees the love a father has for his daughter and vice versa."

~ * ~

"Gigi was out before I could pull the blankets over her. She absolutely adores you." Vivianna sat by Courtland on the sofa. "You're so good with her, Courtland. It makes me think about us having another one." Vivianna rubbed Courtland's shoulder.

"I'm her father. She's supposed to adore e, and I'm supposed to be with her."

"Wouldn't you like to have a son? I know all men long for a son."

Courtland moved his shoulder out of Vivianna's grasp. "My daughters are plenty. They are all I need."

Vivianna ignored Courtland's body language and slid closer. "Then how about we make another little girl."

"Enough."

Vivianna paused. "Okay, Courtland. I'm sorry. We can discuss that later. I don't want to fight with you. I want to end the evening on a good note. You're completely right, fathers are supposed to be good for their daughters. And you are definitely a good father." Vivianna paused inelegantly and waited for the return compliment, which never came. Vivianna turned herself to face Courtland even more. Vivianna leaned forward and gave Courtland full view of her cleavage. "I know things started off a little sideways earlier. And again, I am so sorry it did. I'm hoping we are able to get things back on track."

Courtland rested his elbows on his thighs and his chin in his hands. He stared at the darkness that had embraced the last of the evening sky. "Are you serious with this thing you're doing right now?"

"I'm sorry? I don't understand what you mean."

"You can say that twice more." Courtland mumbled under his breath. Courtland glanced over at Vivianna. "The whole time I've been here you have been going out of your way to brush up against me. Rub my arm. You've giggled at almost everything I said at dinner, and the majority of it wasn't even a little bit funny. You know if you lean over any further, I'll be able to look down your dress and see your toes. And the sad thing is as distant and as off-put as my body language has been you really don't get it. Not one bit."

"Get what, Courtland? I don't understand. I'm doing everything I can to draw you into me. To get you back. Back here with me. You told me I looked ignominious. If you didn't want me then why give me the compliment?"

Courtland palmed his face and deliberately dragged his hand down his face. "I can't even begin to go there with you about that right now. If only you were as smart as you are sexy."

A wide smile ran across Vivianna's face.

"I wasn't giving you a compliment. Vivianna, no one can deny you are a beautiful woman, but beauty is no substitute for intelligence and character. Don't you ever desire to be more than an attractive face?"

"We all have our lot in life, Courtland, and mine is being gorgeous." Vivianna gently ran her nails over Courtland's knee. "Now why don't you let me show you what my beautiful mouth can do? I promise I'll make you forget all about our fight earlier today."

"Christ." Courtland exclaimed. "Vivianna, we have some serious problems between us and what you're trying to do isn't going to fix any of them."

"Oh please, don't act all prudish with me, Court. You're a man."

"You're right, I'm a man, but I'm not a dog on the prowl. A blow job is not how you are going to get me to entertain a discussion about us being anything more than the girls' parents. So cut the bitch in heat act. Makeup sex can't fix what this is, Vivianna. And the fact that you think it can shows just how out of touch with your own reality you are. You're sitting here acting as if I'm not going home in a few. Like I forget Beautiful wasn't here when I got here. Like we didn't argue about it almost immediately. You're acting like we don't have an arrangement. You know damn well I come here to see my girls and not you."

"Then why are you sitting here next to me if it's only about the girls?"

"Being near you is just a necessary cruelty I endure to see my daughters. And I foolishly thought I could talk to you and you would get it this time. Because I'm not going to have done to me what was done to Beautiful's father." Courtland rested his back against on the sofa. "Look, I've said it several times I don't know what happened between the two of you and frankly it's not my business. But what I do know is from the little bits you have told me things don't make sense." Courtland held his hand up to stop Vivianna from speaking. "None of it does so don't even try to defend it. But what I do know is what happened between you and me. What I do know is how you allowed your mother a level of control over your life and our girls. What I understand is things and status mean more to you than even you mean to yourself. You destroyed our family for some stuff and a spot in your mother's will and you have to live with that decision. You have to look at yourself in the mirror. You are going to have to explain all of this to our girls one day. Instead of worrying about me you need to worry about whether or not they are going to forgive you when they find out the truth. Because what you have done to them borders on unforgivable."

"So, you're threatening to take the girls from me. Is that it, Courtland? Well, you can't. You can't take the girls from me. They're mine, so there." Vivianna spat her words at Courtland.

"Vivianna, do you really think I can't fight you in court? I have the means to hire the best lawyers just like you. Or like your mother I should say. You really need to get real about things; one, that dumb-ass agreement you signed isn't worth the ink you used to sign your name. And two, your family isn't the only family who knows a judge or two. I can think one of who would gladly rip that bullshit agreement into tiny pieces. Give me Gigi and revoke your parental rights based solely upon all the bullshit you've done. I could take Gigi and never look back. But where would that leave Grayson? Here with a mother who would hate her more than she already does? Here with an emotionless grandmother who sees her as nothing more as poor-performing stock she can't shake? We both know you would spend your days finding new ways to make Grayson's life hell, because we both know you would find a way to blame Grayson for all it. It tears me up to know I have no legal standing with Grayson. Grayson is the reason why I left Gigi here. That little girl upstairs is a buffer between you and her sister. And Gigi doesn't even know it. That's why I don't unleash hell on your selfish ass. I have to lessen things for Grayson as much as I can. That's what a parent does."

"What do you want from me, Courtland? I'm trying. But I don't know what the hell you want from me? One minute you're angry and the next you're calling me sexy. What is it? What do you want from me?"

"The only thing I have ever wanted from you: be my wife, love me, love my daughters, and stop making Grayson your enemy. I want you to look at Grayson the way I do. You know I'll never forget how Grayson looked at me with her big eyes trying to figure out who I was the first time I met her. She was peeking around the corner, all that beautiful hair that for the life of me I'll never understand why you cut off flowing everywhere. She was perfect, and at that moment she became my Beautiful. I wanted my family not here, but with me living separately from all the *Harrow* bullshit. You just showed me how impossible that is for you. You don't have it in you, Vivianna. But you have made choices that make it very clear you can't provide me with the things my heart and soul crave. So you can stop insulting my mind and my heart by offering me your ass as a tribute to my dick. That part of me is surviving."

"What do you want me to say, Courtland? Do you want me to say sorry? Fine. I'm sorry. I get it, I've made mistakes. Now, can we finally move past everything? I'm tired of you bringing up the past. How many times do I have to say tell me what to say, and I'll say it? You know I've done a lot, Courtland. You don't give me credit, but I have. I have endured all of your lectures about how I did things wrong. How I have made wrong decisions. How much more do I have to listen to before we move forward?"

Courtland snatched his arm away from Vivianna's grasp.

"And as for your dick. You never complained about makeup sex when you lived here. Now you're too good for it? When are you going to stop judging me, Court? When are you going to start seeing I have suffered too? You're tired? You think there aren't things I'm tired of? Well, let me tell you something mister judgmental, I'm exhausted. You have no idea how tiring and sickening it is to listen to the way you make everything about Grayson. I swear I think you love her more than Gigi or me. And Gigi is your flesh. Always putting Grayson on a pedestal. I don't know why you think she's so special. You're just like *him,* always telling me how special she is, how perfect she is." Vivianna rolled her eyes in her petty, self-absorbed nonsensical way. "So tired of it. Well, I've got a bulletin, she's not perfect. I would know."

"Are you finished? I want to make sure you're finished with your tantrum before I retort."

"It's not a tantrum."

"Yes, it is. I wouldn't use the word tantrum if it didn't fit the majority of your actions. You are completely void of any form of comprehension that doesn't involve you being the center of attention."

"That's not true, Courtland. It's not, but there you go again blaming me for everything."

"Damnit Vivianna, would you for once listen. Just listen. You just took everything I said about me, the girls, and especially Grayson and

194

twisted it to make yourself the victim. Let's put this thing between you and me to the side for the moment. Are you aware of the vituperation that you speak about Grayson with?"

Vivianna's expression went blank. "What?"

"Jesus Christ, Vivianna, vituperation, it means venom, bitter criticism, damn. In other words, what you say about Grayson never comes from a place of love. You talk about Grayson as if she's a burden to you. And anytime anyone shows Grayson the love you are determined to deny her you lose it. I don't understand why so are so harsh towards her? Grayson didn't have anything to do with the decisions you made in your early years. She is merely the product of your decisions. There is nothing sadder than listening to you speak with resentment and disgust in your heart when you talk about our daughter. It's not right. She's your daughter. You spent nine months growing her. She came out of you. She is connected to you, and you're throwing it all away over bullshit. You are destroying your relationship with Grayson before it has time to develop. You're supposed to love her now. Build her up now and then spend the teenage years being passive aggressive to each other in that mother-daughter way."

"I want you to think, Vivianna. I mean really think. Have you ever considered for a moment that if Grayson's biological father and I are both telling you the same thing there is a reason behind it? I've never met the man, but the one thing we agree on is Grayson is special. Grayson and Gigi are both special, all children are. But in Grayson, you can see that little extra something that if you cultivate it instead of crushing it, it will develop into greatness. She truly has the potential to be anything in life. You gave birth to greatness, stop blocking her from becoming great."

"Vivianna, your children are supposed to be the most special and important people to you. But just because Grayson doesn't fit this bullshit Harrow standard and you can't parade her around like a show pony you don't care to see how unique and beautiful she is. There is a mind in that little girl that is going to achieve wonderful things. And you as her mother should be her biggest cheerleader. Mothers are supposed to uplift not tear down."

Vivianna didn't bother to offer Courtland a glass of the scotch. She gulped the first two in front of him with no shame and great ease. Hard truth, just like harsh reality, was never Vivianna's thing.

"You are going to end up like your mother and grandmother if you don't stop with the booze, miserable with adult children who tolerate you but don't really want to be around you, little to no friends. I mean real friends and not only deriving pleasure from manipulating others. Is that the sad way you want to exist?"

"What do you care?" Third scotch followed the same path as the first two. "You don't want me."

"Because you're the mother of my daughters I have to care. I will always care."

Vivianna slurred her words slightly. "Yeah, but like I said you don't want me. How stupid is that? You could have me but you're sitting there acting weak. Rambling on about the importance of whatever you were talking about. I stop listening part way through. Why are you still here, to talk? If I wanted a conversation, I would talk to Cora's fat ass. And I never want to talk to her fat ass."

"I just poured my heart out to you. Told you everything and you're standing there half drunk and pissed off because I won't fuck you. You're not embarrassed that I'm disgusted by the way you treat our oldest daughter. You're not even upset that I won't discuss coming back here. That our marriage has crumbled. You're just mad about not getting my dick. How pathetic is that? How pathetic are you?"

Vivianna poured a fourth glass. "Look at me. Take a good hard look at me, Courtland; I can have any man I want. I was just being generous by offering to be with you. But this is how you treat me for trying to show you kindness. I don't have to look nice when you come over here. I do it to make you feel good. Feel special."

"Generosity and kindness. You are unbelievable. I give you credit for one thing: you have this amazing ability to not only make everything about you but think you're doing everyone a favor when you do it. Woman, you are as shallow as the Mississippi is deep. I'm as just as handsome as you are attractive, which means if all I'm looking for is a nut, all I need is ten minutes in a bar and I can have my pick of the women there. I don't need to play the role of your human dildo to get some. I'm just not infatuated with my looks like you, so I don't fawn over myself and I damn sure don't feel the need to go out of my way to remind the world how handsome I am unlike someone I know. When you possess intellect, you don't have to cripple yourself by relying solely on looks."

"Fuck you. I'm not going to listen to more of your bullshit. Fuck you, fuck you and get the fuck out of my house, now."

"Your house?" Courtland scoffed.

"Fuck you, Courtland. You know what the fuck I mean." Vivianna gulped the last of the scotch. "You want honesty from me, well here it is. Your daughters don't need you, and neither do I. Having a man around is overrated. My daughters will do just fine without a father around. So, just go. And when you leave close the door quietly on the way out when you leave so you don't break another one of Momma's vases. She was absolutely disgusted by the way you left last time."

Courtland stood in front of Vivianna. The smell of his cologne mixed with the liquor on her breath and created a toxic scent. Courtland made a point to invade Vivianna's personal space. "My daughters will always need me. And I will always be here for them. Until my final breath, I will be there for them. That's what a father does. Be there no matter what. You can't erase me from their life no matter how hard you try." Courtland grabbed Vivianna by the chin when she looked away. Courtland's piercing stare ate at Vivianna's soul. "As for you, Vivianna, you can tell me all you want that you don't need me but you and I both know you need me and want me. You and I both know your getting off is nothing more than a feeble attempt to show how tough you are. Like a dog that barks out of fear hoping the target doesn't see how scared it is. And yes, Vivianna, you are scared. Scared you don't own the dress or scent of perfume that will make me want you. You're scared you will never be able to get me back into your bed. Scared your ego won't survive being rejected by me. Your games are so childish and translucent. If it weren't reality it would be funny. Don't you ever get tired of playing the tragic Jezebel?"

"Fuck you." Vivianna shook her chin free.

"If I let you, would you? Fuck me that is. I could take you upstairs right now and tear it up so hard that the headboard would sound like it's going to crash through the wall. I could make you scream my name so loud people two miles away would hear you beg me to fuck you harder. I could make you orgasm so hard you would see stars. I could fuck you so well when I finally finish you would plead with me to stay and do it all over again in the morning. You want me. You'll always want me. I know your panties are dripping wet right now for me. "

Vivianna couldn't deny the reaction her body was having. Her nipples hardened and pushed against her bra. Vivianna clinched her thighs as her lower back tensed. She was unaware of her quickening breath as her mouth dried. Vivianna's mind went numb listening to Courtland.

"You want to deny it, but we both know you can't."

Vivianna couldn't pull her thoughts together to offer a snide counter remark. Vivianna's face bore the expression of a lust-filled woman who was desperate for Courtland to make good on his threat. Courtland grabbed Vivianna and pulled her into him as he stared into her wanting eyes. Vivianna felt her womanhood contract. Courtland grabbed a handful of Vivianna's hair. Vivianna willingly tossed her head back. Courtland felt Vivianna's sexual desperation.

"You know what I want you to do for me?"

"Anything." Vivianna forced the passion-filled response from her lips. "Tell me, and I'll do it. Anything for you, Courtland."

Courtland held his lips to Vivianna's ear and whispered in that low baritone growl she loved. "Grow the fuck up."

Rage quickly replaced Vivianna's lust-filled gaze. "Asshole. I hate you. I hate you so much. Let go of me. Let go of me right now."

"When I'm ready."

Vivianna inhaled deeply.

"I would suggest you swallow every drop of spit you intend on throwing. The last time you spit on me was your first and only time. Do it again, and I will be more than happy to forget that I don't hit women."

Vivianna relaxed her posture and mouth.

"Look at that, you might just have a little bit of common sense after all." Courtland released Vivianna from his grasp. "Now I'm ready to leave." Courtland paused before he left. "And Vivianna, after you clean yourself up, do yourself a favor and grab a dictionary and look up the word ignominious." Even though petty was never Courtland's nature he couldn't resist. Courtland pushed over Emily's replacement vase on the way out. Vivianna jumped at the sound of the vase shattering on the floor.

~ * ~

Vivianna sat with her legs curled underneath her drunken body. She destroyed her flawless makeup with a stream of endless tears as she downed several more glasses of scotch. *'Grow the fuck up' he says. 'Be better' the other one said. Who in the hell do either one of them think they are judging me? I could have had any man. Any man. Why in the hell did I choose either one of them? Maybe I don't want to do either. Maybe all I wanted to be in life is an over-privileged brat who grew up to be an over-privileged housewife. Maybe that's all I'm supposed to be. Why the hell am I wrong for not wanting to live in fucking poverty with his black ass? Why am I wrong for giving up custody of Grayson for a better life? I'm not meant to be fucking poor. I'm not built for poverty. And the other one with his worthless endless lectures, why the hell couldn't he just shut the fuck up and stay with me. If fat ass Cora had just kept her overeating mouth shut. He would have nothing to complain about. Nothing. None of this is my fault, and they both blame me. Me. Not Emily, me. Emily did this not me. She cheated on Quincy, I didn't, she made me choose poverty. I hate them. I hate her. And Grayson. Grayson, she made my life hell. Why the hell couldn't she just be light skinned like me? I never get anything I want. Maybe I should let Brenda keep her. Hell, it would be easier on me if she did.*

Vivianna closed her eyes as the brown liquors tumbled down her throat. She then abandoned the glass and drank straight from the decanter. *And the way they both fawn over Grayson like she's special. She's not special. I'm special. I was the prettiest debutante at the ball. I was the one the boys wanted to date in school. I'm everything a man would want. There are women paying serious money to plastic surgeons and hairdressers to look like me. You don't have to know big words like ig-ignor- or whatever the hell it was Courtland said when you look like me. And Gigi, Gigi is going to be just like me. She'll never need those words because she'll have my face.*

Both of them telling me I'm going to end up like my mother. They don't fucking know me. I'm better than my mother. I'm better than Momma, ten times better than her. Momma wishes she was me. Fuck Raymond. Fuck Courtland. I can get another man. Men love me. I'm Vivianna. Men will always love me. Neither one of them knows a damn thing about me. Telling me what I need to walk away from. I would rather have all of this here than either one of them. The decanter made a small thud when it rested on the floor. Vivianna's thoughts slurred into a muddy mess as the booze forced her body to sleep. "I'm Vivianna, and I'm perfect. Absolutely perfect."

Epilogue

The Tragic End to Vivianna

Vivianna swallowed her glass of wine in two gulps. Emily snatched the glass out of her hand before she could pour another.

"Even for you, it's entirely too damn early."

"Hello to you too, Momma." Vivianna slid back on the sofa that bore witness to most of the memories she would rather forget. Vivianna folded her arms across her chest like a defiant teenager.

"Don't Momma me. And don't look at me with that expression on your face either."

"I have a look. I'm just waiting for you to tell me what I did wrong today."

The years had caught up with Emily. Emily's appearance had withered but her tongue was still vicious. Emily lorded over her daughter. "It's not just today, Vivianna. Today just adds to the never-ending list of things you have done wrong."

"Then please tell me what my mistakes are as of eleven this morning. So, I can. I can. I don't even know anymore."

"Of course you don't know. You never have, and you never will know." The cruelness grew in Emily's voice. "You are a pathetic excuse for a middle-aged woman and even a sadder excuse for a daughter. And don't get me started on the debacle you have made out of being a wife and a mother. Everything you touch turns rotten. Both of your daughters are a disgrace. One couldn't find her way out a paper bag if it was open at the ends, soaking wet, and she had two GPS and a travel guide. Her only saving grace is that she was able to marry well. And the other one, the ill-gotten daughter you produced out of your inability to keep your legs closed. That girl spoke in a way after dinner at her house that made trashy women look respectable. And the way you made a complete ass of yourself at her house after Carrington was born. You didn't just humiliate yourself, you humiliated me too. How many times do I have to tell you everything you do is a reflection of me? You acted like a complete savage. Once again you have made me embarrassed to call you my daughter."

"I can say one good thing came out of the endless mess you have created. The ill-gotten one cut you out of her life. Thank God for that. You don't know how happy I was to hear that she's done with you. I'm so happy I never have to worry about her darkening my house again. Finally, something has gone right. She's grown, and your eggs are dried up, so I never had to worry about another one of her being in our bloodline. If I knew then what I know about you now I would have had your uterus removed at birth. You have no idea how exhausting it has been for me being your mother." Emily paced around the room. "There isn't a word to describe your level of failure you developed into, Vivianna."

Vivianna stared down at her wedding rings.

"Stop toying with those damn rings. You make me so sick. Look at yourself, Vivianna. You look like a complete fool parading around in the rings of a man who is never coming back to you. You destroyed your marriage. He ran away from you quicker than your daughter did." Emily threw her hands in the air. "I've tried anything and everything and still you never get better. Why have you made my life so hard? Why?"

"Why did you keep me?" Vivianna's voice was tried and small.

"What in the hell did you just ask me?"

Vivianna dragged her stare from her hand to her mother's face. "I said why did you keep me? If I was such a burden from the womb like you claim. Why did you keep me?"

"You think I had a choice? You dumb bitch. You still don't get it. It was the fifties. I had no choice. No access to birth control, no access to abortion. I was stuck. Stuck with you. So, don't you dare stare e down like I had the option not to be saddled with you. You had all the options; you were just too stupid to use them."

"So, are you telling me there were no adoption agencies back then either? No childless couple you could discreetly auction me off to? Then you could just pretend you don't know me. Like you don't know your half siblings." Vivianna smirked.

"I'm not going to tolerate too much more of your disrespectful mouth. You have no idea what you're talking about. So, don't speak on things you don't know. I don't know where you got your rude mouth from."

"The same place I got my loose ways, I guess. You know, Momma, you're always so quick to remind me of my promiscuous ways. Conveniently forgetting your own. From where I'm sitting it seems to me my inability to keep my legs closed is generational, you know, in the bloodline. Guess you're not so different from me after all. Same damn tragic *bonne à rienne* narrative, just a different woman playing the lead role. Guess we're more alike than even I thought. If you ask me."

Vivianna was numb to the impact of Emily's hand bearing down on her cheek. "I didn't ask you." Emily sneered through her teeth. "I am nothing like you. And you will never be me. You know nothing of my past. Nothing about what I have endured. So, you can shut your foolish mouth up."

"Momma, I know more about your time with Edward Waller than you wanted me to know." Heat engulfed Vivianna's face where Emily had left her palm print. "You constantly throw Grayson in my face. As if you didn't do something similar."

"You have no right to speak about him to me. That's my business, not yours. I'm warning you, don't you ever say that man's name in my presence again. Or you will find yourself on the other side of my door looking for a place to lay your sorry head tonight. You were a burden forced upon me. I never wanted any of this. I never wanted you. He never wanted you. He wanted me to get rid of you any way I could. He never wanted you born. You ruined my life."

"That same way Grayson ruined mine. Like I said, not so different after all."

"No, no, no! The difference is you need me. I have never needed you. But you have always needed. Always needing me to bail you out, cover up your bullshit, even find you a damn husband. And you have never said thank you to me. Not one damn time. Did you even think about saying thank you?"

"How did you want me to thank you, Momma? How? How do you thank the woman who ruined your life? How do you thank the woman who picked you apart every chance she got? I don't know if you're aware, but Hallmark doesn't make a card for that."

"You could have started by doing what I told you. Following the rules. You could have simply corrected your bullshit behavior. But instead, you always had to do the opposite of what I needed you to do. I swear you did it for spite, to humiliate me. And you don't even realize how much of a debt you owe me, Vivianna. You owe me, and you have never attempted to pay me. You have done nothing right. Not even die after birth."

"What?"

"Oh, don't look so surprised. Yes, you almost died after you were born. It was lack of oxygen from the cord being around your neck or something." Emily flung her hands in the air. "But as we both know *you* survived. So, you're fine."

"Wow. You never really wanted me? All the times you told me you didn't. I foolishly thought it was just your anger and Momma being Momma. But you really wished I had died the day I was born?"

"Yes, yes, yes! I already had two children, my one girl, and one boy. I didn't need a third child. I was getting my life back, or so I thought. My fun and my excitement were back and then it was all gone because of you. You stole my damn happiness, my freedom, all of it gone because of you. And there I was stuck. You made me stuck. You have been nothing but a burden. If you had died, my life would be different."

"And you wonder why I drink as much as I do."

"You drink because you're a drunk, a drunk who has ravaged my wine cellar and liquor cabinet. You crawl in and out of bottle after bottle with no dignity or shame. You have attacked two-hundred-dollar bottles of scotch and three-hundred-dollar bottles of wine like the two-dollar-bottle beer you chugged when you were slumming with that thing. You're a pathetic dunk."

"Being a heavy drinker, something else we have in common." Vivianna mumbled under her breath.

"What did you just say?"

"Nothing. Nothing at all."

"That's what I thought, nothing."

"Since I'm such a disappointment maybe I should just kill myself? That's what you have wanted since the day I was born, for me to die. Maybe I'll just throw myself off the roof of the house and break my neck in the fall or better yet, put a gun to my head."

"Kill yourself? Don't be so damn dramatic or common, Vivianna. I would never tell you to kill yourself. What type of mother tells her daughter to kill herself? But I do believe you should never close any doors when making choices in life either."

There was a long lingering pause between the two of them. Neither one of them dared show weakness by breaking the stare. Vivianna's body craved a drink. The insults and truth she and Emily had hurled at each other made her yearn for the taste of scotch and the mind-numbing effects she knew would take hold after the third glass. Emily had the same yearning in her throat and the same desire to forget. Emily wanted the alcohol to drown out her memories of Edward Waller. She wanted nothing more than to beat him back in the dark place in her memory she reserved for him.

"How do you sleep at night?" Vivianna's cold question really didn't require an answer. Considering she knew all too well how a destructive and dysfunctional mother sleeps at night.

"The same way you do, on really expensive sheets." Emily paused at the entrance to the sitting room before she exited. Emily stared down Vivianna with a loathing reserved for one's worst enemy. "Feel free to slither into a bottle of whatever tonight and never crawl out."

~ * ~

How in the hell did I get here? Why do things always happen to me? I was supposed to be happy and loved and envied. Vivianna studied the age in her face. Vivianna acknowledged the quiet lines she pretended didn't exist. Vivianna couldn't deny the dullness in her eyes. She studied the few strands of grey hair emerging from her roots. *Three hours at the damn hairdressers and I still have grey, never-ending fucking grey.*

Vivianna ran her hand over her neck and studied how it no longer looked twenty. *I would give anything to have those years back. I need those years back.* Endless loneliness filled Vivianna's dark soul as it cast a depressed shadow over her face. Vivianna wiped the last of her makeup mask off. Vivianna searched for the self she lost when she returned to Lakeland. Finally realizing how much she missed being the woman Raymond fell in love with, the shock of seeing her austere reflection and raw isolation reflected back at her was a truth Vivianna never wanted to view. *My entire life had been nothing more than a well-dressed shit show.* Vivianna held the bottle tight as the phone rang. She gripped the bottle tighter and tighter with every ring. Vivianna lamented her decision when she heard that familiar sound.

"Hello?" Warmth attacked the part of her she thought was dead.

"Hello?"

Still sounds like…

"Vivianna?"

"How did you—"

"The caller ID. That and anyone else in your area code would have started a rapid-fire conversation with me after the first hello."

Vivianna folded her legs under her. Vivianna released a long exhausted sigh. "Hi."

"Hello."

Vivianna listened to Raymond's breath.

"Is everything okay?"

Vivianna only offered her silence as her response. Raymond could feel her pain through the phone. Instead of how Vivianna had treated Raymond the last time they interacted, Raymond's humanity would not allow him to treat Vivianna with the reckless disregard he had received.

"Can we not do the polite small talk exchange?"

"Yes, Raymond." Vivianna could believe how good it felt to say his name.

"Why me? Why are you calling me after all these years? After everything that you said the last time, we saw each other?"

"Are you mad?"

"You took my daughter and kept her from me for years. Hell, decades. I'm not mad. I'm furious with you. But my anger doesn't answer why you called me."

"Fair enough. Maybe I called because you are the only person who I knew wouldn't slam the phone down on me."

The silence echoed through the phone.

"Raymond, can I ask you a question?"

"Sure."

"What happened to me?"

"Everything you wanted to have happened, Vivianna. While your beginning wasn't in your control everything that happened in adulthood was. Your adult life has been a victim of your ego and arrogance. You are who you chose to be. I told you when we were together years ago, figure out who Vivianna is and be that. Don't let Lakeland define you. I guess you have decided to be a product of Lakeland."

"So, I guess you hate me like Grayson hates me? Like everyone hates me."

"At first I hated you. For a while, I woke up every morning consumed with hate for you. I went to bed every night hating you. But then I let go of hating you. I had to let go of hating you. After I spent the night nursing my hand from putting it through the wall for the third time. I realized I couldn't live my life hating you. I realized I wouldn't have a life if I spent every waking moment hating you. My wife wouldn't have given me a chance to say more than hello to her if I had been miserable and hate-filled when I met her. You've done a lot of damage Vivianna, and most of it can't be undone. But the bottom line is I can't love my daughter and hate you. You are just as much a part of her as I am. As for Grayson, I can't speak for her. It's not my place. And I don't know who everyone is, so I'm not going to speak for them either."

"You still don't water down the truth."

"And I never will."

"Does she talk about me? Grayson. If she does, what does she say?"

"Again, not my place to say." Raymond lit another cigarette. "What do you want from me, Vivianna? I feel like there is something you want to ask or say and you're not for some reason."

"Do you think Grayson loves me?"

"Do you love her is the question you need to ask and answer. Not for me and not for Grayson but for yourself. It's something you need to figure out. Once you figure that out the rest of the answers will appear."

"Would I be a bad mother if I said I didn't love Grayson?"

"I would say it makes sense. Why you did the things you did and treated her the way you did." Raymond contemplated how to answer the question. The anger he pledged to keep at bay while he spoke to Vivianna crept into the conversation. "Yes, Vivianna, it makes you a bad mother. It also makes you a bad person. I will never understand why you did what you did to Grayson or me. You could have left her with me and gone on with your life. You didn't have to put our daughter through all the bullshit you put her through. I would have taken care of our daughter and never asked you or your family for one damn dime." Raymond's voice drifted off. "You damn near destroyed my mother when you took Grayson from us."

Raymond's works shook Vivianna. "I, I, Raymond I don't know what to say." Her voice was small and for the first time, in a long time, humble.

"I don't expect you to know what to say, Vivianna. Like I said we haven't had any contact since that day at Grayson's home. Grayson is beyond grown, so we don't have to deal with each other for me to have a relationship with my daughter. So, what is it? What did you really call me for?"

Vivianna studied her reflection more intently in the mirror. She wiped the stale tears from her face. "He left me. Courtland left me for good, Raymond. He filed for divorce and everything. I know he moved out years again, but I always thought I could get him back. But when he heard what happened at Grayson's house, he ended it for good. I lost my husband, Ray."

"Vivianna, are you serious? Did you really call me over a man? I'm not one of your girlfriends. Moan to one of them about your husband leaving you, not me. It is so fucked up, Jesus, when are you going to grow up? You're too old for this, Vivianna. Too damn old." Raymond snapped.

"You're just like him, always attacking me. Always telling me to grow up."

"Well, maybe you should take our advice and grow the hell up. I can't believe you wasted my time with this." Raymond exhaled hard. "Calling me over a man. All that does Grayson love me talk it was just a way to keep me on the phone. I can't believe I was dumb enough to fall for your bullshit. I can't believe you didn't call to say I'm sorry. To say I fucked up, but over a man? I swear, Vivianna, the day you stop thinking with your vagina is the day you stop existing."

"I never asked you any of this."

"You're right, you didn't ask. You took. For your own selfish needs, you took."

"You know what, Raymond, I think it's best I end this and go."

"If that's how you feel then leave."

~ * ~

"Vivianna. Vivianna." Brenda shook her motionless body. "Vivianna." Brenda's screams grew louder and louder. Brenda grabbed the bottle. "No, no, no. Don't you do this. Please don't do this. Come back, come back. Wake up. Wake up. You have to wake up. Damnit, Vivianna wake up." Vivianna's head flopped back and forth as Brenda violently shook her. "Please wake up."

"Brenda, what has gotten into you? I can hear you bellowing down the hall!"

Brenda's voice was labored and stressed. She looked over at Emily as she slapped Vivianna several times on the face, desperate to get some type of response. "It's Vivianna. She took these. I don't know when. I found her lying across the bed and she won't wake up. I don't know what to do. She won't wake up."

Emily's voice was flat and emotionless. "She took the whole bottle?"

"Yes, Miss Emily, the whole bottle." Panic overwhelmed Brenda.

"Then throw away the bottle and call the funeral home."

"But she still has a slight pulse."

Emily let out a long exaggerated sigh. "Damn."

About the Author

Tamara White lives in Illinois and is married to her husband, Dennis. Tamara is also a mother of five and had two dogs Sheba and Grayson. Tamara also teaches at a local community college. In her spear time, she enjoys photography, trips to the zoo, and reading.

Grayson
Shattered Existence Book 1

The Harrow family is a family that has spent generations hiding behind the illusion of perfection and lineage. Grayson thought she had escaped the dysfunction of the Harrow Family until the shock of an unplanned pregnancy forced her to return to Lakeland. Grayson must confront her color-struck mother, Vivianna, about her childhood at Lakeland and the real reason why her biological father was never a part of her life. Grayson learns how twisted her mother's version of love is, and how the truth is more complex than she could have ever imagined. Her husband David is there to support her every step of the way, and when Grayson reconnects with her sister, Gigi, she learns the price Gigi paid for being their mother's favorite.

Chapter One

"You know the only reason she likes you is because you're white."

"I know." David pulled Grayson to him and kissed the top of her forehead, as the Lincoln limousine sleeked effortlessly up the winding country estate road. "I've always known."

Grayson shifted her gaze away from the mammoth weeping willow and oak trees that lined the drive leading to her childhood home, Lakeland. Grayson searched David's face in vain trying to find the humor in his words. Grayson prayed his casual response was nothing more than another failed attempt at one of his God-awful jokes. "You're serious?"

"Yeah, why wouldn't I be?" David's chuckle exposed his deeply-set dimples.

"And you're fine with that? It doesn't bother you at all that my mother doesn't give a damn about you? What you like? What you don't like? How you treat me? Are you happy? Hell, are we happy? You're fine with Mother thinking of you as nothing more than unproven breeding stock rather than seeing you as my husband. The man who loves me and takes care of me." Grayson's tone had a recalcitrant edge to it. The edge in her voice let David know she was tired of dealing with all the crap that came along with being a Harrow. Grayson rolled her sultry onyx-colored eyes behind her soft eyelids and thick lashes. A hint of Grayson's buried southern accent peaked through in her response. Grayson's voice only showed its roots when she was either too tired, or too pissed off to care that someone might hear her speak in her true vernacular.

David let out a loud boyish laugh. "Unproven breeding stock! Wow, that's a new one. I've been called a lot of things but never breeding stock. Hell, I could be *proven* breeding stock if I could get a weekend alone with you." David kissed the top of her head, and whispered, "Just you and me; no work, no cell phones, just one long weekend in bed, and a couple of bottles of cheap wine."

Grayson pulled away slightly, and ran her fingers through her hair. It was one of her many nervous idiosyncrasies. Lakeland and the business of being her mother's daughter could send her anxiety through the roof. "I am so tired of all of this. I don't understand how you can be so calm knowing that's what she thinks about you. David, you let her off the hook too easily." Grayson returned her gaze to the trees. "The comments she makes are out of line, and you know I'm telling the truth. You let her get away with too much. You have to put her in her place. Mother needs to know she can't just say anything to you or about you. She needs to know she just can't—"

David's Louisiana drawl tickled his words as he spoke. "Baby, listen to me. I can't let your mother off the hook because I never had her on the hook. Nor do I want to." David turned Grayson's shoulders so she faced him again. He lifted her chin up so his blue eyes could meet her worried gaze. "You know why I don't let your mother get to me? Because

I know it's what she wants. She wants to antagonize me to the point I lose it with her. Your mother knows once I lose, she has me. And she can rain misery down on me anytime she wants. I'm not going to let her own me, Gray. I refuse. And you need to stop letting your mother control you. Grayson, you get so worked up when it comes to your mother. Do you know that just the mention of her name sends you into an emotional tailspin? You've got to let some of this stuff go. It's not healthy to obsess about her the way you do."

"So, I'm just supposed to be meek, keep my mouth shut, and let her get away with everything she does?"

"No, I didn't say that. I'd never ask you to do anything like that. What I'm saying is," David curled the corner of his lip down in frustration, "you give her too much pull in your life. You let her get in your head. It's a choice you make. Don't let her get to you. Don't entertain her bullshit; it's simple."

"Says the guy whose childhood was a Norman Rockwell painting. But as the woman whose childhood was Norman Rockwell strung out on vodka and Valium, I'm here to tell you it's not easy to just let go. Mother made sure she did enough damage to keep me stuck. For as long as I can remember my mother has treated me like a stain on her perfect blue-vein society family tree. She treats me as if I ruined her life," Grayson scoffed. "I didn't choose any of this shit. That woman never gave a damn about me. I'm nothing more than the collateral damage left over from her past. She never wanted me, but she didn't get rid of me either. It's like she hated me too much to let me go. I swear we're like a dysfunctional version of the Addams Family."

David's lips turned up in a soft masculine smile before he pulled Grayson back into his arms. He knew there was nothing he could say in the next few minutes that would change her mind or the situation. David let a pronounced sigh escape from his slender lips. The robust smell of peppermint gum and the slight sway of the limousine as they traveled up the long drive made Grayson's stomach turn. *No, no, not now. Please not now. I'm not ready to have that conversation either.*

"Just remember you're here for answers, not a fight." David wrapped his strong arms around her, and drank in her scent. The tighter he pulled Grayson in, the more the peppermint assaulted her senses.

Grayson swallowed the pooling saliva in her mouth as fast as she could. Over and over she swallowed, but the clear liquid filling her mouth was never ending. *If this damn car doesn't get to the house soon, the breakfast sandwich I ate is going to be all over this damn floor.* Her stomach turned over again, and she felt a sour taste overtake her mouth. *This kid is determined to make its presence known whether I want him to or not. Hell, one more thing in a long list that hasn't gone as planned. It would be a miracle if anything in life actually went the way I wanted it to go. Maybe I should tell David I'm pregnant. Because if marrying into the Harrow Family hasn't run him off, a baby shouldn't. I hope. I'll look at him and say congratulations, not only are you going to be a dad, you are now forever connected to the most dysfunctional Black family south of the Mason-Dixon line. But, if I tell him now, then it just adds another layer to the bullshit—gives Mother something to gloat about. She'll find a way to take credit for me being pregnant. As if she had anything to do with it. And I don't even know if I'm going to—* Grayson caught herself mid thought.

David stroked his wife's arm as he allowed a barrage of curse words to fill every available space in his brain. It hurt him to see his Grayson so tormented. He wished he could liberate her from her painful past. David often felt like a failure as a husband because he couldn't make the nightmares in her head go away. "Baby, she was young. Our youth allows us to make decisions, and do things age and wisdom would never allow us to. At least that's what my Mawmaw used to say."

"Being young is no excuse. I was her child, and she treated me like, like the flu. You know what I mean. You really don't want it, but if you get it you cope and suffer through it, and you try not to get it again." Grayson swallowed the sourness her stomach produced, and prayed it didn't rush up again.

"Baby, it's not—"

"Mr. and Mrs. Taylor." The limousine driver unknowingly interrupted their painful discussion.

Oh, thank God. Grayson slid out of the backseat. The sound of her strappy Manolo Blahnik stilettos on the pebbled road made her pause. Their move to the land of concrete had made her forget how ear deafening the pebbled stones were. Lakeland's loud road was always too eager to tell everyone's business. It wasn't the staff you had to worry about telling on you; it was the damn road.

Grayson took a moment to soak up the quietness of the afternoon before they headed inside. The country air tickled her nose. Grayson had forgotten how clean air could smell. The sweet smell of the honeysuckle lingered over the slight breeze and settled her stomach as it occupied her lungs. She enjoyed how the crisp air danced on her skin, and brushed away the city of Boston's lingering aroma. Grayson turned her eyes towards the estate she had grown up in, and saw Lakeland in a way she never had before.

The unusually harsh winters over the past few years had abused the hand-made clay shingles and caused a distinct discoloration. The landscaping was neat, but not kept to the same standard it had been when her grandfather was alive. Grayson knew her grandfather would have never allowed the forsythia bushes to expand and move about the grounds freely. He would have demanded the gardeners control the beautifully bright yellow shrubberies and conform them to the Harrow standard. Wild is for the wilderness, Grayson's grandfather would have said. Grayson smiled at the absence of the ancient oak tree she'd fallen out of when she was ten. The enormous oak tree with the giant knothole had shaded her bedroom, and helped her sneak out when she was sixteen to Elizabeth Brownsworth's end of the year party. The white-washed bricks demanded a thorough cleaning, and the cliché, *Gone with the Wind* pillars pleaded desperately for a fresh coat of cloud-white paint. Lakeland looked miserable. It was as if Lakeland knew her final chapter was already written.

Lakeland is really showing her years. Grayson stared at the midnight-black, heavily ornate front door with the bulky lion head doorknocker, and equally obnoxious doorknob she swore she'd never enter again, every time she walked out. Grayson picked up her laptop bag and started her pilgrimage towards her past.

"Relax," David whispered from behind her. "Everything is going to be fine."

Her mother, Vivianna, opened the front door and stood in the archway like a Grand Duchess impatiently awaiting the arrival of her audience. "Grayson, put the bag down!" she snapped in an egotistical tone.

"We don't carry our bags. We have them carried. Has city life caused you to abandon your upbringing? Ladies of means do not carry bags."

Five seconds. That's how long it took Grayson to go from a strong, accounting firm executive, to the shy, chocolate-skinned, frizzy-haired, correction-shoe girl of her past.

"Mother," Grayson retorted in the stiff flat tone she reserved for addressing Vivianna. "So nice to see—"

"Never mind all that." Vivianna motioned them towards the front door. "Inside quickly. No need for some of us to get any darker than we already are, darling." Vivianna paused in the foyer to admire her creamy beige skin in the mirror before entering the sitting room. She never passed on an opportunity to admire what she perceived as her greatness. "Grayson, I don't see how you're able to endure. I don't know what I would do if my skin was permanently darkened by the sun." The physical differences in Vivianna and Grayson went beyond skin tone. Vivianna was thin in stature. She never had an issue maintaining a hundred and ten pounds on her five-foot three frame. Her nose was narrow, her lips thin, and her eyes were almond shaped. People, mostly women, assumed her green eyes were fake, but they were indeed real. Vivianna was everything a color-complex-struck Black man found irresistible. She was their must-have. Grayson, on the other hand, possessed curves for days, full lips, and a round face with a button nose to match her high cheekbones. She had the type of body hip-hop artists paid homage to in their lyrics, minus the chocolate-colored skin.

"Come, Grayson...sit. I want to know how things are going. Was the flight enjoyable? I hope you flew first class. I've heard people in coach can have an odor to them."

Grayson rolled her eyes behind Vivianna's back. *And so it begins.*

Grayson tried desperately to situate herself on the overtly ostentatious sofa. Her lack of comfort symbolized her life at Lakeland. Everything in the formal sitting room was a throwback to an era most Black people wanted to forget. With the exception of the photos of Black family members, the room screamed Old South. Everything in the room fell into two categories: Antique and expensive as hell, or just plain expensive as hell. Her grandparent's large formal portrait adorned the mantel over the fireplace. The Steinway grand piano, which wasn't touched unless her Aunt Cora was home, engulfed most of the far end of the room. Antique rugs, imported from every part of Asia and the Middle East, covered the over one-hundred-year-old wood floors. Grand photographs of her younger sister Gigi on horseback, and in her debutante attire, lay in glamorous frames. They easily overshadowed the two pictures of Grayson in the room. It was one more way the Harrows made Grayson feel like an unwanted guest no one had the heart to ask to leave.

Brenda, the longstanding housekeeper, who had taken over as head housekeeper after her mother died, walked into the room carrying a tray of wine glasses and a carafe of Vivianna's early afternoon favorite. She exchanged a telling glance, and huge smile with Grayson. "So nice to have you home, Grayson."

Even though Brenda was closer to Vivianna's age, she was in essence Grayson's surrogate older sister. The two were tighter than two pieces of bonded paper when Grayson was there. Grayson lived for those rare occasions when Vivianna allowed her to spend time with Brenda and her family. As impoverished as Brenda's family was, Grayson often wished she were one of them instead of a Harrow. It was the moments of love and laughter she experienced with Brenda that allowed her to leave Lakeland in a semi-functional state. Without Brenda, Grayson would have lost her mind, or much worse. Brenda was Grayson's seraph. The two of them would have entire conversations with nothing more than looks and giggles traded between them.

Grayson's slight head movement rejected the wine glass Brenda sat on the baroque coffee table. "I'm going to pass, Brenda. Thank you for thinking of me, though."

"No wine? Grayson, you're not one of those Islam people, are you?"

"No, Mother. I'm not Muslim." Grayson chuckled faintly at the way her mother could be exceedingly offensive with absolutely no effort. Being around Vivianna was like stepping into John Jake's *North and South* trilogy with an all-black cast. "It's just that, it's eleven o'clock in the morning, Mother."

"Good. It's bad enough we have to tolerate your cousin being a vegan at the family barbeque. I don't know who told you eleven is too early to drink, but in Paris we drank wine at all hours. You do remember, don't you?" Vivianna inhaled her first glass of Chardonnay.

"You don't forget being thirteen and buzzed all day, Mother."

Even though Vivianna only half-heartedly wanted a relationship with Grayson, she despised the closeness Brenda shared with Grayson. In Vivianna's mind, Grayson was her daughter, and therefore her possession. Vivianna shook her glass, and hissed in her rude, dismissive tone. "And Brenda, it's Mrs. Grayson. *Mrs.* First names are only for family. Don't make me remind you again." Vivianna lifted her glass. "You've said your hello. Now fill my glass on the way out."

"Mother, you don't have to be so harsh. Brenda is a person of her own mind, and not your property. It wouldn't hurt you to use a kinder tone, and say please and thank you."

"Really, Grayson. Do I look like my age has caught up with me like your Aunt Cora that I have to say please and thank you? As for my tone it is what it had always been. Besides, Brenda's people have worked for our family for decades; she knows her place. The help always know their place." Vivianna winked at Grayson.

"And every plantation had a big daddy, but that doesn't make it right."

"You're vulgar."

"On occasion. But most days I'm just city-living rude." Grayson smiled with that toothy grin Brenda had fallen in love with when Grayson was a little girl. "Brenda, it's just Grayson like it's always been." Grayson threw Brenda one of her *we'll chat later* winks, as Vivianna locked eyes on her next target.

"David, my dear son-in-law, I haven't forgotten about you." Vivianna shooed Brenda out of the room.

Shit.

"Will you be taking the job at the university in the fall? It would thrill me to know your answer is yes." Vivianna flashed an ultra-white smile.

"Vivianna—"

Vivianna winked at David. "Mom."

David cleared his throat before he spoke again. "Vivianna, as much as I appreciate you setting up the meeting with the president of the university, I'm going to have to decline. I enjoy teaching high school

English."

"Lovely. I know the deans at a couple of prestigious secondary academies. I could call and—"

David quickly interjected. "Thank you, but no thank you. I'm happy where I am. I like my kids."

"That's adorable. But you are so talented, David. I hate to see you wasting your genius on the future drug dealers and strippers of America. I mean, really, what good can come out of the public school system?"

"Mother! There is nothing wrong with attending public schools. David went to public school, and he's wonderful. There are plenty of people who go to public schools and turn out just fine. There are lessons you learn when you are a public school kid that escape you when you come from privilege."

"Grayson, darling, there isn't a single lesson worth learning that comes from living a third-world public school lifestyle in a first-world country. Besides, David knows I'm not talking about him. I'm talking about people *like* him."

"Mother."

"Grayson."

"Sweetheart, it's fine," David flashed a conciliatory smile at his mother-in-law. "Your mother means well in her own special, and very much injudicious, way." Grayson glared at David. She hated how he could maneuver his way out of her mother's vortex with ease.

"Vivianna, as much as I would love to keep discussing the distaste you have for public school kids who aren't me, but are like me, I'm going to have to pass. I need to find a quiet place to grade my papers. Besides, it gives you two some needed alone time. You ladies don't confabulate enough. And, I make it a point not to palaver unprolific conjecture with parochial personage." *That's right, this public school kid got a damn near perfect score in English on the SAT.* David swallowed his glass of wine in two gulps, after he pecked Grayson on the cheek. "See you upstairs, sweetie."

Vivianna may have had the best schooling, but her lack of retort showed how her parents' money couldn't buy her real intelligence. Vivianna held her tongue until David was out of earshot. "Really, Grayson, only you would pick a financially-challenged bleeding heart who enjoys associating with commoners to marry. Next, he'll want to adopt some mutt from the pound, or worse one of those little foreign kids from one of those countries where they have too many of them. Please tell me you're not considering anything of the kind?"

"No, Mother, we're not getting another dog." Grayson maintained her flat tone.

Vivianna's tone turned cold. "Don't play with me, young lady. I could care less about a damn dog."

"Fine, I'll call the adoption agency when we get home. I'll tell them to cancel my order for little Pablo. I'm within my thirty days, so I won't lose my deposit. David and I will just adopt a nice chocolate baby from the U.S. instead."

"I hope you don't expect me to find your low-class humor entertaining." Vivianna softened her tone. It was an act she could turn off and on like a switch. "As annoyed as I am with your antics, and the bleeding heart you married, I take comfort in knowing he will be able to assist you in producing the correctly-colored grandchildren: two beautiful grandchildren and no more. God knows, you don't want to look like a breeder, like your cousin Deborah. I swear she is going to keep dropping those little half-whatevers onto the planet every couple of years until her uterus falls out. I just thank God you didn't have any children with your first husband. The last thing I need is to be burdened with little pickaninnies running around referring to me as Ma Mere. Dear God, I'll never understand what you saw in him anyway." Vivianna rolled her eyes in an exhausted manner.

"He was a good man, Mother."

"He was a Black man. Too black for my taste."

"What does that have to do with anything? What exactly are you saying?"

"I'm saying there's no reason to limit yourself with a person like your ex-husband. I'm sure his appearance would have been fine for some working-class woman who was looking for love. But we're Harrows; we have an image. We can't be seen with just anyone. Looks are everything. You were raised aware of that fact. Grayson, while we're on the topic of blackness, how many times do I have to remind you to stay out of the sun? You get darker every time I see you. You're starting to make *me* look dark.

Did you forget we're colored, not African?"

"Colored? How progressive of you, Mother."

"I refuse to be African American. With the exclusion of you, our family is far too light, and we have too many European ancestors, to ever be African anything. God only knows who came up with that slave term."

"Slave term, really, Mother? Since when did identifying with one's ancestors become slavish? You never miss an opportunity to stand on the wrong side of progress, do you? I don't even know what to say. It's like you're determined to stay stuck and you refuse to become socially aware. There are books to teach you the importance of African History, African-American history, social injustice and the institutional social constructs that have plagued people of African descent all over the globe. You've heard of the phrase 'stay woke,' meaning to be aware of the racial changes around you? Well instead of being *woke* you are clearly playing team *stay asleep.* You would rather exist inside racism's oppressive bubble than break it and actually live. I am so sorry my darkness has been such an inconvenience for you. I'm amazed you have survived the struggle."

"No need to apologize, Grayson. We all have our crosses to carry." Vivianna's self-absorbed nature didn't allow her to hear cynicism in Grayson's words. "I was just plagued with more than most. But grandchildren to adore will smooth things over."

"Wow, I don't know whether to be fascinated, astounded, or offended that you think I'm going to produce grandchildren for you to adore. I mean you'll adore them as long as they don't do something stupid like hug you or call you granny."

"You'll give me what I want. Like—"

"Like what, Mother, your well-trained chattel property? Once a plantation owner's great-great-great granddaughter, always one. Is that the idea, Mother? I mean isn't that the 1915's *Birth of a Nation* point you're desperate to make? With your limited knowledge and appreciation for African Americans and African-American history on full display, the only thing missing from your oppressive, bigoted rhetoric is a *South shall rise again* bumper sticker on your Lexus, and a Confederate flag on the wall."

"Watch your mouth, little girl. I'm your mother, not your friend."

"You're right. I should watch what I say. I wouldn't want my words to get the Negros wound up and start an uprising—like our ancestor, the slave woman whose name still remains unknown. Because as hard as you and Yaya have tried, you can't erase her from the family tree; you can't erase her from your blood. I mean, she *is* the reason why you are the great-great-great granddaughter of a plantation owner. Quite scandalous, how her daughter ended up with Lakeland, don't you think? But that's another bedtime story for another time. Let's change course because as much as I would love to keep discussing the dissimilarity in our melanin concentrations, theoretical grandchildren, my low-class attitude, and our less-than-perfect European ancestors, I actually need to converse about something with you, other than your yearning for the good ol' days."

Vivianna contorted her face to show her displeasure in Grayson. She responded to Grayson's rant with fluff because she knew she didn't have the intellect to debate color with her. "We can discuss anything as long as it's not distressing for me. I do have other things to do besides deal with you and your need to disgrace my family." The elongated, overdramatic sigh Vivianna produced pissed Grayson off. It was Vivianna's nice nasty way of saying, *I don't really care about your problems.*

Determination oozed from Grayson's gaze as she locked eyes with Vivianna. "I'm sure you do, Mother. Even though I can't think of anything. Not a single thing, but like they say, details are just details. Now, to the real reason why I'm having a conversation more than two minutes long with you. Mother, I want my father's name, his *whole* name. That means first, middle, and last. I want it. I'm entitled to it."

"Entitled," Vivianna scoffed as she placed the glass down. "Please, you're entitled to nothing. Besides, he doesn't want you. Never has and never will," Vivianna snapped.

"I didn't ask you if he wanted me. I asked you for his name."

"He doesn't want you."

"Then let him tell me he doesn't want me. Let him hurt my feelings and tell me he never wanted me. Frankly, at this stage of my life, I would prefer to hear it from him, instead of always hearing it from you."

Vivianna's tone turned nasty and toxic. "You're not getting that barely human piece of garbage's name. It's bad enough I have had to tolerate you resembling the slue-footed, bubble-lipped ape. I won't tolerate you dragging him from under whatever rock he lives under. I won't allow you to bring him back into my life. I have suffered enough because of him. I will not! I'm warning you, if you bring him up again, I won't be as polite as I am now. He is the biggest mistake of my life, and I will not relive it. I have a right to not have him in my life."

"First of all, I'm not dragging him into your life. I'm bringing him into mine." Grayson leaned forward on the edge of the sofa. "Second, you have no right to withhold his name from me. I'm a grown woman, and wanting to know my father has nothing to do with you." Grayson's voice cracked as she fought back tears. The war between Grayson and her mother over her father had consumed the majority of her life. She was exhausted from fighting it. Grayson was desperate to find her father. Her need grew greater with every passing year. She didn't know anything about her father, but she knew Lakeland was never meant to be her home. She wanted to let the tears roll down her face. But Grayson refused to give Vivianna the pleasure of seeing her cry again. "You have no right." Grayson balled her fists up and slammed them on her thighs. "Absolutely no right."

"I have every right." Vivianna pointed a French-tipped acrylic nail at Grayson. She had a look of victory on her face. "You're the one who has no right. My past is mine and mine alone. I am not going to waste my time reliving it so you can chase some silly little girl dream. I can do whatever I want with my past. And I choose not to share it with you." Vivianna's eyes overflowed with revulsion and anger. She raised her voice loud enough to make Brenda pause as she walked by. "I rescued you from him, gave you a father figure who makes more in a week than that low life is worth. You owe me a thank you, but all I get is your selfish disrespect."

Grayson's head shook in repulsion. She used her internal voice to speak to the baby as her stomach churned. Vivianna couldn't become privileged to her secret. Grayson matched her mother's tone. "My God, Mother. When are you going to stop making everything about me about you? This isn't about you. It's about me. My father and I had nothing to do with you. All I want is his fucking name! Why can't you just give me his fucking name! Jesus Christ. Why are you so fucking—"

"I don't know who the hell you think you are. You don't speak to me that way! There is no why, there is no who. There's only you learning to leave things that don't fucking concern you alone." Vivianna gritted her teeth. "You're not getting his name. Not now, not ever. So, I would suggest you get a life and move on."

"How do you live with yourself? Don't you ever get tired of making everything about you? Doesn't it get old wreaking havoc just so you can stay relevant? It's as if you know once I have his name I'll be through with you, Vivianna."

Grayson's last comment struck a chord with Vivianna; which made Vivianna resort to what she had always done: Insult Grayson's physical appearance. "You're lucky I'm too much of a lady to smack those over-sized lips off your obscure face. You are nothing more than an over-privileged darkie, who doesn't appreciate being given an opportunity to be something more than black." Vivianna stood up and smoothed her skirt. She grabbed her almost empty glass of wine. "If the whole purpose of your visit this weekend was to ask me for his name you should have stayed at home instead of coming here and wasting my time."

Grayson sat stock-still as her mother took her triumphant exit. It was always the comments about her looks that hurt the most. Grayson had no choice in the way she looked, but Vivianna punished her as if she did. The Harrows treated dark-skinned African Americans as *those people,* and the Harrows prided themselves on not being those people. Grayson's appearance was a glaring reminder *they* were *those people.* And how it didn't matter how many European ancestors you had, or how little melanin you had; the one-drop rule was still the one-drop rule.

Grayson sat still and let her mind race faster than she could run while her soul absorbed Vivianna's invectives. *Why me? I am so tired of the universe fucking me over. How bad did I fuck up with God that she allowed me to be born to this woman?* Grayson swallowed hard as she thought about her little girl self. How she'd once prayed to God to make her light skinned like her mother. Grayson knew if she had been born light, Vivianna would have been kinder. Vivianna would have loved her the way she loved Gigi.

Grayson's thoughts quickly turned from self-pity to rage as she had one of her long conversations with whatever god could be listening, if one existed at all. *That's just one of a long list of unanswered prayers. You allowed her to do anything and everything she could to make my life hell on Earth. You stood by and watched as she treated me like I was less than human. The worse she treated me the more life worked out for her. And you have the nerve to expect me to say thank you for my life. Praise you and give you ten percent of my wealth. I'll wipe my ass with that money, and toss it in the trash before I give a dime to you. All I want is his name. You can't be bothered to step up and make her give me that. You want me to be thankful, fine. Thank you for absolutely nothing. Thank you for not rescuing me. Thank you for making her life as easy as possible and mine as hard as hell. Thanks for making sure I spend the rest of my life feeling like a piece of a person. Thank you and kiss my ass.*

Grayson's only mollifying thought on the subject of her father came from an innate belief her father loved her. It was a pull she couldn't explain or shake. Grayson's conviction about her father's love left her at odds with Vivianna. Grayson held her truth close to her heart. It always soothed her when she was at her lowest points. As a little girl, Grayson pretended he was off on an adventure and couldn't get back. Her father was everything from an explorer who traveled to places one couldn't find on the map, to a soldier who was off saving the world. The special love she felt for a man whose face she couldn't identify if her life depended on it wouldn't allow her soul to believe her father had voluntarily deserted her in perdition.

~ * ~

Grayson paced feverishly back and forth in her childhood bedroom. The floor creaked slightly as she moved around the room. David sat on the bed, his papers spread out around him, watching her. "I am so tired of this bullshit with her. It's never ending. I'm just sick. Sick of it all." Grayson folded her arms across her chest. "There is no need for any of this. I don't understand. Why does she have to be so cruel? Or better yet, what the hell did I do to deserve being saddled with her as a mother. I swear some days I wish she would just die. It's not like she has anything to contribute to society. My mother is a walking, talking, breathing waste. I'm convinced that the only reason she's alive is because God can't stand the thought of me being happy. If there is a God."

"Baby, don't speak such things. My Mawmaw said when you talk about God..."

Grayson interrupted his lecture. "David, *please.* Look, I loved Miss Hanny, and she loved me like I was one of her own. But I can't listen to one of her stories about life, and God, and everything happens for a reason, and how truth will prevail and faith will see you through. Not now. Now I just want to be angry. I want someone to hate—someone to blame. I want someone, anyone, to feel my pain. To hurt the way I hurt every time I'm near Vivianna."

David looked down at his worn sneakers before he spoke. "I know you do, but I want you to know God doesn't hate you or love seeing you suffer." He had said the phrase to Grayson countless times, and nothing ever changed for the better. David had a twinge of doubt about there being truth in his words, or if God even existed at this point. He was at a loss for words that didn't belong to his Mawmaw. "It can't be bad forever."

"You know something else about the Almighty?" Grayson scoffed at the title. "She's got a really twisted way of showing me She cares. If She cared—I mean truly cared—Vivianna wouldn't exist anymore. I mean, come on! Would it really be so bad if she just died? It's not as if her death would be some great loss to the world. One less over-privileged, aging drama queen roving the planet. When does the great Almighty get off the sidelines and actually do something?" Grayson fumbled over her words in her tears. David sat on the edge of the bed. He studied Grayson's movements as she expelled her vexations. He had seen her frustrated before, but this time it was frustration on a whole other level. "When do I stop being her collateral damage? How long am I supposed to be held hostage by her? I'm tired of being so damn tired of this. All of it."

"Hey," David reached out and drew her down on the bed. Grayson sat, but she wouldn't let him put his arm around her. "Stop it. I'm going to hold you. Whether you want me to or not. I'm not going to let you talk like that."

"David!"

"No, Grayson, no. Look, I know you don't like Vivianna. Hell, you probably even hate her."

"'Probably' is an understatement," Grayson scoffed.

"Enough." David's tone made it very clear he wasn't going to allow her to continue to speak ill of her mother. "Hating her and wishing her dead isn't going to do anything but bring you down to her level. I won't watch my wife go down that road. It's not who you are. You're better than that. You're the better woman, and I *need* you to act like the better woman I know you to be."

Grayson shook free, and threw her hands up in a melodramatic wave. "She wins again. I have to take the high road, while she plays in the gutter. It must be nice to be a complete jackass and still have the favor of the universe—still have everything go your way. She keeps my father's name her secret, and I get nothing."

"Stop. I mean it. You know that's not the way things are. Your mother lives in her own special hell." David pulled Grayson's face towards his. "Your mother's not happy. Not truly. Look at her life. She doesn't have a real relationship with her oldest daughter. What she does have with you can only be described as cruel and cold. You're her flesh, and you can't stand her. That's hell for a mother not to have the love of her child. She may not show it, but trust me she's miserable." David leaned his head against the side of her head. His lips grazed the side of her head as he spoke. "It's not good for you to be like this. It damn sure ain't good for us either." Grayson's last explosion had forced David's hand. He reconciled within himself that Vivianna's antics had run their course. David realized he could no longer sit on the sidelines and patiently wait for Vivianna to do the right thing. "I'm gonna fix this, okay? I promise."

"Yeah," Grayson forced herself to answer. Grayson conditioned herself years ago not to believe in the things people promised her. She discovered it was easier to hold onto disappointment than the hope that anyone would do right by her. It didn't matter David had proven to her over and over he was the exception in her life. She continued to hold onto the idea that one day he would disappoint her like everyone else.

"You don't believe a word I'm saying to you." Grayson shot him a guilty look. "It's okay that you don't. I'll just do what I've always done. I'll prove you wrong and fix it. I'll make it all better like I always do." Grayson's attempt at a poker face was a complete failure. "That's the smile I've missed on your beautiful face. I need you to keep that smile on your face while I fix it. Give me space, and let me make it better for you." Grayson nodded her response. David lowered his voice a little more. "I know this is probably going to be hard for you. But I want you to try and relax a little while we're here." Grayson threw David a condescending glance. "I know; I know considering everything going on it's going to be difficult, but I need you to try. I mean it. Try and take a nap."

"I'm not tired. I'm too mad to sleep, and the last thing I want right now is a nap."

"Well, those bags under your eyes say different."

"Really?"

"As a matter of fact, they say you should be madly in love with the idea of taking a nap right now."

"Only because I find you cute, I'm I going to let that comment about the bags under my eyes slide." Grayson shook her head softly. "You're lucky I find you cute."

"You're lucky I find you cute," David mimicked her with a goofy grin smeared on his face.

~ * ~

Grayson reluctantly took David's advice. She retreated to the one place on Lakeland that always lulled her into a sense of calm and sometimes sleep: Her favorite willow tree. Grayson loved the location of her special tree. It was close enough to the house she could faintly hear someone calling for her, but far enough away she could lie and say she didn't hear them. Grayson's tree had a large base and thick trunk, which made it easy for Grayson to lean against, and no one who looked over would see her. When the breeze was just right, the sound of the leaves gently swaying back and forth would serenade Grayson to sleep.

"What is it about you and this damn tree? When you're here, you're always under it with a damn book asleep. You think no one knows you're under here, but we all know. You're not clever. Hell, if it was a man, you'd be cheating on David every time you visit." The sound of her sister's high-pitched voice ripped Grayson out of her much-needed and undisturbed slumber. Gigi was too proud of her southern roots to hide her accent.

Grayson let out a deep sigh as she woke up. "It's comfortable, and usually pretty tranquil." Grayson stressed her words as she arched her back and stretched.

"I don't know what could be so comfortable about sitting under a tree, like you're homeless. Really, Grayson, you look like one of those homeless women you see in the city, but with nicer clothes. No offense, but you do." Gigi's light brown barrel curls flopped back and forth as she nodded her head.

Grayson glared up at her younger half-sister who, by design, developed over the years into an exact replica of their mother. "I wouldn't expect you to understand something like solace, Gigi."

"I know what solace means. I got straight A's in English. I just don't understand this tree thing. It's bizarre. If you want to sleep, go in the house and lay in the bed."

Grayson sighed patiently. "Gigi, you know that feeling you get when you're in Prada or shopping for a new pair of Louboutins?"

A huge, perfectly-capped grin sprinted across Gigi's fair face. "Yes."

"The tranquil feeling washing over you, while you're remembering your last shopping spree, that's how I feel when I'm sitting here."

Gigi plopped down next to her sister. She tried to find the feeling of bliss Grayson swore existed. "Well, if you say it's the same. I'm trying to feel it, but all I can think about is the dirt on my jeans, and what animal peed here before I got here." Gigi scrunched up her face.

"Never mind, Gigi. Trying to get you to understand why I like sitting under my tree, is like trying to get you to understand poor people and government cheese. It ain't gonna happen."

"Grayson, cheese comes from the store, not the government."

Grayson nodded her head as she spoke. "Yes, it does, Gigi. Yes, it does. Game set match. We're done. Thank you and goodnight." Grayson attempted to stand up, but the combination of dizziness and nausea forced her back down.

Gigi looked alarmed. "Grayson, are you okay? What's wrong? Something's wrong? Tell me. You're not sick, are you? If you are, don't cough on me."

"No, I'm not sick. I'm fine, Gigi. Just fine. You don't have to worry about me getting you sick," Grayson snapped. "If I did forget to cover my mouth and cough on you, trust me you wouldn't catch anything from me."

"Well, the funk in your voice, and the way you damn near fell on me, tells me something's wrong. Tell me what's going on with you."

"What's going on with me has absolutely nothing to do with you. You can go back to planning your next shopping trip in your head. Shouldn't you be heading back into the house with the drapes drawn, anyway? You and Mother are like vampires when the sun is out."

"Ouch. I didn't know being concerned about my sister would mean we'd end up in a juvenile sparring match and right back at each other's throats about nothing. I thought we had moved past all those good times."

"Whatever, Gigi, you're concerned about me as much as I'm concerned about the last shit my dog took. We've never gotten along. So, let's not break with tradition and start now. Hell, the only reason we didn't kill each other as kids is because we didn't have the ability to hide the body." Grayson rolled her eyes as she stared off at the wooded area.

"I can't argue with you. We fought like wild dogs as kids —I'll give you that—but we don't have to do it as adults. Like it or not, I'm your sister, there's no do over, you can't swap me out for a pony, I'm here. I know something's not right." Gigi slid a little closer. "Look at me. We may not have a traditional sister relationship, but I love you. We're not close, but I care. I really *care*. Please, Grayson, tell me what's wrong."

Grayson debated on whether or not to tell Gigi. Grayson had spent her entire life trying to like her sister, but she couldn't bring herself to do it. She feared that if she showed her vulnerable side to her sister, Gigi would dehumanize her the way their mother did. "Really, I'm fine; there's nothing to talk about." She went into her tough executive mode, but Gigi grabbed her arm before she could attempt to stand again.

"I call bullshit. You're so far from fine, Grayson, it's not even funny."

"Well, you should sleep well tonight knowing my life is an utter wreck right now."

"You're acting like I enjoy watching you suffer?"

"You did and still do." Grayson pushed Gigi's arm off of her. Gigi's actions and words made her recoil. "Oh, don't look shocked, Gigi. You have always enjoyed watching me suffer. Remember when I was nine, and Mother cut off all off my hair because she said it was too long. Mother said long hair was for light-skinned girls, and I was too dark for my type of hair. My hair was in the middle of my back. She cut it up to my ears. You laughed your ass off. Or how about the dark brown sweater you had when you were a teenager? The one you called your 'Grayson brown sweater?' Or the stupid straw hat Mother insisted I wear when I was outside in the summer because she said I couldn't afford to get any darker? You loved seeing me suffer in that ugly ass hat. I spent my entire time here bring told what I couldn't be, where I couldn't go, what man would or would not want me because I wasn't light like you. I was the one who was told to make sure I got good grades so I could take care of myself because men don't take care of women who look like me. And you're the one who gets to walk around saying dumb shit like cheese comes from the store and not the government. You have no idea what I went through here, while you walked around here being miss perfect. You want to know what's wrong with me? It's everyone in this shitty family, that's what's wrong with me. Happy now?"

"Poor, poor Grayson. Don't you ever get tired of playing the poor, defenseless chocolate drop who grew up in a family of light skin?"

"Fuck you."

"No fuck *you!* I'm tired of this shit!" Gigi spat back in her ultra-feminine voice that never sounded quite right when she raised it, or swore. "I called that sweater my Grayson-brown sweater because it was a beautiful shade of brown like my sister. And as for your hair, I didn't know why Momma cut your hair. I laughed because you have big ears, and I didn't realize how big they were until your hair was short. Cut me a bit of slack, I was fucking five. And as for that stupid hat I didn't know why you wore the damn thing. I just knew it was big as hell, and you always had the damn thing on. I am so tired of hearing you cry the dark-skinned blues. You know, it wasn't easy for me either, Grayson. You think there weren't things I was denied. You think there weren't opportunities that were taken away from me.

"Try walking around in hundred-degree heat with hair almost down to your ass. All I wanted to do was cut it up to my shoulders, and Momma said no because no one would think I was pretty with short hair. Or better yet try being around men who only want to fuck you because you're so damn light." Gigi made air quotations around the words "so damn light." "And on top of wanting to fuck you, they hope they get you pregnant. Not a day goes by that someone doesn't ask me *what are you?* Or tell me how exotic I am. Tigers are *exotic*. Orchids are *exotic*. I'm not exotic. I'm just Gigi, a Black woman with light skin and green eyes. You have no idea how hard it is when men see you as nothing more than the lead in their erotic fantasy. Every activity Momma put me in she did it under the guise of wanting me to attract the right kind of man. So that meant no science club, no Future Leaders of America club. I only rode horse because Momma said it was the sport of kings and people of means. Momma was beside herself with joy when I met Sebastian at one of my events. In our own ways, Grayson, we both caught hell for looking the way we do. I just never unleashed on you about it. I never made you feel like less than me because you didn't understand what it was like to be me. All I have ever wanted was to be your sister. I don't give a damn what color you are. Just be my sister."

Grayson sat stunned. For the first time she saw her sister as something other than a superficial high yellow bitch she made her out to be in her mind. Gigi became less perfect and more human to her. Grayson saw the hurt in her sister's eyes and realized they were ore like opposite sides of the same coin, rather than two women on the opposite end of the color spectrum.

"Now, we can sit here all day playing who suffered more, light skinned or dark skinned, or you can let me in, and we can talk. We can have a real conversation. Like the ones we should have been having all this time. We go too long in between visits and phone calls." Gigi placed her hand on Grayson's. "Please, let me be your sister."

As much as Grayson wasn't completely sold on the idea of confiding in Gigi, she knew she couldn't keep internalizing her fears. Her hamster-on-a-wheel routine wasn't working.

"Tell me." Gigi nudged her softly. "Unless it's going to make me an accessory to something; then keep it to your damned self. I wouldn't last five minutes in the penal system, and those outfits aren't cute either." Gigi let out one of her bigger than the world laughs, as Grayson rolled her eyes. "I'm just kidding, Grayson, tell me."

"I can talk to you?"

"Yes."

"No, Gigi, I'm serious. If I can't talk to you, tell me now."

"Yes, my old sister can talk to me about anything." Gigi leaned in an over-exaggerated style.

Grayson let a much-needed laugh slip. Her laughter gave her a sense of release and comfort. The endorphins released allowed Grayson to believe, if only for a moment, everything would be all right. "Bitch. I'm only four years older than you."

Gigi batted her eyes at Grayson. "Four long, *long* years."

In that moment, and for the first time, Grayson and Gigi felt like sisters. This was the moment they had both longed for; there was no envy, no favoritism, no light skin, and no dark skin. Just the two of them being the sisters they would have been, if it weren't for Vivianna's malevolent behavior.

Grayson let out a deep sigh before she spoke. "I'm pregnant."

"That's wonderful!" Gigi's eyes lit up. "David's walking on air, isn't he? And I know Momma's thrilled. Have you told Yaya?"

"I'm not keeping it."

"First of all, you're carrying a *baby* and not an it. And second, yes you are."

"No, I'm not..." Grayson trailed off in a half whisper.

"Yes."

"I can't."

"Why?"

Grayson curled the corner of her lip, and Gigi glared at her. "Because I don't want it. Okay? I don't want this baby, *my* baby, to go through what I did being a part of this family."

"What do you mean?" Gigi countered. "Barring our unnecessary bullshit arguments we had, we had a good childhood. We had the best schools. Our passports were full before we could drive. We lived a life most people daydream about while they look through magazines that mirrored our reality.

"We had things. But it's Mother's love I wanted. You had it. I didn't. You were the light one. The one Mother loved more. You were the one she wanted. I mean *really* wanted. You were the one who fit in around here, not me."

Gigi rolled her green eyes. "Grayson, not this shit again. Didn't we just go there? We flung 'fuck you' back and forth and everything."

"It's more than that. Gigi, hear me out. Please. You were the one who looked like Mother, not me. And that made you the prized one. I was the dark one. The one who made the family look bad with my coarse hair, full lips, and ample figure. I was the one without a father. I was the one our aunts, uncles, and cousins whispered about at family gatherings. The one pushed to the side or in back of the family photos. Everyone always went out of their way to explain to everyone who married into this family why I was the one without the father. They all went out of their way to make sure everyone knew why I didn't look like everyone else. I don't want this family treating my baby the way they treated me. The truth is there is no guarantee this kid will come out light with straight hair. Or worse—and this scares me more than all of this family crap—is that I end up treating it the way I was treated, as some twisted resentful thing because it does come out light with straight hair." Gigi arched her eyebrow in disapproval of Grayson's use of the word "it" again. "I mean the baby, my baby, the way Mother, and the rest of them treated me. I don't want to heap any of this crap on a kid."

"No father? Grayson, please. Daddy loved you like you were his. Really his. Hell, there were plenty of times *I* was jealous of the way Daddy catered to you. He always hugged you first, said goodnight to you first. You got to go through his pockets and grab as much change as you could first when we were little. As for Momma, I never saw any of that between the two of you—I swear. I never did. I knew you and Momma weren't really close, but I thought that was because you guys didn't get along. Some mothers and daughters don't. As for the rest of the family, I never really paid attention to them." Gigi spoke in a half whisper, "Was it really that bad?"

"It was a hundred times worse. I spent my entire childhood knowing I wasn't wanted. I was just tolerated. That's why I can't keep this kid. I wouldn't be able to live with myself if I raised a child that felt unloved and unwanted like I did."

Gigi's tone turned stern and demanding. "Then *don't*. I swear, could you be a little more self-absorbed?"

"Self-absorbed?"

"Yeah, self-absorbed. You're so busy manufacturing the *what if,* you don't see how wonderful things are for you right now. You have the opportunity to have a baby, a beautiful and wonderful baby. It's an opportunity some women would sell their souls to have. But you're too caught up in feeling sorry for yourself to understand how perfect this baby is. I would give anything to be you right now."

"Oh please, you and Sebastian are going to have more kids than you know what to do with. If you two can be in the same time zone long enough to make it happen."

"His traveling isn't an issue for us. I can tag alone whenever I please. We're not going to have kids because we can't." Gigi lowered her tone. "Because I can't."

"Are you sure?" Gigi threw Grayson a side eye in response. "I mean I know you're sure, but are you really sure. Wait, I shouldn't have asked that question. What I meant to say is have you guys seen a fertility specialist? Things have come a long way."

"We saw a specialist. We got a second and a third opinion and after months of poking, prodding, and false hope they all said the same thing my gynecologist did. The chances of me being able to conceive are almost nonexistent, and if by some miracle I did get pregnant, I probably wouldn't carry the baby past the second trimester. I could try, for the sake of trying, but the thought of going through all of the pain, and not having a baby at the end of it is something I can't handle. I'm tired of people asking me when Sebastian and I are going to have a baby."

"At first, I used to lie and tell people we weren't ready, and then I made the mistake of telling a couple of people the truth. You should have seen the pity in their eyes. Like, I was somehow not a whole woman because I couldn't get pregnant. I got an abundance of unsolicited advice; everything from homeopathic remedies to sex positions to try. It got so bad one of my girlfriends didn't invite me to her baby shower, because apparently she was afraid I would bring the mood in the room down. What did she think I was going to do, give a slide show presentation about my infertility at her shower? This is my barren uterus. These are y jacked-up fallopian tubes. Now, I just lie and tell people I don't like kids. I've been called selfish a few times, but I would rather people think I'm selfish than pity me."

"Gigi, I don't know what to say. I want to say sorry, but I know sorry is not enough. It would sound shallow and stupid if I said it. I never thought something like this would happen to you. I mean, it never crossed my mind that one of us wouldn't be able to have kids. There are certain things you never think about. Like, can I have kids, you just always assume it's a gimmie you can until someone tells you no, you can't." Grayson's words were all over the place. "Gigi, if I had known, I would have never started this conversation with you. I feel like a real ass now. How's Sebastian doing?"

"He's okay. He hasn't left me, yet," Gigi let a weak smile creep across her face as she scoffed. "I mean it's been a rough few months, but I'm accepting it. I think he's accepting it, too. I am a little scared though."

"Scared Sebastian is going to leave?"

"I don't know. Not really. He said he's not leaving, but nothing is a hundred percent. Maybe I'm a little worried about him leaving but not scared. I wonder if I'm enough for him; just me, no kids. I don't know if he's really absorbed the idea of there isn't going to be any large family photo hanging above our mantel like his sisters have, no one to teach things to, no toys to put together, no big holiday dinners. All of his sisters have girls, so as of right now his family name dies with him. And his family is way more into tradition and lineage than ours. I'm a little concerned work is going to become his substitute for children, and instead of us growing together we grow apart. But what scares me, I mean really scares the shit out of me, Grayson, is me becoming one of those women who walks around with one of those tiny dogs, dressed in a ridiculous outfit—pushing it in a stroller, calling it my baby, and letting it sit on the dining room table and eat. I actually saw a woman when we were on vacation last year cutting up chicken and feeding it to this little whatever thing like you would feed a toddler. Thank God I can't stand cats, or I would run the risk of having thirty of them running around the house. You know what, now that I said it out loud, it all scares the hell out of me, Gray. I never expected to be here, so I don't know what to do now that I am. In a way you're right; my life was supposed to be perfect."

"It could be worse."

"Worse really. How!?"

"You could become one of those weirdos who walks around with a baby doll."

"What the hell are you talking about?"

"I have a friend who's a divorce lawyer, and one of her clients—you know what? It's too long of a disturbing story to tell. Just promise me no dolls. Maybe you guys could adopt? There are plenty of babies and kids in need of a good home. You can be a fantastic mother without having to experience stretch marks and morning sickness. Biology doesn't make you a mom, it's how you treat a child that does."

"Sebastian won't. He said if he can't have one of his own, he doesn't want someone else's."

"But it wouldn't be someone else's; he or she would belong to the two of you. You guys would be the baby's mom and dad. That would be your son, or daughter."

"I know. But he doesn't see it that way. Sebastian said he's not taking care of another man's responsibility." Gigi took Grayson's hand in hers. "Now, you know why I'm so against what you're thinking about doing. You're experiencing something I would give anything to experience." Gigi's eyes watered. She took a profound breath as the tears crept from the corners of her eyes. "Grayson, being there for my nieces and nephews is the closest I will ever get to motherhood. That baby is going to have more love than he or she knows what to do with. Between you, David, and his young, adoring, and spectacularly fabulously stylish auntie, that baby is going to be spoiled on a massive scale." Gigi crinkled her nose. Grayson let out another gut deep laugh. "You laugh, but there are kids who would sell their parents to have an auntie like the one I'm going to be."

"I know, Gigi, I know."

Grayson slid closer to Gigi. "I never knew how hard it's been being you."

"No harder than you being you, Gray."

"Just think I always wanted to be the one everyone adored."

"And I wanted to be the one who faded deep into the background."

Grayson and Gigi sat drifting back and forth between sisterly conversation and comfortable silence for well over two hours. The division that had been created between them as children dissipated as they laughed about old boyfriends, bad fashion choices, and the things their husbands did that annoyed them. As their conversation died down, it circled back to the unavoidable elephant and the source of the division between them.

Gigi rested her head on Grayson's shoulder. "Why do you think

Momma stays here? I mean Daddy makes enough money to give her a lifestyle like this someplace else. And even though Yaya is in her late seventies she doesn't need anyone's help. She never has. Brenda and the rest of the staff are here for her. Our mother is a grown-ass woman, and she lives at home."

"I guess it's safer if Mother stays. The last time she left, Mother showed back up with no husband and me. Needless to say, that's not the Harrow way. I think our mother is one of those women who can never be trusted to live her own life. At least if Mother is here, Yaya can catch most of the pieces before they fall."

"I guess."

VISIT OUR WEBSITE
FOR THE FULL INVENTORY
OF QUALITY BOOKS:

http://www.roguephoenixpress.com

Rogue Phoenix Press

Representing Excellence in Publishing

*Quality trade paperbacks and downloads
in multiple formats,
in genres ranging from historical to contemporary romance,
mystery and science fiction.
Visit the website then bookmark it.
We add new titles each month!*

www.ingramcontent.com/pod-product-compliance
Lightning Source LLC
Chambersburg PA
CBHW051945220626
47052CB00004B/808